NECESSARY EVIL &the GREATER GOOD

By Adam Ingle

To my father,

who will never get to read this.

And my mother,

who will.

Contents

Chapter 1

The Beginning of The End

They sat in silence watching the sun as it peeked over the horizon of the planet Earth. They had done this a thousand times before, but this one felt different – or it would, in retrospect. To say this was the first day of the rest of their lives was both cheesy and not entirely accurate. If anything, this was the last day of their old lives. A semantic argument, perhaps, but to the Angel and Demon sitting on the solar array of a GPS satellite slowly orbiting over Australia, it was an important detail.

"Someday soon this will all be a twisted, agonizing Hellscape of pain and suffering," said Mestoph as he made a grand sweeping gesture across the Earth from sunrise to twilight.

The pristine blue oceans, the puffy clouds, and the green and brown smudges of land all began to glow red and boil away. Great arcs of fire lined the mountain ranges as the rocks themselves began to burn. Even from ten thousand miles up, they could see the waters swirling and dancing in frenzied, boiling excitement. Explosions pocked the surface of the Earth, fluming up and making tiny mushroom clouds.

Just as Australia was being left a dark grey-black ruin of ash Leviticus sighed, snapped his fingers, and the illusion returned to normal. Mestoph just smiled.

Mestoph was short for Mestopholes, a bastardized version of his son-of-a-bitch father's name: Mephistopheles. Mephisto was one of the greatest demons Hell had ever seen. He had brought misery, pain, suffering, and death to humans for thousands of years. He was especially well known for getting humans to willingly sign their souls over to Satan in exchange for worldly delights and granting wishes. There were always catches to the deals that the humans either were too naïve to comprehend the ramifications of, or simply didn't care. Mestoph, on the other hand, wasn't well known for much of anything, other than not living up to his father's name. Being the spawn of such an ancient and revered Demon as Mephisto came with a few perks, like free refills in the Hell Industries cafeteria and plenty of slutty little Hellbound groupies, but it also came with more than its share of expectations.

When Mestoph's father opted for early retirement at the age of 10,000, people started to expect big things from him – especially Satan. The unfortunate truth, for both Mestoph and Satan, was that he just didn't have it in him. Mestoph was a son-of-a-bitch in his own right, but so was every other Demon in Hell. Mestoph didn't have his father's hate, anger, and rage. And Mephisto would never have been caught enjoying a sunrise with his Angelic best friend.

"Agonizing Hellscape of pain and suffering?" asked Leviticus. "Is that the official Hell Industries PR copy, or are you getting sentimental?"

This was a game they often played. Mestoph would try to get Leviticus to condemn humanity to a Hellish ruin, while Leviticus would try to get Mestoph to admit that he secretly enjoyed roller skating or hot chocolate. Mestoph wasn't going to bite this morning. Instead, he continued to watch the sunrise until he couldn't tolerate the light. The bright rays of the rising sun reflected off his dark, almost black skin and he closed his eyes for a moment to take in its warmth. When he opened them again, he stared into the glimmering sun; there was nothing this bright and beautiful in Hell.

To an observer, it would have looked as if two normal human friends were watching a peaceful sunrise –albeit in outer space. Mestoph was a dark black man with his black leather trench coat draped over the solar panel behind him while Leviticus was an olive skinned man in a crisp, clean, baby blue ankle-length thawb. The difference was that a normal human wouldn't be able to feel the warmth of the sun in space, or hear the person next to him gasping for the air that was rushing uncontrollably out of his lungs, but since they were not of this plane, the rules didn't really apply to them. At least some of the rules didn't.

Just before Mestoph figured blindness would be inevitable and permanent, he slid a dark pair of sunglasses on and smiled, brushing his tightly braided dreadlocks behind his shoulders. Leviticus, being an Angel, was used to the constant and unyielding glare of God's aura. There was also the actual Holy Light that lit Heaven in a permanent hour-before-sunset glow at that angle that blinded people driving down the interstate after work. On top of that, there were the unusually oily and glistening Angelic beings and all the other really obnoxiously bright things that seemed to inhabit Heaven in an unexplainably high density.

"I've been working on a plan," said Mestoph.

Leviticus arched a single brow but said nothing. He knew that Mestoph would, slowly and in his own time, spit out whatever it was he had been scheming. They had been doing these sunrise meetings for over a thousand years, and about once a century or so, one or the other of them concocted a harebrained plan to get the best of God, Satan, or both. Inevitably, "getting the best of" meant some kind of con to get exorbitant amounts of money or vacation time on Earth. More often than not, these plans would fall apart before they had ever gotten off the ground. The few that did manage to get anywhere always ended with them getting caught early on or overlooking some seemingly inconsequential detail that would cause them to fail so spectacularly that the failure itself—and the resulting shame and embarrassment—was considered punishment enough. That was if their grand scheme even registered on anyone's radar.

This plan would assuredly be no different, but it was tradition and tradition must be upheld. The truth was that the limited chance of success was probably the only thing that kept them going. If they were to actually succeed, they would probably be just like a dog that suddenly regretted ever catching that car it was always chasing.

"We've spent our entire lives working toward The End of the World, and we're no closer than we were the day you and I met," Mestoph said. He paused and let out a little sigh. "I'm tired—and I'm fairly certain you must be too—of busting our asses for something I'm not sure I even believe in and definitely don't care about anymore."

The End of the World was the ultimate goal of both Heaven, Inc. and Hell Industries. Each wanted to have the upper hand and the most souls when the time came, which meant that both sides spent an unbelievable amount of time and resources toward thwarting and stalling the plans of the other. Progress toward The End of the World therefore stalled to a near halt. Humans kept on living their lives, oblivious to the fact that their fates and immortal souls were nothing more than a tiny percentage point in the seemingly eternal struggle for market share dominance by the Higher Powers. At current count The End was 1000 years overdue, and there was no longer any time wasted on calculating an ETA (or Estimated Time of Apocalypse), not even a symbolic one for the sake of morale. Nowadays, the End of Times version of the Doomsday Clock permanently flashed 12:00 like the VCR that still sat on top of the television at just about everyone's grandmother's house.

"So I've been working on a plan to get us kicked out of The Afterlife, but not banished to T or C for Eternity, with enough money to get us settled and just wait out the eventual End," said Mestoph after another brief pause.

Leviticus looked at Mestoph with his head still slightly tilted, thinking about what he had said, especially the "T or C" part. T or C was the tiny town of Truth or Consequences, New Mexico. This was the physical point on Earth in which Purgatory was located. It was not, contrary to popular opinion, in New Jersey. This wasn't quite the normal once-a-century plan that they cooked up. This one was serious and sounded like it could get them in serious trouble. The thought of spending the rest of humanity's existence in T or C was worse than an eternity as a slightly disgruntled cubicle jockey. Mestoph was right, however, in that he too was tired of it all. Being an Agent of Heaven, a fancy title for an employee of Heaven Inc., was different than residing in Heaven. It wasn't Eternity in Paradise; it was a job— a boring and tedious job of late, and one he couldn't just quit. Mestoph was in the same boat down as a Shadow for Hell Industries.

Heaven and Hell, for the most part, worked just like humans imagined. Each person's version of Heaven or Hell was a little different, and within reason it was catered to them when they arrived. As such, a masochist wouldn't spend an eternity being whipped and beaten in Hell since they'd enjoy that far too much. On the other hand, a masochist in Heaven could get a little taste of pain—or a big one if they wanted—whenever they felt the need. A big, sprawling pleasure or pain palace with a population higher than anyone would care to count doesn't run itself. As a result, both Heaven and Hell were run by giant, bureaucratic conglomerates. They both had Boards of Directors, but unlike most businesses they had little ultimate power. They had power only in so much as God or Satan let them. They each had Marketing, Public Relations, Research and Development, and even Human Resource departments. If it was found in your average

Fortune 500 Company on Earth, it was probably implemented to some degree in the Afterlife. Despite all the manpower and nearly unlimited resources, neither Heaven nor Hell had a lot of direct influence on humanity or Earth nowadays. This wasn't always the case, as a quick scan of the Old Testament would prove.

Leviticus thought for a moment longer and then looked seriously at Mestoph. "Alright, what did you have in mind?" he asked.

Marcus realized he was staring at her again. Despite knowing this, he couldn't stop doing it. He had been coming to this coffee shop nearly every day for over a year, and yet he rarely said more than three sentences to Stephanie, the raven-haired, elfish barista who was the object of his desire. He liked everything about her: from the fact that she was so short that she barely came up to his shoulders—and he was by no means tall—to the geeky thick-rimmed rectangular glasses that framed her almost too large eyes that were striated with bands of green and gold. Her dark hair flowed just past her shoulders like an obsidian river. On warm days, when the coffee shop had the windows open and the fans on, he could smell a hint of jasmine. He knew it was probably her shampoo or maybe even some lightly applied perfume, but in his mind he liked to imagine that it was her natural scent.

"Hi, Stephanie. How are you doing?"

One.

I can do it this time, he thought.

"I'm good, Marcus. How are you?"

"Not too bad, just need a little morning Joe before work."

Two.

His palms began to get clammy, and he could feel anxiety rising up in his gut as his stomach began to tighten.

"Well, here you go. Ready for another day," she said with a smile that made Marcus want to grab her and kiss her.

"Thanks, have a good day."

Three.

His mouth was a desert, his mind was a sandstorm. He walked off with his coffee and small bag of bread, and he waved back to Stephanie awkwardly.

The status quo had been upheld—another three sentences in the books. He left Stephanie the Barista at the Bean Counters coffee shop, once again without having said a single word about how he felt, how he found himself thinking about her while he was working, or even a few words about the weather. Maybe tomorrow.

Marcus left the coffee shop and found Sir Regi sitting with his little doggy-size goggles in the sidecar of his old 1942 Indian Scout motorcycle where he had left him. Sir Regi was a very well behaved dog, which was surprising given the typical nature of a Scottish terrier. Scotties were notoriously territorial, feisty, and stubborn dogs. Sir Regi, which was short for Sir Reginald Pollywog Newcastle III, had shown up sitting in Marcus's sidecar one day after work with a note and a collar. The collar had borne his ridiculously long name, while the note had simply read "Your new dog." There had been no one around, no one claiming the practical joke. He had always wanted a dog, but the commitment and responsibility had frightened him a bit. Marcus told himself that he would keep Sir Regi until he found the dog's owner, but weeks and then months had gone by and no one had put up signs looking for a lost dog. That had been three years ago, and they had been best friends ever since.

Marcus would vent his frustrations with life in general,

and his non-existent relationship with Stephanie in particular, to the small dog. Sir Regi always sat listening with rapt attention and would often seem deep in thought and even frustrated on Marcus's behalf. Marcus liked to think Sir Regi was frustrated with his inability to share his sage wisdom. Sometimes Marcus worried about the amount of personification he had bestowed upon Sir Regi over the years, but most of the time he was just glad to have a loyal friend who didn't think he was completely pathetic.

Sir Regi barked happily as Marcus walked over to the bike and tossed him a heel of day-old sourdough that Stephanie had given him. She always saved up leftovers for him, ever since Marcus had mentioned Sir Regi's love for sourdough bread. The dog happily munched on it as Marcus rode to work.

Sir Regi didn't so much go to work with Marcus as he rode to the general locale where Marcus worked and hung out in the parks nearby. Marcus often found himself staring off into oblivion, thinking about the little dog-sized adventures that Sir Regi must have while he toiled away at work. Sometimes it would be as simple as figuring out where an enticing smell came from, and others would be as complicated as the Scotty being a high-ranking member of a secret dog adventurers group that protected ancient secrets and artifacts of canine lore and legend.

When he wasn't busy saving the world for all dog-kind, Sir Regi would meet Marcus at his motorcycle at noon and the two would have lunch together. Sometimes they would share a sandwich at a bench in the park across the street. When a coworker invited him to lunch, which honestly hardly ever happened, they would eat at a cafe or coffee shop where they could sit outside. Sir Regi would come with them and quietly eat whatever Marcus slid to him under the table. Today the weather looked like rain, so Marcus would probably eat at his desk, leaving Sir Regi to fend for himself. Sir Regi was a very resourceful dog; Marcus was convinced that the dog had a regular circuit of people that fed him while he worked, so he wasn't too concerned.

Marcus pulled the olive drab Scout into one of the midget-sized motorcycle parking spots in front of his office. It was an old motorcycle that had been through more in its life than Marcus probably ever would, so he didn't think a little rain would hurt it. Marcus took off the old pair of WWI aviator goggles he wore when riding, since the Indian Scout didn't have an actual windshield, and Sir Regi pawed off the tiny pair he very obligingly wore as well. The two said their goodbyes, and Sir Regi bounded up to the park across the road as Marcus went in to his office.

Marcus's job, like most things in his life, was fairly mundane. He was a small cog in a large machine that developed custom financial software for other companies. The job of the cog named Marcus was to test obscure combinations of functions to make sure that when the software hit the real world it didn't self-destruct because a woman with a lime green Volkswagen Thing tried to refinance a loan on a Friday the 13th by a Wisconsin girl named Bethany, or that the computer didn't restart every time the girl in accounting pressed F12. Whenever he came across one of these rare bugs, which Marcus called Smurfs because of their near impossibility to catch, it was his job to find out why it happened and how to keep it from happening again.

The quality of Marcus's day could easily be discerned by the number of coffee cups in his trash can. On a normal, easygoing day he would have a max of three cups of coffee. One to get him started—usually the one Stephanie made him—and then two more late in the day to hold him over until quitting time. A bad day could have as many as five cups before lunch, with the rest of the day spent within close proximity to the coffee machine and its lukewarm, syrupy-thick burnt coffee at all times.

It was currently a quarter till eleven, and Marcus had just thrown his fourth cup into the waste basket. Considering how mundane his job was on paper, it always amazed him how stressful it could be in reality. He had already uncovered two instances of what had been dubbed The Superman Virus, in which tiny fractions of each transaction would go unaccounted for. It was better known in the rest of the world as salami slicing or penny shaving, but Marcus liked "Superman Virus" better.

On their own, these rogue fractions were insignificant, but in a high enough volume over a long enough period of time, they could turn into rather substantial sums of money. This was rarely, if ever, intentionally done, since it was nearly impossible for the malefactor to funnel the money anywhere useful due to various oversights by banks, governments, and the software itself. Regardless, it was a huge pain in the ass to track the source and then fix. Thus, Marcus was overdosing on coffee to keep sharp. One slip of a fraction was just that, a slip. Two wasn't yet a pattern, but it was definitely a red flag. If he found three, he had to send out an alert to his superiors, which would likely result in an all-night lockdown while the development team went back through every line of code in the software.

In the seven years Marcus had worked for the company, this had only happened three times, and it had always ended up being deemed a fluke. Last time it had taken a group of fifteen programmers about twelve hours to scour tens of thousands of lines of code. Adding to the tedium and confusion was the fact that everyone wrote code a little differently, which meant someone unfamiliar with another programmer's style would spend just as much time deciphering it as checking for evil schemes to embezzle millions.

After a couple hours of diligent scheme thwarting, Marcus shifted into neutral, having found nothing further out of the ordinary. It was time for a late lunch, so Marcus took a peek outside to check the weather. It was dark grey out, but the rain had held off so far. Constituting one of the day's major decisions, Marcus chose to risk it and eat outside with Sir Regi. He would stay near the office, however, in case a down-pour poured down. Marcus bought a hotdog and some chips from one of the vendors near the building and sat side-saddle on his motorcycle. Every few bites he would pinch off a piece of bun or a chip and toss it to Sir Regi, who gobbled it up quickly.

"He's perfect," said Mestoph as he and Leviticus watched Marcus from a bench at the edge of the park.

"This guy? If he were any more boring and mild mannered, he'd be dead," said Leviticus.

Mestoph gave him a look that said that was the whole point. Leviticus thought about it; they were looking for someone under the radar, and it didn't get much further under the radar than this schmuk. Marcus couldn't possibly be on the To-Watch List of anyone in Heaven or Hell, making him the perfect pawn for their plan.

"So what's his incentive to do what we want?" asked Leviticus.

Mestoph sighed. "Have you not been paying attention over the last few days? He would do anything for that girl at the coffee shop. He pines for her like I do for an eighteen-year old single-malt."

"And how do we get her?"

Mestoph smiled. "That's the most beautiful part of the plan."

While Mestoph and Leviticus had been talking, Sir Regi had been doing simple tricks for the bits of food that Marcus had been tossing him. He had been standing on his hind legs when the little dog's ear twitched and he became distracted. He dropped down on all fours and turned to face the two men who were walking by. One of the men, a tall, lean black man with long dreads, turned and winked. At first Marcus thought the man was winking at him, but at second glance he was obviously winking at Sir Regi. The little Scottie let out a low, deep growl. Startled by the unusual outburst from Sir Regi, Marcus looked back up at the passing men, expecting some kind of danger. He saw the black man whispering something to his friend, an olive-skinned man wearing some kind of Middle-Eastern looking robe. The robed man looked shocked and exclaimed "Really?" in response. They looked back toward Sir Regi, and the man with the dreads nodded toward the dog, and then they quickly walked off. Sir Regi still seemed unsettled.

"Now what?" asked Leviticus, once they had gotten a block away from Marcus and his dog.

"Now we need a Prophecy,' said Mestoph.

"There's always a Prophecy," said Leviticus, with a scowl.

"And an Omen," added Mestoph.

"Fuck."

When going over the basics of his plan with Leviticus, Mestoph had intentionally left two specific details out of the conversation. If he had told Leviticus about having to *steal* a Prophecy and an Omen, the Angel would have flipped his shit. This was understandable as Prophecies and Omens were the most protected, valuable, and powerful items in all of Heaven and Hell, respectively. Now that Leviticus had become invested in the plan, he was much more likely to hear Mestoph out.

To understand the usefulness of these two pivotal documents, one needs to understand what they do. Omens

18

and Prophecies are equal and opposite in the way they perform. They both act as binding contracts or personal laws that add predetermined milestones in history: either global or singularly personal. Where the two differ are the types of things they cover. To put it simply, Omens cause bad things while Prophecies cause good things. The lines can blur a bit as some good or bad things are rather subjective.

Omens and Prophecies are used sparingly, at least these days, for two reasons— both involving freewill. As a part of the Ancient Agreement between Heaven and Hell, the two entities, then made up solely of God and Satan, vowed to give humans the freedom of will to make or break their own lives. They would wait until death to be judged and sent on their merry or not-so-merry way. The second reason Prophecies and Omens are rarely used is because of the oversight of Freewill International.

As the battle for the End of Times began to ramp up about two thousand years ago, both Heaven Inc. and Hell Industries began to enact Prophecies and Omens left and right, some affecting drastic, broad, sweeping changes, and many contradicting one another. These unfair and unethical changes came to the attention of highly evolved humans of scrupulous moral character from various religions and walks of life such as Gandhi, Mother Theresa, and Larry King. These highly attuned—and usually unbelievably old—humans came together to form the watchdog group later known as Freewill International.

It's kind of like what would happen if the Justice League was run by the Swiss.

Because they still resided on Earth, whether dead or alive, they weren't bound by the Ancient Agreement like God or Satan were and could meddle directly in the affairs of humans. This meddling was strictly a last resort tactic as the threat, only realized after their one great interaction, was usually more than enough to keep Heaven and Hell in line. That one great interaction was named Judas Iscariot. Freewill International weren't big fans of God's attempt to use his son to try and grant blanket amnesty to everyone in one fell swoop, giving every saint, sinner, and in-between a free ride to Heaven and throwing off the balance. In the end they showed God and Satan what one well-placed whisper could do.

Because of the perceived power and constant vigil of Freewill International, both Heaven and Hell put great measures in place to keep themselves and each other from throwing Fate and Freewill completely out of whack. These days it took a considerable amount of wheeling, dealing, and a unanimous vote by their respective Boards of Directors to get a Prophecy or Omen signed. Despite the difficulty of stealing one of each, Mestoph had a plan to make things a great deal easier. In the case of the Prophecy, they would take advantage of the laziness of God and the Board of Directors of Heaven, Inc.

In anticipation of the End Times, when God would need access to Prophecies that were ready to go on short notice, the Research and Development team of Heaven, Inc. had been working on a little thing they called Secure-Signed Prophecies. These were basically form-filled Prophecies that were put on pages of E-Ink paper with a wireless connection so that God could fill in the blanks like a Mad Libs story and then send an email to the Board telling them to put their digital signatures on the Prophecy. This negated the need to call in scribes, arrange a board meeting, and follow the formalities entailed in getting approval to wipe a measly city off the face of the Earth. If the destruction of Sodom and Gomorrah had been as difficult then as it would be now, it probably wouldn't have happened at all.

The security for the R&D department was a great deal

easier to subvert than that of God's office, where the plain old blank pen-and-paper prophecies were usually stored. Mestoph had a pal who was a Hell Industries spy planted in the R&D department, a lowly administrative assistant that owed him a few favors and was pretty loose-lipped after a night of heavy drinking.

Stealing an Omen would be a little more complicated, but seeing as Mestoph wasn't quite as averted to violence and underhandedness as Leviticus, he was okay with having to take on the greater of the two risks. Unlike Heaven, Inc., Hell Industries had no such convenient project in the works. Breaking into Satan's office was out of the question. The security was far too tight and advanced for just Mestoph to overcome; and he had no intention of hiring or bringing into the inner circle any more people than necessary. Instead, Mestoph would have to find an Omen elsewhere.

Satisfied that they had the good beginnings of a plan, the two shook hands to symbolically seal the deal and agreed to get back together as soon as they could both quietly sneak away from their domains.

Chapter 2

Make your own destiny...or steal a Prophecy

Leviticus sat at his desk and stared at the monitor. He was just one of thousands, maybe even millions of Angels sitting in cubicles at that very moment, working away at the day's tasks. Most of his coworkers actually seemed to like their jobs. Most of them hadn't been at it nearly as long as he had, but even the few that had still seemed to believe in what they were doing. Leviticus wasn't sure when he had stopped believing, but he knew it had been a long, long time ago. He no longer went out with the other Angels after work to drink and talk about the good work they had done, the little coups they had scored in the name of righteousness. He faked it just enough to stay below suspicion and did his job just well enough to keep it. After all, it could always get worse – even Heaven needed janitors.

Today he wasn't even pretending to work; he just couldn't bring himself to care. Bits and pieces of Mestoph's plan kept swirling around in his head, making it hard to concentrate. All he could think about were Omens and Prophecies. Mestoph had been right: he was tired, sick and tired. Worse still, he was sick and tired of being sick and tired. Leviticus had once been a major player on the world stage, hobnobbing with Jesus and his apostles, doing the work of the Lord and feeling good about it. But the glory days of plotting and scheming on Earth in the name of the Lord were long behind him. After Judas, things just hadn't been the same. With their orchestration of that great betrayal, Freewill Industries had shown that they could play the same games too. And if they so chose they could play them better.

Once upon a time, Leviticus had been Jesus's forward

reconnaissance during his Spreading the Word of the Lord tour, checking out cities and towns to see how desperate they were for a miracle, how gullible they might be and how they would react if something completely unexplainable happened. The last thing they needed was to find a receptive town only to have them freak out when Jesus did one of his patented parlor tricks and string him up. Not that it hadn't ever happened. They'd had to sneak out of Bethphage like thieves in the night because they had been accused of being thieves in the day for stealing a donkey. It seemed that claiming the Lord needed it was not an acceptable form of currency in Bethphage. They did, of course, steal the donkey on their way out.

Jesus was arrested in Ephraim for being a warlock after he made a dead chicken dance—in hindsight they probably shouldn't have used a cooked one that people had already eaten from—and Leviticus and Judas had to break him out of jail before they stoned him the next morning. The townspeople would have stoned him that night, but they were too busy vomiting reanimated pieces of chicken.

They all had to sneak out of Caesarea Philippi after a string of suicides were attributed to Jesus. He had given a sermon while floating off the edge of a nearby cliff, stating it was his faith in God that kept him aloft. He had meant it to be metaphorical, but when a dozen bodies were found at the bottom of the cliff the next day, it wasn't hard to find someone to blame.

After they had been run out of enough places, they had realized they had to keep that sort of thing to a minimum or the rumors of his failures would outpace the rumors of his miracles. There were only so many small, backwater towns back in that day that you could wipe out before people started getting a bit suspicious. That was before CNN and the internet, when there were such things as secrets and privacy.

23

Judas' betrayal was a complete surprise to everyone in Heaven, Inc, and a bigger surprise to Jesus himself. They had been close friends, and he took it very personally. The two of them hadn't spoken since; when he got back to Heaven, he made sure Judas never worked in the upper echelon again. That's not to say that Heaven, Inc. didn't spin it all the best way possible. It *had* helped jump-start a whole new religion, which to be honest was what Jesus and his apostles had been trying rather futilely to do the whole time. However, let's not confuse getting most of what Heaven, Inc. wanted with having the plan backfire on Freewill International. They had proved without a doubt that despite the fact that they didn't have divine or otherworldly powers, they could play on our level—and they could play well. It was a big coming out party for them and it set them up for life.

Nowadays Leviticus sat in front of a computer screen and looked for things. Not *just* things, but things that made sense. He looked for patterns, trends, and shifts in just about everything. He was looking for what he called investment opportunities. He scoured newspapers, local news channels, social networks, and occasionally eavesdropped on coffee shop banter. If he noticed the sentiment toward a particular politician was shifting, or that people were suddenly becoming interested in locally grown produce, or if people were tired of shows about nothing but doctors fucking, then he would write up reports for God to check out every morning and decide where to shift their focus.

God would arrange for a sex scandal involving one politician to draw attention away from another one of his that was falling behind in the polls. God would plant the seed of an idea in a filmmaker's mind that a documentary about the evils of the agriculture industry was needed, and plant another seed in an organic farmer's mind who was rather savvy in the art of public speaking and could slip a few "Thank Gods" and "Praise the Lords" innocuously in his interview. Individually they would only count for fractions of a percent gains in the hearts and minds of the public, but a few fractions here and there, day in and day out added up.

Or they would, if there weren't someone in Hell Industries doing exactly the same thing. Some days Leviticus was ahead of the game, and some days his counterpart, whom he liked to imagine was a mind-numbingly boring demon named Carl who had gone to Hell for tax evasion, came out ahead. It was yet another example of the futility of everything they did, and the unending stalemate that had stricken progress toward The End.

Being a member of Team Jesus had gotten him the job he now loathed, but at the time it had been a big win for him. Leviticus had jumped up from ramen noodles to steak overnight. He moved from a small, windowless basement apartment to a swanky, top-floor pad in one of the nicer urban areas near the center of Heaven Two thousand years later, he was still in the same spot, working just hard enough to keep his head above water.

It wasn't until Leviticus had met Mestoph on one of his rare on-Earth assignments—Leviticus was trying to stop an uprising in Kenya while Mestoph was trying to start it— that he found someone else felt the same way. After weeks in a stalemate, they had met at a Demon bar in the middle of the desert to talk things out since. After a few drinks, they had both been complaining about how pointless their jobs really were. It had shocked him, and at first even worried him, to find a kindred spirit in a Demon, but seeing as everyone else had swallowed the Heavenly Kool-Aid without a question, he couldn't be picky about where his friends came from.

Thinking of all the times they had bitched and moaned about how much they hated their jobs made Leviticus a bit melancholy and more than a bit angry. Finally, he sighed and jumped to his feet.

"Fuck this!" he said, louder than he had intended, and walked away from his desk and his job. A few of the Angels in the cubicles surrounding him looked up from their work, giving him a confused or disappointed look, but then felt it was probably better if they didn't pry. They hunkered back down to business and pretended they didn't see him storm off, mumbling to himself.

Leviticus spent the next hour walking aimlessly through the headquarters of Heaven, Inc. Though he wasn't sure why, he took a detour by one of the supply closets, where he picked up one of those white, disposable haz-mat bunny suits, a large fire extinguisher, and an a gas mask (the World War II kind with the long hose that had a scrubber attached to the end) and walked with unknown intent but fully protected from any hazardous waste he might encounter when he got to wherever he was heading. He nonchalantly interrupted a department meeting when he used a conference room as a shortcut. The people in the meeting just stared, mouths agape but silent. He wondered if that was what happened when people went postal; they just suddenly found themselves with a gun and a pile of bodies, sparing only the cute receptionist so she could say what a quiet person they were when the news anchor interviewed her.

Leviticus finally realized where he was going. He cursed out loud as he found himself standing in the long, gleaming white hallway that ended in the Research and Development department of Heaven Inc, where the Prophecies were housed. The labs were soundproof, fireproof, bulletproof, waterproof, and Demon-proof. He might as well try and steal the Ark of the Covenant or Mary Magdalene's virginity— although supposedly that had been stolen more than once. The thought of stealing a whore's virginity brought a slight grin to his face behind his gas mask, but the sobriety of the situation hit him, and his scowl returned. It was the same scowl that had popped on his face the second Mestoph had told him about stealing the Prophecy.

"Steal a Prophecy, Leviticus." said Leviticus, in a high-pitched mimicry of Mestoph's Demonic accent, which sounded kind of like a mix of Creole and South African with a dash of German: in other words, exactly like Klingon. Leviticus wondered how people had described the Demonic tongue before *Star Trek*. He shook his head, trying to focus. As ridiculous as Mestoph's plan was, it was his only hope for getting out—and hope was something he hadn't had in a *long* time. He needed a break, even if it was only the bleak hope of actually getting out of the End of the World business. Leviticus took a step toward the door, and then another, until finally he was walking down the long hallway.

His footsteps echoed loudly in the stark, bleached white hallways. So loudly he just knew someone would hear him at the guard post on the other side of the thick glass doors that lead to the R&D department. Up until he opened those doors, he could always turn back. Once he was in, there was no calling it off; he would be punished whether or not he stole even so much as a stapler.

Only the highest ranking Angels in the Heaven Inc. hierarchy were allowed inside the department. Whatever they did in there, it was not for mortal eyes or rank-and-file Angels like Leviticus. Even those who worked in R&D were allowed only severely limited and monitored access to the general population of Heaven for fear of letting secrets slip. Most mingled, married, or fooled around within the R&D pool, which created a semi-incestuous, House of Plantagenet-style twisted but elite circle. How Mestoph had learned about the Secure-Signed Prophecies was beyond Leviticus—and probably beyond Mestoph, for all he knew.

His thoughts had taken him all the way to automatic

sliding-glass door that lead into the R&D department. He punched the code Mestoph had given him into the keypad, and the magnetic locks released and the door slid open. Leviticus was pretty sure he didn't want to know where or how Mestoph had gotten the code. Now, only a manned security booth and a second set of doors stood between him and labs. The security guard, who had been watching some weird Japanese game show that involved being blindfolded and sticking your head into a box of bugs or Jell-O or something else equally pointless on one of the security monitors, glanced at Leviticus and turned back, nonplussed. It was a second or two before the guard turned back around, the perplexing image having taken a while to register in his rather simple brain. Leviticus stood in front of the security guard wearing the now foggy gas mask and paper bunny suit and was carrying the fire extinguisher in one hand and the hose in the other. Leviticus pointed the hose at the guard before he could push an alarm, pull a gun, or scream, and released a thick, white gas that quickly filled the anteroom.

The guard had been trying to stand, and the noxious Halon chemicals finally suffocated him just as he reached his full height. He crumpled back to the ground in a sad little arc. Leviticus reached over and turned off the monitor with the annoying game show. At the same time the guard's soul, wispy and mostly transparent, rose from his body and up to eye level with Leviticus.

"I was watching that, asshole," said the guard just before he faded away.

If the guard had been a decent person, he would be back in Heaven and on the job in no time, but Leviticus decided not to think too much about that now. He dropped the fire extinguisher, stepped over the body of the guard, and stared at an array of buttons at the security console. After poring over the buttons, none of which were labeled, he finally found a buzzer underneath the desk. Hedging his bets that it was more like a pawn shop in a seedy neighborhood than a silent alarm in a bank, he hit the button.

The second glass door slid open. The door quickly whooshed closed again after he stepped through, leaving Leviticus to suddenly wonder how he was supposed to get back out. He would have to worry about that on the way back.

After he had walked around a few corners, he ripped the long, trailing hose off of the gas mask so that he could finally get some air that wasn't hot and damp. He would keep the mask itself on in hopes that he could hide his identity from the security cameras and any staff who might be hanging around to get in some late night brown-nosing or just stealing office supplies. If he actually did run into anyone, he was almost certainly screwed since he knew he wasn't supposed to be there, and they definitely knew he wasn't supposed to be there. Leviticus wasn't much of a fighter and didn't figure he could take out anyone in hand-to-hand combat—and wasn't sure he wanted to—before they pulled an alarm or just shot him themselves. For all he knew, everyone in R&D was an ex-Swiss Guard, carried an SG 552 Commando assault rifle, and was just itching to spill some holy blood.

He tried to put such thoughts out of his mind as he navigated his way through the maze of hallways, offices, and conference rooms that made up the enormous Research and Development wing. Mestoph had sketched out a relatively accurate map for him, but it only had the direct route he needed to reach the Prophecy Research Lab. He passed by doors with seemingly innocuous signs on them such as Origami Papal Hat Development, God's Glorious Light Tanning Bed Testing, and one rather long sign that read: Completely Innocent Stuff That Couldn't Possibly Harm Anyone But You Should Still Stay Away Research. Then there were the more ominous or confusing ones like Time-Traveling Monkey Paradox Reduction, Wildlife Weaponization Foundation, and Vaginal Exorcism Training.

Along the walls were various trophy cases with awards for All-Saints Softball tournaments, Angels of the Month, and Wii Bowling League—the kind of thing that probably littered the trophy cases of any large company on Earth. However, there were also certificates of congratulation and small plaques of merit covering a wide range of oddities. There was one that said Least Number of Resurrections, which had a bronze Angel holding his own severed and haloed head while giving a thumbs up. Another said Most Fatal Wounds Caused By Non-Standard Office Supplies; that one had a giant bronzed carrot comically impaling an Angel. Next to that was a Best Satan-So-Fat Joke award with a morbidly obese, bronzed Satan atop a small wooden base. There was even a Best Use of Skylab Before It Crashed award, which had a small caption that indicated the winning idea was a Kegerator.

There were also safety-oriented signs and banners that listed the number of days since an unintentional Apocalypse had been averted (which currently read *one*, though the record was in the triple digits). Another sign showed the number of days since the last Transporter accident (also at one) with a tally of total accidents underneath that had been covered up with cardboard. Leviticus took that to mean it either could no longer count high enough or the number was just too embarrassing. Finally, there was an odd one that was a small chalk board on an unlabeled door that said "Number of Days Since Santa Rampage" (it was at thirteen, with the previous record being twelve) that looked like it got erased relatively frequently.

After a while Leviticus stopped reading the signs and plaques because they seemed either too ridiculous or too disturbing to be true—or so he told himself.

He looked down at his sketchily sketched map of the R&D department and realized he was at the X that marked the spot. In front of him was a stark white, unmarked door, but on the map it was labeled as the lab he was looking for. He looked at the map again and retraced his route, just to be sure. He was hoping he was wrong.

The stark door was stark in its starkest possibility. In fact, at this moment it wasn't even a door, just a white, solid metal rectangle. There was no knob, handle, keyhole, lock, latch, keypad, button, or even a drive-through speaker to yell at. It was at this point that Leviticus considered abandoning the plan—the plan that had passed the point of no return ten minutes prior—and going home to await his impending arrest. Then he heard a noise that told him he wouldn't have to do much waiting. Echoing down the hallway, though how far he couldn't tell, was the unmistakable sound of footsteps.

Leviticus froze. He'd been fairly convinced he'd get caught to begin with, and this just proved his suspicion. As the footsteps got closer, his survival instincts kicked in and he began to look for a place to hide. He went down the hallway, trying several doors before one finally opened and he slipped in, closing the door and locking it behind him.

He looked around the long, narrow room that seemed to stretch out further than the eye could see. It was filled with row after row of thick-glassed vats containing a nearly transparent blue liquid that looked like a thick version of the cleaning solution barbers stuck their scissors and combs in. Suspended within the liquid of each vat, of which there had to be thousands, was what appeared to be a living and breathing Santa Claus. Running to each vat were various tubes, some with fluids flowing in and some with fluids flowing out. In one tube was a single wire that every so often would arc with electricity, which in turn would cause the Santa Claus to twitch mildly.

Although they all wore the trademark red clothes and hat, no two Santas appeared to be alike. They were all of varying size, build, and color. A few had what seemed like randomly substituted appendages: snakes instead of arms, a toaster instead of a head, pogo sticks instead of legs. One looked more like a Swiss Army knife than Santa Claus, with its left hand being a corkscrew, the right a can opener, its legs a fork and spoon, and in place of its head was the empty spot where a pair of tweezers or toothpick should've been—but, like most Swiss Army knives, it was missing. Leviticus wondered where it could have gone since it wasn't anywhere in the vat.

He listened at the door for the footsteps. Instead, as he put his ear to the door, the handle jiggled. Leviticus jumped back, startled, and assumed a fake karate pose. Behind him, one of the more normal although rather short Santas began sloshing around in his tank. Leviticus could hear keys in the door now, and he began looking around for some place to hide. A few rows away was an enormous, muscular Santa wearing red Santa pants and typical Santa hat but without a shirt so as to show off his incredibly ripped abs. Leviticus ran for that vat and slid behind it, hoping the bulk of the Santanator would hide him. The door opened and a guard dressed in what looked like riot gear walked through; several of the Santas twitched as he came in. Leviticus noticed that he carried a large, futuristic looking rifle that was probably devised specially for the R&D guards.

The guard walked in and looked around, eyeballing several of the Santas with an oddly pleased smile on his face. He locked the door, set his riot helmet and rifle against the wall near the door, and then turned back toward the rows of Santas as he rubbed his hands together in a look of glee that made Leviticus nervous. He was about 5' 10" with a build that suggested he had been in excellent shape about ten years ago but had let things go recently. He had a short, but not quite buzzed, haircut that was typical of military types, but with a goatee and mustache of deep reddish brown that showed he was a little more lax than your average special-ops wannabe. Despite having lost his ripped physique, he still had the habit of walking with his arms and chest puffed out like a bulldog as he drifted from one vat to another. He was probably the kind of guy who, while he was alive, spent all his time talking about what a big shot he had been in high school. The guard tapped a vat at random, causing an eagle-headed Santa to flinch.

Leviticus suddenly recognized the creepy smile as that of a kid who enjoyed torturing neighborhood cats and dogs. The guard made what seemed like a well-rehearsed tour of his favorite Santas, tapping and knocking on the glass as he passed. He, of course, stopped in front of the massively muscular Santa behind which Leviticus was hiding. Leviticus slid down, trying to make himself smaller, and hid in the tangle of tubes. The Santanator twitched and jerked more rapidly as the guard approached. The guard pulled a pronged baton out of a holster on his belt. He hit a button built into the handle and a loud, clicking arc of electricity shot between the prongs, sending Santanator into a slow, sloshy fury.

All of the vats were secured to the floor by four large bolts, one at each corner of the base. As the Santanator moved in the thick liquid, the vat jostled slightly, and Leviticus noticed that the bolts had loosened considerably, probably a result of a long history of the hulking Santa being teased and tortured by the guard. Leviticus tried to twist the nut off the bolt with his bare fingers. It was still tight enough to make it difficult to unscrew bare handed, but in between rounds of taunting and sloshing he was able to get one and then a second nut unscrewed.

The guard's taunting escalated, and the thick blue liquid

33

began to slosh out of the top of the vat where it was open to the air. The guard stuck the tip of the stun baton into an overflow pipe. An enormous and sickening smile grew on his face, and then he pressed the button to send a jolt of electricity into the highly conductive fluid. The Santanator let out an eerie, bubbly scream, braced against the walls of the vat, and jerked back and forth.

Leviticus wasn't sure how far this game would progress and what would happen when the guard tired of taunting this particular Santa. He felt this was his only window of opportunity to take matters into his own hands. He decided to give chance a little help and timed a full-shouldered shove against the vat.

The movement caught the attention of the guard who let out a dumbfounded "Whuh?" but his sudden attention to detail was too late, as Leviticus and Santanator had pushed the vat past the tipping point. It began a free fall that seemed to happen in slow motion. As a wave of thick blue liquid spilled over the edge of the vat, Leviticus thought it was an image of David and Goliath in reverse. A sick, sadistic David and a tortured, genetically altered Goliath in red velvet pants and a fur-trimmed hat.

Leviticus shook the image from his mind as the vat hit the hard tiles and shattered, leaving a slick-wet monster Santa Claus covered in glass shards curled up on the floor. Leviticus looked down at the Santanator and then up at the guard, who followed suit by looking down at the hulk and then up at Leviticus.

"What have you done?" said the guard, scared, confused, and outraged all at once. His swirl of emotions didn't last long as Santanator stood up, grabbed the guard by his head, lifted him off the ground, and then smashed him against the next nearest vat in rapid succession. Leviticus heard a sickeningly wet thump-crush and then a piercing shattering as the guard's head collapsed and the vat of the Swiss Army Santa spider-webbed and shattered, sending another wave of the blue stuff out across the floor.

Leviticus jumped back, bumping into the vat behind him, and stared at the unfolding scene. Santanator turned to look at Leviticus and paused for several seconds, which seemed eternities each, and then smiled.

"Merry fucking Christmas!" it said and then took off running toward the door, taking it off its hinges with a shoulder and continuing down the hall. Leviticus stood as still as possible as the Swiss Army Santa began to jump and jitter on the ground where it landed, trying to get up. Since it had no real arms or legs, it skittered as the various tools swung and flailed until finally, by pure dumb luck, it managed to jump upright on its fork and spoon legs. Instead of walking, it rolled around like a cartwheeling child, bumping into anything and everything as it went. Leviticus couldn't tell if it could see where it was going or if it was blindly moving around the narrow room. Finally, the Swiss Army Santa built up some speed and rolled toward the door; however, it missed by several feet, and the sharp-hooked can opener arm impaled itself into the wall, where it struggled to free itself.

The sound of an alarm brought Leviticus out of his paralysis. Santanator had no doubt finally brought the attention of security down on him. Feeling his chance to steal the Prophecy being yanked away from him, Leviticus came up with a quick plan. He pulled off the easy to remove pieces riot gear from the body of the former sadistic security guard, which was mostly just the vest, tactical cargo pants, and a thin navy blue jacket with "Security" written on the back in big yellow letters, replaced the hoseless gas mask with the riot helmet, and grabbed the futuristic rifle.

As Leviticus picked up the futuristic rifle, which hummed with a subtle vibration as if it were purring softly,

Swiss Army Santa managed to leverage its spoon leg against the wall and jerk itself free. It dislodged with enough force to throw it backwards into the nearest Santa vat, shattering the glass and freeing yet another Santa. It revved up its cartwheeling and this time made it out of the door, missing Leviticus by only inches. Left standing in the shattered remains of the newly broken vat was a tiny Santa with the disproportionate body of a dwarf but the head of a normal-sized human. Slapped somewhat crooked on that head was a mouth at least three times larger than normal. It was currently smiling at Leviticus.

After a minute of the two staring each other down, the tiny, cartoonish Santa opened its mouth, which seemed to suddenly take up more surface than it had head for. Hidden inside was a jet engine. This was not immediately apparent to Leviticus, because he had never expected to see a jet engine within the mouth of anything, let alone a two-foot dwarf Santa Claus. As the rotor within the Santa's mouth began to turn, the concept became much clearer and more frightening, and Leviticus expected the diminutive Santa to hurtle forward at some insane speed nearing that of light, or sound at the very least. Instead, the opposite began to happen as tiny bits of debris near the Santa were sucked up and into its mouth. The tiny engine quickly gained speed, and soon larger items were being pulled toward the nexus of swirling debris that disappeared into the mouth of the Vacuum Santa.

By the time the danger that he was in finally dawned on him, which was easily excusable considering the absurdity of everything that had happened in the last several minutes, Leviticus was already sliding toward the Santa's mouth on the slick blue liquid all over the floor. He managed to grab onto one of the tubes leading into a vat with one hand as his feet were swept out from under him. The suction had grown to the point where the tube had gone taught, leaving him flailing

36

wildly in the air. The tube was slippery with vat goo, and Leviticus could feel himself slowly sliding closer to the turbine Santa.

Not knowing how much more suction the Vacuum Santa was capable of, and even less sure of his ability to continue hanging on to the slippery tube, Leviticus did the only thing he knew to do—he killed Santa Claus. Leviticus leveled the rifle and pulled the trigger. He squeezed his eyes shut as he squeezed the trigger and had a brief moment of disappointment when he heard absolutely nothing. Not *pew-pew*, nor *bang-bang*, nor even a Heaven-shattering *kaboom*. Instead there was silence, absolute and complete. Not even the sound of the roaring engine of Vacuum Santa could be heard.

When Leviticus slammed down on the floor in a splash of blue goop, he finally opened his eyes. In a straight line from his feet and all the way to the end of the long room was a path of debris and ashy dust, as if a giant bowling ball of energy had hit Vacuum Santa and then kept going. This imaginary bowling ball of doom had not only turned everything it touched into dust, but also left a wake of slightly less destructive destruction, in which vats and the various apparatus that supported them were shattered and twisted into pretzely, knotted shapes. Flopping around on the floor were dozens of stunned Santas, as well as many that remained motionless and likely dead. At the thought of an army of mutant Santas rampaging through the halls—So *that's* what the sign meant, he thought—Leviticus bolted from the Hall of Santas, wishing that Santanator had not busted the door off the hinge. He ran down the R&D hallway, where the sound of the alarms rang in his ears, again reminding him that a full security force would be there any moment.

Once again he stood in front of the stark white door, which had been his whole reason for coming. Leviticus pushed on the door and nothing happened. It didn't even give in a little like most doors. He tried pushing harder but was met with the same result. Pushing turned into pounding and pounding turned into him running full tilt at the door with his shoulder like the Santanator, only to find himself stopped suddenly and painfully.

"Please open?" asked Leviticus, but the door neither opened nor replied.

"Open, damn you!"

Again, the door did nothing.

"Fine, you want to do this the hard way? But you're going to regret this," Leviticus warned the door, though he hoped that he wasn't about to make a tragic mistake.

Leviticus aimed the futuristic rifle at the door and paused, giving the completely inanimate door one last chance to comply, and then pulled the trigger. Again there was total silence, one so loud that it drowned out the klaxon of the alarms. This time, however, Leviticus did not close his eyes, which allowed him to see a large green ball of swirly, glowy energy grow at the tip of the rifle and then hurtle toward the door at an amazing speed…only to hit the door and then fall straight to the floor with no effect. The swirly-twirly ball sat on the floor, motionless except for its internal swirling and twirling.

"Oh come on!" Leviticus screamed.

In a mild tantrum, he went to kick at the ball of energy.

It wasn't until he was committed fully to the kick that he thought kicking a ball of energy that had taken out a room full of Santas in bottles was probably a really bad idea. Luckily for him the ball dissipated, and his foot connected, poorly and at a painful angle, with the door. At the force of the rather feeble kick, the door creaked and then slowly toppled over into the room. Leviticus looked around, a small part of him hoping that someone was around to witness his amazing feat of strength.

In reality, the ball of energy had hit with incredible force, but unbeknownst to Leviticus the projectile was designed specifically for Santa suppression and to not cause any damage to the infrastructure of the R&D department. Regardless, there's no way to negate the laws of physics, even in Heaven, and the substantial force of the impact was enough—though just barely—to weaken what *was* an unimaginably strong and secure door.

Leviticus marched into the lab with an air of righteousness, as if he were Caesar marching triumphantly into Rome after victory at the Battle of Munda. He strolled over to a pedestal where three glass scroll cases rested on velvet pads beneath a glass display. Within each scroll case was a rolled-up prototype of the Secure-Signed Prophecies that he and Mestoph were after.

The Santa rampage had been a rather fortuitous event, considering the acquisition of the rifle. Leviticus had no idea the rifle was the only way he could've gotten into the lab without a code. Nor did he know that if the alarms hadn't already been blaring when he smashed the display case and swiped a single scroll, they definitely would be now. He slid the glass case underneath his riot vest and turned around to see a security guard walk into the room.

"All clear?' the guard asked a panicked and bewildered Leviticus.

"Uhh...yeah," he said hesitantly as Leviticus realized he was not, in fact, busted. "...All clear. Only minor damage."

"Alright, continue your sweep of the corridor." ordered the guard, clearly his superior—for the moment at least.

The guard turned and walked further down the corridor with. Leviticus followed soon after. He saw the Superior Officer take off at a full run as a giant purple lizard with a Santa hat and ill-fitting red pants scurried down an intersecting corridor. A screaming guard hung on to the lizard's neck. Leviticus took advantage of the distraction and went the opposite direction, back toward the way he had entered R&D. Once he was certain the way was clear, he, too, took off into a full run, letting off another shot of the futuristic rifle as he neared the sealed-off area of the guard post. The green ball swirly-twirlied its way down the corridor and smashed through the glass on his end of the guard post. The concussion that followed shattered the glass wall, and door to the guard booth, and obliterated all the equipment in the room. When the energy ball hit the opposite wall, it thudded to the floor and stopped.

Leviticus peeled off the pieces of stolen guard apparel, making sure to stick the scroll case deep into the pockets of his robe, and threw them into the green energy ball that still sat swirling on the floor. He'd become rather fond of the rifle and felt a pang of remorse at having to part with it. *No evidence*, he thought and tossed it into the energy ball as he ran off.

Behind him, a small supernova bloomed out from the center of the glowing energy orb, the result of all the unstable ammo within the rifle reacting and chain-reacting, and ripped a small, mostly innocuous hole in time.

Leviticus ran down the hallways of headquarters with an enormous smile on his face, jumping up to hit exit signs and clapping, hooting, and high-fiving people as he passed. He was living high on adrenaline and excitement, like a kid who had just won his high school championship. He felt free and alive like he hadn't in at least two thousand years, and the thought that he might be able to feel this way forever prolonged the euphoria all the way out the front doors of Heaven Inc., hopefully for the last time.

God sat at his desk in an office that looked like it could have been a smoking room in a Victorian mansion, backlit by a large window that looked onto the rainbow farms of Heaven. Peter sat opposite God in one of two extremely comfortable chairs that Herman Miller had made for God when he first arrived. The chair was an odd mix of 1950's euro-mod and 17th century French that worked well with each other and the formal opulence of the rest of the office. Peter was in charge of Research and Development for Heaven Inc. and looked like he should play a Roman senator in a Masterpiece Theater rendition of *Titus Andronicus*. He had the extremely short, bowl-cut black hair, the prominent bent nose, and the British accent that were all mandatory to get into a PBS production of anything Roman.

God looked like your grandfather. Good or bad, God looked like everyone's grandfather.

Peter had just finished filling God in on the situation. He looked out the window and saw hundreds of little people—actual little people, as in midgets, dwarfs, leprechauns and so on—climbing up and down ladders to inspect the light readings and structural integrity of each rainbow. God had only nodded in understanding when Peter had finished. Several seconds had passed, and he hadn't started yelling. God wasn't mad at Peter; it could have happened to anyone. God leaned back in his dark brown leather chair, which was dotted by large, brass buttons. The seat creaked in a soft and melodic way that pleased God. He steepled his fingers in front of his mouth and looked up at a tapestry on the walnut paneled wall that depicted The Fall of the Angel Lucifer. The artist, an old woman who had lived during the 11th or 12th century—God couldn't remember anymore—had portrayed

Satan as a leathery looking half-bat, half-man creature that He had always thought was a little unfair to Lucifer. Not unfair enough to change it, but He still felt that people misunderstood His relationship with Satan. After all, He had His uses. This thought gave God an idea, and He leaned over the intercom on his Brazilian tulipwood Louis XIV desk.

"Mary?" God asked.

"Yes, God?" came a scratchy voice on the other end of the intercom.

"Mary, can you get Peter on the phone?"

"R&D Peter or St. Peter?"

"You just let R&D Peter into my office five minutes ago," said God.

"Yes?"

"And you haven't seen him walk out," explained God.

"So…?"

"St. Peter," God said, sounding somewhat exasperated but trying to hide it.

God looked up from the intercom at R&D Peter, who only shrugged.

"She's your son's girlfriend. Or one of them."

"My son, in all his glory, is like a one-man rock band on tour. The groupies, the parties, only he hasn't performed in two thousand years," said God. He sighed. "You part a sea and suddenly you're a miracle worker."

"Wasn't that Moses?" asked Peter

"Huh?"

"The Red Sea. That wasn't your son, that was Moses," explained Peter

"Oh…then what did Jesus do?" asked God, genuinely bewildered.

"Died for their Sins?"

"Oh, yeah. Well, that *is* kinda something," said God

"Wasn't that the point, Sir? You sent your only son to

die for mankind."

God shook His head. "No, I sent my only son because he was getting in the way. Showboating and upstaging me at board meetings."

"Well, I hate to be the one to break it, but that kind of backfired," said Peter, laughing uncomfortably. There was a long, awkward silence. Peter wasn't sure if he had insulted God since conversation with Him was full of such odd pauses. When you've been around for all eternity, prompt responses aren't really a priority.

"God? St. Peter is here to see you" blurted Mary's voice from the intercom.

"Send him in," commanded God.

The buzz of the intercom died. Then a lock clicked, two panels of the wall slid apart, and in walked a gorilla of a man. He was well over six feet tall and at least 220 lbs. of bristling muscle. He was wearing a well-tailored suit of fine black wool with subtle silver pinstripes. His salt-and-pepper hair was slicked back in a way that made him look like a finely dressed Russian mobster gorilla. St. Peter was Chief of Security for Heaven Inc, and no one got in without his say so.

God stood up and gripped St. Peter's massive hand. The pressure of the saint's grip made Him wince slightly.

"God, Peter," said St. Peter as he nodded to each and took a seat, barely fitting in the chair. "What can I do for you, gentleman?"

God nodded to R&D Peter, who said, "Well, we think there's a breach in security."

St. Peter's brow arched and his muscles tensed visibly beneath his suit. He took a deep breath and then spoke, "No one gets in unless they're on the list." he said seriously.

God and R&D Peter glanced at each other. God spoke up, "Yeah. And you do a great job. Problem isn't the incoming but the outgoing."

St. Peter looked back and forth between God and R&D Peter. "But the list, it's only for who comes in. No one ever mentioned anything about keeping them in. This is Heaven, not prison—or Hell Industries."

"True. But it's not so much who got out, but…what," said God.

"The Titans!" exclaimed St. Peter, standing up and almost out the door already.

"Sit down. The Titans are under the ocean where we left them" said God. St. Peter reluctantly sat back down, relaxing only slightly.

God pushed a button on his desk, and one of the walls slid open to reveal a large monitor. The grainy security footage showed a robed Angel with a gas mask walk into a guard booth and kill a man with a fire extinguisher. The footage blinked from one vantage point to another as the figure walked down the hallway. The footage skipped a large chunk of time, and suddenly alarms were going off and the Angel was now dressed in parts of a security guard outfit and holding what St. Peter assumed was a GLObE, or Geodesic Laserized Object Emitter. The figure shot the gun and then kicked the door down, which looked impressive on film. The next camera showed the inside of a lab, where the figure smashed and then stole a large glass vial.

R&D Peter turned toward St. Peter. "As you can see, a Prophecy has gone missing." He said. St. Peter's arm swung so fast that R&D Peter nearly rolled backwards out of his seat, afraid he was about to get punched.

"Protocol: St. Peter 12 Red," St. Peter said into a hidden microphone on the cuff of his sleeve. Alarms went off a second later. The dimly lit office suddenly went incredibly bright, and the large window overlooking the rainbow farm went black as barriers slid down over the glass.

"Sweet Fuck!" God screamed, "Cancel the lockdown; it's

already gone."

St. Peter sighed. "Cancel St. Peter 12 Red. Authorization: God Is Good" he said to his sleeve.

The alarms immediately went silent, the lighting dimmed back to normal, and the barriers raised, showing once more the brilliant rainbows growing in the light mist that surrounded the Farm.

"We think we know who took it. What we can't figure is why and how he did it. Also, we don't know where he is now," said R&D Peter.

"Give me a name." said St. Peter.

"Leviticus," said God.

"Luh...vit...uhh...kus..." St. Peter said, grinding syllables through his clenched teeth.

"Now St. Peter, we know you and Leviticus have had run-ins in the past, so don't use this as justification to get revenge. There's probably a really good reason for what he *might* have done," said God.

"Yeah, St. Peter. We *think* he did it. We're not sure. That's your job. Find out, without a doubt, and then find out why," said R&D Peter.

St. Peter took a deep breath before speaking. "If I can prove he did it...can I kill him?"

God and R&D Peter looked at each other and laughed.

"Well, of course. If he's guilty, ice the fucker." God said, holding his fingers like a gun, gangsta sideways.

R&D Peter sighed, grateful that St. Peter hadn't asked about the missing footage. Not being privy to everything that went on in R&D had always been a sore spot for St. Peter. Plus, he didn't want to have to explain all the Santas.

Chapter 3

Braggadocio

Stephanie followed her grandmother down the dark, wooded path. The old woman turned occasionally to make sure she was following, but as usual said absolutely nothing. It was dark and the moon was blotted out more often than not by clouds, but there was a soft ambient light emanating from her grandmother that kept Stephanie from breaking her neck on the various roots, rocks, and branches that reached out from the path to trip her up. The gentle breeze was crisp but not cold, and blew her long black hair softly behind her. The old woman looked back again, a slight smile on her face, and beckoned more emphatically.

Finally, and for the first time ever, they reached the end of the path, or at least this part of the path. It opened to a circular clearing with a small family graveyard at the center of it. It was surrounded by black gothic wrought iron fencing with heavy chains and intricate tassels connecting ornate posts capped with lifelike iron ravens. Directly in the middle of the cemetery was a headstone with Stephanie's name on it. The birth date matched what she had always known to be her birthday, but the death date was marred and eroded to the point that she couldn't discern anything more than the fact that the month had an R in it.

Her grandmother smiled as she pointed at the headstone, motioning her to come forward, but the smile slowly turned into concern and then terror as she gazed at something behind Stephanie. Grams opened her mouth to scream, but nothing came out, and then she disappeared, scrambling and clawing at the headstone as she vanished, leaving Stephanie by herself in the clearing. The feeling creeping up the back of Stephanie's neck quickly corrected her: she was not alone after all.

Slowly, Stephanie turned around and glimpsed a large, dark figure against the backdrop of the woods. Its shape was hard to discern because she couldn't seem to focus on it for more than a split second. Whatever it was shifted and moved faster than her eyes could adjust. Stephanie felt cold and tingly, and a fear she had never felt before grew in her chest. She was shaking, but her body wouldn't do what she told it. The shifting form was sliding, maybe even floating, toward her, and she could make out the hint of feathers and wings. The creature, which she could now tell was as black as the deepest trenches of the sea, spread a series of three pairs of large, rapidly fluttering wings to reveal a pale, white face with an unusually elongated jaw and neck.

Stephanie still couldn't move, even as she felt its cold, damp breath on her neck. The creature's mouth opened wide, so wide that it didn't seem to ever stop opening, and Stephanie knew that it meant to drain her like a vampire. Just before it struck, Stephanie heard what sounded like a cross between the noise of an arc of electricity and that of paper ripping, and she felt as if she were momentarily being pulled inside out through her own belly button.

A swirling and shimmering green gash in what Stephanie could only think of as Space and Time appeared, and Stephanie stumbled out of the rip. A different Stephanie. A Stephanie not herself. The other Stephanie was wearing what looked like an old World War II gas mask and holding a futuristic rifle. "Shit, more Nephilim," said Other Stephanie as she shot the black-winged fluttery vampire-bird-thing.

As Other Stephanie pulled the trigger and a big green light sprang forth from the barrel, Stephanie bolted upright in her bed. She was back in her bedroom. She was covered in sweat and was breathing heavily. She looked around, and a slow calm began to fill that cold fear that she had felt only moments before. After several seconds, she was satisfied that the nightmare was truly gone and her world had returned to normal

She often had dreams in which her grandmother lead her down paths of enlightenment, literal and figurative. She'd taken Grams' death rather hard, and these continued visits were something of a consolation. She wasn't sure if the connection was directly between her and Grams, or if it was because Stephanie was living in Grams' house, which she'd inherited. The bedroom was almost exactly the way Grams had left it when she died. This was still Grams' house, not Stephanie's.

She wasn't sure if she didn't change the house out of respect for Grams, or out of fear that making it her own would be admitting her grandmother was definitely gone. She also worried that the act of settling into the house would also mean settling for good. Stephanie had had always dreamed of living an adventurous life, only coming back to Grams' now and then to gather her thoughts and finances before she set off again to destinations unknown.

She had seen many things on the dream journeys with Grams that had exhilarated her, but they were no substitute for a life of her own. Stephanie had also seen disturbing things with Grams. Certain minor events that had yet to pass, like the death of a distant relative or a surprise change in weather—Grams had always been very concerned about the weather— but never anything like the creature in the dream. Gram had been scared, and then that ghastly black-winged vampire had banished her. At least Stephanie had shown up to save herself.

Mestoph appeared in the alley next to the coffee shop in a puff of black smoke. The alley was empty save for a stray cat digging through the trash. It darted away, startled by the cork-popping sound and sudden gust of wind from Mestoph's teleporting. Just as the smoke cleared, there was another loud pop and a cottony puff of thick white smoke that quickly dissipated into the gloomy grayness of the day.

Leviticus had a ridiculously big grin on his face.

"You look like some perverted kid who just got fondled by his favorite uncle," said Mestoph.

Leviticus shook his head, slightly amused and slightly disgusted. "You'll never guess what I did," he said.

"Finally got your first touch of a real woman's breast, and not that water balloon you like to fondle in the dark?"

"Aww, isn't that sweet, projecting your deficiencies on me," said Leviticus.

"Alright, Virgin Mary, tell me what cute little misadventure you had on your field trip," said Mestoph in a sickly sweet maternal voice.

Leviticus pulled out a gleaming glass vial wrapped in intricate chrome filigree and flipped it in his left hand with a cocky and overly self-satisfied look on his face. "Behold, a Prophecy!" he said, after some minor legerdemain of spinning and rolling the vial in one hand.

"Nope. Not falling for it," said Mestoph.

Leviticus looked down at the vial, crestfallen, and sighed. Just as the Demon was beginning to let a small smirk of victory creep onto his face, Leviticus tossed the vial toward Mestoph. It tumbled and flipped in slow motion as uncertainty began to show on Mestoph's face. He made a sudden, last moment dash to grab the vial, nearly tipping it to the ground with his effort. Mestoph looked down at the beautiful vial which, as if in response to his lingering doubt, gleamed brilliantly in the meager light of the narrow alley.

"Holy shit!" said Mestoph.

"Holy Shit indeed. Now put that away before someone sees it," said Leviticus as he sauntered past Mestoph and out of the alley.

Mestoph and Leviticus sat at a small cafe table at Bean Counters, which had quickly become their makeshift headquarters. Aside from being a convenient and cozy location with higher-than-usual quality coffee, it was also the crossroads at which their human marks, Marcus and Stephanie, intersected. They sat quietly staring at their cups of coffee, Leviticus blowing on his plain, black cup of joe and Mestoph swirling some sugary sweet concoction that was topped with whipped cream and caramel.

Their friendship had worked so well for so long because neither felt the need to constantly fill every moment with some pointless bit of drivel about how one or the other had gone grocery shopping or walked the dog—not that they'd ever done either of those activities, since they had no need to do so in the afterlife and neither had lived a mortal life on Earth. Instead, they were satisfied to let the meaningful, important things simmer and stew until they were ready to talk. After fifteen or twenty minutes of sipping and stirring, Leviticus finally broke.

"You do realize that I'm not going to let this go for a very long time?"

"What's that?" asked Mestoph.

"Oh, is that how we're going to play it? You know exactly what I'm talking about. I got the Prophecy, and you haven't even gotten close to getting the Omen," said Leviticus.

Mestoph stared down at the liquidy lumps of whipped cream that had survived his endless stirring. He took a long, noisy sip of the triple-shot caramel mocha macchiato, swished the drink that could barely be called coffee inside his mouth for several moments, swallowed, and let out a satisfied sigh.

"I figured I would make sure you could hold up your end of the bargain before I risked my life. Your part was the one most up in the air because it required a lot of skills that frankly you just don't use in your daily afterlife. Therefore, there was no point going further until you pulled through," said Mestoph.

Leviticus smiled and shook his head.

"You know, the sad thing is I think you're right. But that doesn't negate the fact that I pulled through before you could even *plan* what you were going to do if I was successful. Face it, I'm just better at this than you are," said Leviticus.

They let another long pause pass between them as each pondered their next move, like they were playing a game of chess.

"You had a lot of inside help. I killed a great spy and drinking buddy to get you information that would have otherwise made your task impossible," said Mestoph with a minor triumphant smile.

"Oh, yeah! Blame the fact that Heaven has better security than Hell. If that's your defense, then you should have an Omen on hand just for the Hell of it," said Leviticus.

Mestoph screwed his face up as the Angel sunk his entire argument. While he was squirming, trying to avoid admitting defeat, he caught a glimpse of their star performer— and his little dog too.

"Hey, look who just showed up," said Mestoph.

"Don't change the subject."

"No, really. Our new best friend is here."

Leviticus looked over and saw Marcus, with Sir Regi in tow, standing in line at the counter. They let the man and his dog get their coffee, including his bumbling ritual with the barista, and then settle into a comfortable seat before they made their move. It was a Saturday, and if history proved correct, Marcus and Sir Regi would be here for the better part of the morning.

Marcus sat in an overstuffed reading chair in the corner of the dark, wood-paneled coffee shop, rendered even darker by the gray gloom coming in through the plantation shutters. He was reading a particularly interesting—at least to him— book on the early days of the Federal Reserve. Sir Regi was curled at his feet. Neither Leviticus nor Mestoph were quite sure how to approach the dog without drawing the attention of his master. They resorted to staring and clearing their throats, without much success. It turned into a passive-aggressive showdown: Mestoph and Leviticus kept staring at Sir Regi, who in turn kept staring back.

Leviticus and Mestoph weren't really sure what they were expecting to accomplish by sitting around glaring at a Scottish terrier. Granted, they knew his secret, and once Mestoph had cued Leviticus in on it they both understood his value. They also knew exactly how they planned to get what they wanted out of him. The problem was that they couldn't afford to let the cat out of the bag, so to speak, and give away the dog's secret.

"Are we just going to sit here and stare at that damn dog all day?" asked Leviticus.

Mestoph had been deep in a trance, staring at the dog, and was surprised to find himself jolted back into reality.

"The little bastard is a hypnomancer!" exclaimed Mestoph in a loud whisper—the kind that if anyone really wanted to listen, they wouldn't have to put much effort into it.

"Do the thing," said the Demon.

"What?" asked Leviticus.

"The thing," he said again, gesturing emphatically toward

the dog.

"Oh!" said Leviticus, finally getting it.

Leviticus smiled slyly at Mestoph and then turned to the dog. His eyes locked onto the dog's and then began to jerk and flutter like they were having their own private seizure. His vision blurred and then it felt like the space in between him and the dog shrank while the rest of the coffee shop stayed the same. After a moment the room went black, and only Leviticus and Sir Regi were spotlit as if they were part of a soliloquy in a Shakespearean play.

"It's about fucking time!" said the tiny dog in a thick Scottish accent.

"I'm sorry?" said Leviticus.

"I've been waiting for the better part of an hour for one of you scunners to get a clue. It's only after I nearly scramble the brains of that daft Demon friend of yours that he figures it out."

The dog trotted over, followed by his spotlight, and hopped up on the table. The two spotlights merged and created one large splotch of bright white, creating a harsh chiaroscuro effect. At the edge of the circle, the features of Mestoph's face could barely be seen. The dog turned to face the Demon, let out a low purring sound, and a tiny spotlight shone on the top of Mestoph's head. It grew for a few seconds, then popped and joined with the main circle of light like two soap bubbles merging. Mestoph suddenly came to life and joined the small, private conference of a dog, an Angel, and, now, a Demon.

"I told you he was an Angel," said Mestoph to Leviticus.

"Alright, so what do you two fucktards want? If you're just being eejit tourists, you've seen me, so now move on. If you've got business, let's get with it. I've got plenty of napping to do," said the dog.

"Are you really...you know...P-pro—" stuttered Leviticus.

"Whoever I am or was is of no consequence now. I'm Sir Regi, and that's all you need to know."

Mestoph looked down at the dog's collar and stifled a chuckle. "Sir Reginald Pollywog Newcastle III?"

"You'll call me Sir Regi, or you'll call me nothing at all! If you got nothing to offer, I've got fuck all for you, and I'll be pleased to have you move on," barked Sir Regi.

Leviticus looked over to Mestoph, raising his brow. The dog's attitude could end up being a liability, but Mestoph simply nodded.

What Leviticus and Mestoph described to Sir Regi was a simple deal, though obviously only a small piece of the overall plan, which involved very little actual work from the dog. All they really needed was a snitch. Their plan had to be big and serious enough to get them in trouble with the Powers That Be, but they needed someone to turn them in at just the right time so that things didn't get too far out of hand. In return for snitching on them, Sir Regi would in favor with God and potentially get readmitted into Heaven. Everyone would win.

"You do realize," said the dog, "that at some point you'll have to clue me in on what you're actually doing?"

"Well yeah, but you don't really expect us to give you all the details now, do you?" asked Leviticus.

"Yeah, do you think if Hitler had told everyone up front that he wanted to kill a few million Jews and take over the world that we'd have gotten to have World War II?" asked Mestoph.

Leviticus and Sir Regi looked at Mestoph, equally perplexed and appalled. "You didn't read *Mein Kampf,* did you?" asked Sir Regi.

"And you do realize that World War II was a bad thing?" added Leviticus.

"Ok, sure. It had some bad sides, too," he said.

"Alright, now that we've once again celebrated Victory in

Europe, you have to answer at least one question—why me?" asked Sir Regi.

Once again Leviticus looked at Mestoph, and once again Mestoph nodded. Leviticus explained that they needed someone off the grid to use as a vessel until the time was right to blow the lid off of everything. Sir Regi surprised them by balking at their use of Marcus. Mestoph wondered if he hadn't taken up the role of a faithful dog a little too whole heartedly.

"Is this plan of yours going put Marcus in danger?" asked Sir Regi.

"Not if you do your job right," said Mestoph.

Sir Regi walked back over to his master, and the spotlight disappeared. When the light returned to normal, Mestoph and Leviticus reoriented themselves and looked around. People who had been mid-sip or in the midst of talking finished their gulps or sentences as if no time had passed. The Demon and Angel walked out of the front door and darted around the corner toward the alleyway. Mestoph paused and looked over his shoulder; he had the feeling someone was watching. The streets were empty, and he couldn't see any eyes peeping at him from surrounding windows, so he shrugged it off and followed Leviticus into the alley. He gave Leviticus a mock salute, and Leviticus flipped him off in return. Seconds later the alley was filled with a gray mix of different smokes.

Once the Angel and Demon disappeared, St. Peter stepped forward from the shadows across the street and smiled. "I've got you, you little bastard," he muttered to himself. There was no way he could get clearance to take out Leviticus, at least not without more proof than a clandestine meeting with one of Hell Industries' senior demons. He could, however, call in one of his double agents and work his way from Hell back to Heaven until he had enough evidence to satisfy God.

He pulled a brushed steel phone from his pocket. The phone rang a few times, and then a voice that sounded like someone slipping in and out of puberty answered.

"Atreyus here."

"I've got a job for you," said St. Peter.

Chapter 4

There's no such thing as a good Omen

Mestoph paced back and forth in the living room of his messy but comfortable apartment. He would pace the length of the long built-in bookshelf, perform a snappy about-face that sent his dreadlocks flapping wildly, and then pace the length of the bookshelf again. He mumbled heatedly to himself, but little of it was intelligible. Occasionally he would plop down, exasperated, into his overstuffed and well distressed leather reading chair. It wouldn't be long, however, before he was back up and pacing again.

He aggressively paced to his old ice-locker style 1947 Westinghouse refrigerator. He jerked the door open and a cold wave of frosty air and condensation roiled out. Mestoph grabbed a Rogue Dead Guy, his beer of choice, slammed the door shut, and popped the cap off with the bottle opener mounted on the door of the fridge.

Mestoph had a love for everything that represented the Atomic Era. From the restored fridge to an old avocado green couch with buttoned back cushions, on which he had spent many nights sleeping, the whole apartment looked like it was snatched straight out of the 50s. He had an artist friend who took old magazine ads and painted them large, only replacing the smiling pinkish faces of the perfect Caucasian Atomic Families and replacing them with various people of color and ethnicity. His personal favorite, which adorned the wall of his living room, was a redux of a Chesterfield Cigarette ad from the 40s that swapped a wholesome blonde in a two-piece bathing suit reaching out to offer you a pack of refreshing Chesterfields with a curvy black woman in a cleavage popping bikini. Mestoph stopped briefly to take a swig of his beer and admire the painting before he was back to pacing again.

"God damn it!" he shouted as he plopped down onto the couch, which groaned arthritically. It wasn't a reproduction or conjuring; it had really been through more than fifty years of asses and was showing its age. Mestoph groaned, too. He had been trying to come up with a plan to steal the Omen that would go undetected. He was sure that security at Heaven Inc. had noticed the theft of the Prophecy by now, but he had no way of knowing what their response would be. If a Prophecy *and* an Omen went missing at the same time, he could be fairly sure there would be a swift and harsh reaction. Most likely involving a declaration of emergency, sending Heaven and Hell into a state of martial law until the goods were recovered, and the offenders—well, the offenders would be dealt with in a manner that fit the severity of the situation.

Then it happened, quite suddenly, like a cheesy connect-the-dots epiphany on a cop show with writers too lazy to actually make a logical chain of evidence that leads the investigator to the guilty party. Mestoph sat on his couch, looking around his apartment, which seemed more like a museum installation for an era he never lived through than the abode of a living, breathing person. Or demon. And just like that, his mind went from *museum* to *hall of records*. Specifically Hell Industries' Hall of Records. The Hall contained every major, and many minor, piece of paper that had ever been produced by the underworld conglomerate. From press releases to expense reports to meeting minutes— and yes, even Omens. They were spent Omens, having been drafted and set into motion before being filed, but Omens nonetheless.

They were seen as mostly harmless because they were essentially spent ammo, and as such the security protecting them was considerably less than that of Satan's office. However, like any empty shell casing it could be reloaded and used again with the right tools. It would involve forging the physical document as well as the digital copy of it, which is where the real power was these days. Mestoph was no forger, nor was he a hacker, but he happened to know someone with a grudge who was both. All he had to do was get his hands on a sparsely worded Omen with some wiggle room and he'd be back in action.

Mestoph jumped up, sending his beer tumbling to the floor, and grabbed his gun and trench coat. You couldn't have a heist without a trench coat.

A few minutes later he was peeking around the corner of the hallway that led to the entrance of the Hall of Records. There were two guards dressed in standard security guard uniforms standing on both sides of a pair of old wooden doors with wire-meshed glass like those from a high school built in the 70s. They were both big guys, but one was muscle big, like he could have been a professional body builder or a superhero before he died, whereas the other was fat big. The kind of fat that doesn't get made fun of at school because he didn't necessarily have to be strong to win a fight, he just had to put his weight into it, and then it was all over but the crying.

Muscle Big was in the middle of telling Fat Big an elaborate joke. Mestoph leaned back against the wall, took a deep breath, and tried to make the sign of the cross just in case that kind of thing worked down here, resorting to the *spectacles, testicles, wallet, and watch* mnemonic to do it properly. He pulled the pistol from the inside pocket of his trench coat and popped around the corner just as Muscle Big got to the tongue-twisting punch line.

"So I got a fuck for a duck, a duck for a fuck, and a buck for a fucked-up duck," he said as Mestoph squeezed the trigger.

The gun made a spitting noise that sent a dart into Muscle Big's neck. Fat Big guffawed, while Mestoph made a judgment call and spit two darts at him. The poison in the darts acted fast, and the two security guards dropped to the floor in a stupor that Mestoph hoped would last at least an hour.

Mestoph stepped forward and took a closer look at the two guards on the floor, noticing that Fat Big not only still had a smile on his face but that his eyes were still open. Muscle Big was staring straight up at the ceiling as well.

"Shit, I think I killed them," said Mestoph, mostly to himself.

He nudged Fat Big with his shoe, but there was no grunt and no movement other than the undulation of his stomach in response to the nudge. This already wasn't going as he had planned, but he could only shrug and move on. He was committed to his plan now, whether or not it was a good idea. He wished the two Bigs good luck in their re-sorting by the galactic computer and hoped they ended up with better jobs the next go-round. Then he dragged their bodies into a shadowy corner of the Hall of Records. It took a considerable amount of time, considering they both weighed at least 300 pounds each, being almost double Mestoph's weight individually. Once the bodies had been stashed and searched—the Demon pocked the sixty bucks he found in their pockets—he surveyed his surroundings.

The Hall of Records was an enormous room that rested deep in the boiler-room warm bowels of Hell Industries' HQ. It was like a never-ending version of the Parthenon, complete with monstrous Doric columns that ended long before they could ever dream of reaching—not to mention finding—the ceiling. The epic frieze that rested atop the exterior columns depicted a concise history of Hell. The frieze extended farther than Mestoph could see, but at the front of the hall it showed the fall of Lucifer on one side and the building of the first structures of Hell, all of which were anachronistically medieval looking, on the opposite.

Aside from billions of trivial and uninteresting Hell Industries documents, the Hall of Records also contained every Omen that had ever been passed since the creation of man. From Omen 001, the temptation of Adam and Eve, they were all represented here. A swarm of Imps kept everything clean, if not orderly, but they kept bankers' hours. Once the little hand reached six and the big hand reached twelve, they scurried to their little holes and did whatever Imps did in their spare time. It was now three a.m. in Hell, and the place was deserted.

Hanging from the empty blackness that was, presumably, the ceiling were signs that designated the various areas of the immense hall or gave general directions to other sections. The nearest sign hung, seemingly from nothing, over a pentagonal counter and declared it to be the Information Desk. Dozens of smaller signs hung from the Information Desk sign with little info icons and arrows pointed in various directions with numbers beside them. Mestoph assumed the number was a distance of some sort, but had no idea if it was paces, miles, or even light years. The hall was so immense, any and all seemed possible.

Mestoph walked up to the Information Desk, hoping to find a computer or map. He was surprised to find instead a nude, corpulently obese person was seated—or possibly even standing, for all he knew—behind the counter. Multiple layers of fat draped down on top of each other and pooled around the inside of the information desk to the point that Mestoph wasn't sure the creature had legs or feet. He stared at the creature for several seconds, trying to figure out how to address it since he couldn't and didn't want to figure out what sex it was.

"What are you doing here?" it asked in a voice both guttural and nasal, which was more feminine than it was not.

Mestoph walked around the counter and noticed that her surprisingly dainty wrists were chained to the desk just within reach of a keyboard. The chains were completely unnecessary, as the woman had to be at least a thousand pounds and wasn't going anywhere without a crane and a miracle. It was Hell, however, and he was sure the shackles were more psychological than practical.

"Um, yes. Uh. Excuse me...miss?" He stumbled over the last part, still uncertain, "Yes, I'm looking for the Omens section." Mestoph tried to instill a little more confidence at the end than he had started with.

The woman screwed up her eyes, and he couldn't tell if it was doubt or hyperopia.

"And why the fuck should I help you?" she asked in a flabby voice full of contempt and a definite Southern drawl.

"Maybe because it's your *fucking* job."

Mestoph was trying to out-bitch a classically trained bitch. After a few seconds, he realized she just wasn't going to reply to him at all. She continued to stare in his general direction and nonchalantly scratched at an enormous fold of fat hanging from her chest that he realized was actually one of her breasts.

"Do you know who I am?" asked Mestoph, trying to hide his disgust.

The woman squinted in various ways, indeed trying to figure out who he was. She gave up and squeezed both eyes tightly closed to reset whatever focus she had left.

"All I can tell is that you're short and you ain't white. You could be Sammy Davis, Jr. or His Excellency, President for Life, Field Marshal Al Hadji Doctor Idi Amin Dada, Conqueror of the British Empire in Africa in General and

Uganda in Particular and the Most Ubiquitous of all King Of Scotland," she said, spitting it out in one long, uninterrupted stream as if she were vomiting the words. She panted heavily, sweat forming on her brow as she finished.

"Huh?"

"You know, the former President of Uganda."

"Umm, yeah. I'm not Idi Amin. Or Sammy Davis, Jr."

"Well seeing as them's the only darkies I give a shit about, I couldn't give two fucks who you are," she said.

Mestoph, who'd had his hands in his pockets this whole time, ran his finger over the trigger of the gun and strongly fought the urge to shoot her between the useless, rheumy eyes. The truth was that he only had nine darts left in the clip, and aside from the fact that he might need them yet, he also wasn't sure nine would be enough to kill the super-sized cunt. Nothing less than death was worth wasting his time.

Then something piqued his interest.

"Why just those two? Of all the black people in the world to put aside your blind hatred for, why Sammy Davis, Jr. and Idi Amin?" asked Mestoph.

"Cause they cracked me up. Them's were some crazy-ass ni—"

Mestoph had spent some time working both sides of the Civil Rights movement during the late 50s and early 60s. In one town he would enrage the nervous and ignorant white locals by sleeping with their wives until they ended up murdering him, which gained the movement sympathy and traction. In another town he would make waves by inciting the civil rights workers into a fury that would lead to rioting, pillaging, and general violence. This would make the supporters of the movement look militant and act as a justification to the way white people treated the African Americans.

To Mestoph, this was just another day on the job. He didn't see himself as a race traitor since he didn't really have a race. Sure, he was black, but he wasn't of African descent. Strictly speaking, he wasn't even human. It wasn't until Mestoph spent time in the Mississippi delta during the Freedom Summer of 1964 that he got a taste of what it meant to be black in America.

During that summer, he was working for the Council of Federated Organizations in Clarksdale trying to register black people to vote. The delta area of Mississippi was unusually hateful and aggressive toward blacks, even considering the generally racist mentality of the Deep South at that point in history. Working to give black people confidence and respect by way of registering them to vote created an unbelievable amount of unrest, which made the area ripe for Satan to pick up a few good souls. Mestoph was there in the guise of an educated black man from the Lower East Side of Manhattan. He had always been relatively well spoken and even managed to stay polite and mild mannered during his time there. Despite keeping a low profile, he was still a target for some of the members of the local KKK, who also happened to be members of the sheriff's department.

He was alone one night, trying to finish up some paperwork at their makeshift office in the locker room of the Coahoma County Agricultural High School gymnasium, when the lights went out. Moments later, he was hit over the head with what he assumed was a baseball bat, and then it was lights out for him as well. When he woke up, he was in a wooden chair with his wrists and ankles bound by barbed wire.

Over the course of the next three days, Mestoph was

repeatedly tortured until he passed out. Every time he woke up, he was greeted with water, some kind of slop that looked like it was meant for farm animals, and three men in crisp white robes and pointy white hoods. By the time he passed out again, those robes would be covered in blood and sweat, but they were always nice and clean when he came back around.

The thing that confused Mestoph during the three days he was beaten, burnt, prodded, and stabbed was that they never asked him anything or make any demands. They didn't tell him to get out of town or even threaten his friends and family—not that he had any. The only thing they said, just before each punch, kick, cut of a knife, or sizzle of a brand, was the word *nigger*.

Finally, after three days of nearly continuous torture, with breaks only for him to regain consciousness and his assailants to regain their strength, Mestoph died. It wasn't the first time he'd died, and not even the first time he'd been tortured to death. It was, however, the first time he ever wanted revenge. Satan pulled him off the job, likely sensing his new personal stakes in it, and he never got a chance to pay a visit to those three cheerful white guys who killed him.

"—ggers."

Before he even realized what had happened, the gun was out. His hand was as steady as it had ever been, and he felt disconcertingly calm as he stared down the barrel of the gun. He followed it to the dart that was sticking out of the woman's eyeball. Her eyes crossed as she tried to stare at the dart, and then she looked in Mestoph's direction and began to laugh. If was a condescending laugh that was so deep and guttural it sounded like it should be coming from a man the size of a building instead of this woman who weighed as much as a dump truck.

Rage overtook Mestoph's calm, and he leaped onto the counter. He planted one foot on what he could only assume was one of the gelatinous woman's many breasts, leaned down and grabbed her by the hair in one hand, and jammed the dart with the palm of the other until it was lost in her cavernous head. He saw a slight twinge in her face, and then the pupil of her remaining weepy eye dilated. She now had the same vacant stare as the two security guards.

"Guess I'll find it on my own," Mestoph said, jumping down and dusting himself off.

Three hours later he regretted killing the woman at the information desk, racist or not. He had been wandering the Hall of Records, and now not only did he not know where the Omens were, but he had no clue where he was either. He had seen a sign with an information icon—the little italicized "i" inside a circle—over an hour ago and had followed the arrow, which had a "3" beside it. It had definitely not been three paces, and he was beginning to feel reasonably sure it wasn't three miles either. He was on the verge of following his old rule of thumb of just taking left turns until he got to where he wanted, which had served him surprisingly well over the last three millennia, but was spared the need when he finally spotted a small circular information terminal up ahead.

There was a bright beacon of light emanating from its top, and Mestoph realized he had probably passed a dozen of those in the distance since he had set out to find the Omen. He sighed but gave it no more thought, as it wasn't going to solve anything. He was at this one now, so everything would be okay. He hoped.

Even when he zoomed out the map to its limits, it

seemed endless. There was a blinking info icon in the center to show where he was, and a quick scan told him he was nowhere near the Omens. They didn't even show up on the map. There was a search box and an on-screen keyboard, so he typed in "Omen" and tapped the search button.

The terminal queried for a moment, asking him politely to "Please wait while we determine the best route."

He waited several more moments, tapping his feet in impatience. The terminal cycled through a few pleasant phrases, starting with "Please wait while we ask a friend."

Mestoph sighed.

"Please wait while he asks his mom."

"Come on, you piece of junk!" Mestoph shouted at the screen

"Hmm, she didn't know either. Let me check previous queries of the same nature. I appreciate your continued patience."

"I'll show you patience when I tear you apart once piece at a time and dance on top of your mechanical corpse," said Mestoph through gritted teeth.

The message stayed on the screen for several minutes. Finally said it changed to "Fuck if I know" and went back to the main map.

At this point Mestoph was tired, sore, thirsty, and feeling frayed by the stress and murdering. He kicked the machine repeatedly, yelling, "Tell me where the Goddamn Omens are or I'm going to find your friend and his mother and turn the mother inside out to use as a condom to fuck your friend and then rip his dick off and watch him bleed out and then use his dick to piss on you until you short circuit, you overly polite piece of shit!"

There was a deep rumbling and the map on the screen instantly drew a short green line that pointed directly behind him. Mestoph turned around and saw that a large stainless steel and glass capsule had popped up out of the floor only a few feet behind him. A door swished open from the previously seamless tube to reveal a plush white leather seat that was lit by a soft, warm glow. It looked like something out of a 70's architecture and design magazine. Mestoph stepped in and sat down, and the door whispered closed. There was a momentary sucking sound, and then the capsule dropped away into the floor with a whoosh.

The capsule hurtled at an amazing speed through a system of thick, transparent glass tubes, which sprawled, branched, and forked like a hundred cans of silly string had exploded. The seat was built like a Ferris wheel bucket so that no matter how many loops, curves, and switchbacks the tube took, Mestoph was always right side up swaying lightly but smoothly with the motion. It was a good thing, as he imagined vertigo and vomit would have hit him within a few seconds otherwise.

The pneumatic tube took Mestoph deeper and deeper into the depths of Hell Industries' sub-sub-sub basements, until he finally broke through what was obviously the bottom of the bottom—except the capsule kept going. It descended through the strata of basements and bedrock, into a vast sea of magma dotted with small islands of rock or hardened lava and rock columns that had been created from the meeting of unimaginably long and snaking stalagmites and stalactites.

Mestoph imagined that this would have been the part of Dante's tour of the Inferno where he pointed off into the distance asking "What's over there?" and Virgil would just say "Fuck if I know. Now, let's check out that gift shop."

The freefall had gone on for long enough that Mestoph was no longer marveling at the endless expanse of tidal lava and was instead wondering if he had chosen unwisely when he had jumped into the capsule. He breathed on the glass and played a game of tic-tac-toe against himself. Before he could finish his game, he realized that he was running out of tube. He had been hurtling downwards toward the endless ocean for long enough that when it suddenly became obvious that the pneumatic tube ended and he was about to plow through the glowing surface and deep into the sea itself, it came as something of a shock. In a panic, Mestoph jumped to his feet, though he wasn't sure what that was going to do, as the tube hit the surface of the magma.

Nothing happened. In fact, the capsule hardly jostled as it dove beneath the molten sea; the glass windows were unscathed, and it was still the same pleasantly cool temperature it had been up in the Hall of Records.

After a few moments, the capsule entered another tube through a door that dilated like a camera shutter, and the familiar hiss of suction returned. When he was sure he wasn't going to be flash-fried, melted, or suffer some other gruesome lava-related death, Mestoph sat back down and finally breathed again. Calm once more, he sat down and tried to pass time. He was still too nervous to touch the glass, which was glowing a bright orangey yellow, to finish his game of tic-tac-toe. It wasn't necessary anyways, as moments later the tube pulled into what could only be described as a small subway station. The glass slid open and Mestoph stood back up and stepped out.

The station was about fifty feet wide, seventy feet high, and a hundred or so feet long with walls that were covered in glossy white acoustic tile for the first third and then curved into a barrel-vaulted ceiling. In the center of the vault was a long, narrow glass window that ran the length of the station and allowed the bright glow of the magma to shine. Although it was bright, it didn't throw light very far. For that reason, and possibly to complete the subway station feel, the place still had fluorescent lights. In the center of the platform were two sets of three interconnected orange plastic chairs, placed back to back so that each set of three faced the opposite direction.

The air in the station swirled, coming out hot and dry from the pneumatic tube, causing the hanging lights to sway slightly. The hissing from the tubes faded and then stopped. The air inside stilled and quickly took on an acidic, oily taste and smell. It felt slightly damp, too. Mestoph imagined the dampness was the trapped sweat of the Imps or lesser Demons that had built this place however many eons ago, which had created a tiny, isolated evaporation/precipitation cycle. In reality it was a carefully controlled humidity system to counter the vampiric, moisture-sucking property of being beneath an ocean of magma. If it weren't for the moisture, any paper documents, the plastic chairs, and even the tiles would dry out, the walls would crack, and the magma would quickly reclaim this small bubble of habitable space. The oily taste, on the other hand, was much closer to Mestoph's imagination than he'd have cared to know.

Other than the capsule he had arrived in and the plastic chairs, the only other thing in the station was a small metal door with a sign that read "Authorized Personnel Only." He walked over and looked carefully at the door. Seeing no obvious traps or security measures, Mestoph authorized himself to open the door. He turned the knob, wincing as he did. The door simply opened with a little squeak from disuse. Inside, Mestoph found a long, low-ceilinged room that looked like a closet that had forgotten to stop. He couldn't tell exactly how far back it went because it was full of row after row of tall filing cabinets. The cabinets stood four abreast in two sets of two, with a small path in the middle. Mestoph opened the top drawer of the nearest one and found it full of newly minted and executed Omens. They were signed by the board of directors, had an elaborate wax seal at the bottom bearing the Official Crest of the Office of the

Prince of the Underworld, and underneath that was the immaculate signature of Satan. The "S" was illuminated as a serpent and the rest was a slow, loping trail of thick black ink.

The Omen he held was from only a few weeks ago. It precisely described a coup in Kenya that, much to Mestoph's chagrin, had actually failed miserably due to the last minute intervention by Freewill International. The coup had been a pet project of his. Mestoph had assembled an impressively gruesome band of rebels who would have swept through the Kenyan jungles, absorbing or abolishing tribes as necessary, until the accumulated army had reached Nairobi. As long as an all-out conflict erupted, the outcome of the bloody revolt was inconsequential. It only served as a smokescreen for a hostile takeover of the governing body of Kenya.

The rebels had been poised to launch the first of their attacks when Freewill International caught wind of the build-up of forces and interceded, citing the Ancient Agreement and forcing Hell into arbitration. The result was that not only could they not have their revolution, but because of the instability that had been created amongst the rebels and tribes, they would have to take good faith measures as well. That good faith would come in the form of an AIDS awareness campaign and an education initiative on condom use. The meeting with Satan over that particular SNAFU had been an intense and uncomfortable one, but Mestoph had managed to salvage things at the last minute by suggesting they use defective condoms.

Mestoph put the Omen back into the filing cabinet. A quick look at the other Omens in the drawer showed that they were filed chronologically, so anything in that cabinet would be too new and therefore verbose to serve his purposes. They needed something older, preferably an Omen that hadn't been scanned into the digital system yet. Hell was a bit behind the times and had just recently begun building a visual, searchable archive of Omens. Mestoph was already going to have to have the database record changed in addition to having the physical document forged; he didn't want to have to worry about manipulating a scanned image as well.

He walked further into the large closet, passing a dozen or so rows of filing cabinets, before picking another drawer at random. He pulled out an Omen near the back and looked it over. It was from the late 1980s and was a lot less wordy, but still not what he was looking for. He checked the drawer below it, and after opting against several others, he found exactly what he was wanted. The paper had started to yellow and was tattered around the edges from being shuffled around over the years. The Omen was dated 1981, and all it said, in plain lettering in the middle of the document, was "Union Strike."

Mestoph set the Omen down, opened his trench coat, and pulled out a large poster tube from the deep pocket he had dubbed the Highlander Pocket, named for the propensity of the sword-wielding characters from the popular movies and TV series to pull a full-sized katana or claymore from out of nowhere. In reality, it was probably closer to being a Redneck Pocket, more likely to hold a shotgun than a sword. Regardless, Mestoph rolled up the Omen, stuck it in the tube, slapped a shipping label addressed to a Mr. A. H., and shoved the tube back in his Highlander Pocket. Mestoph closed the filing cabinet and walked back to the front of the room. Unsurprisingly, there wasn't a mail slot down there, so he would have to drop it off on his way back home.

When Mestoph returned the subway station, it took a moment for him to register the fact that the pneumatic capsule was gone. There was no reason for it to be gone unless someone else had summoned it to come down. It was a small station, with only one tube leading in, and Mestoph had a hard time believing that the system was programmed to leave stranded everyone that visited. Unless he had seriously pissed off the information terminal—a distinct possibility—then there was someone on their way down.

Mestoph tried to figure out how long the ride had taken, but he had been both so astounded and overwhelmingly bored by the trip that he had no idea. He knew he had only been in the filing closet for a max of fifteen minutes and assumed it had taken at least that long to get down. If the return trip was the same length, he should have at least fifteen minutes left before the capsule returned. Which meant he didn't have a whole lot of time to find a hiding place.

He hadn't given the station a thorough look when he had arrived because there wasn't much to look at thoroughly. There was the platform that made up the majority up the station. There was also a small recess where the capsule docked, and where he would be thoroughly squished if he tried to hide. Hiding under the chairs wouldn't do anything but make him look stupid. Beyond that, the only other place was the filing closet where he had gotten the Omen. Hiding in there would only buy him a few minutes of sanctuary since there was nothing in there but rows of filing cabinets. Granted, there were seemingly endless rows, but how far would he have to go before he was reasonably sure whoever was coming would stop looking before they got to him?

He was beginning to feel the first cold, prickly hints of panic when he noticed the room had suddenly gotten drafty. Hot, dry air was rushing in from the pneumatic tube. The capsule had to be close.

If Mestoph left another dead body, this time right outside the scene of his crime, he would have Nephilim after him before he could even celebrate his victory. Desperate, he pulled out his dart pistol and shot out all the fluorescent lights hanging from the ceiling. Despite the glow of the lava, the station became surprisingly dim. Nothing even close to dark, but enough to make it hard to see into the far corners. The wind was picking up quickly, and Mestoph made a dash for the corner nearest to where the tube came into the station. He hoped that whoever exited the capsule didn't look behind them as soon as they got out.

There had been just enough time between hiding and the capsule arriving for Mestoph to realize exactly how bad his plan was, but by the time he thought of making a mad dash for the filing closet it was too late. The capsule slid smoothly into the station and up to the platform. The door opened and warm light flowed out, illuminating the half of the station where the door to the filing closet was. Out of the capsule stepped a tall, skinny man with long, mangy reddish brown hair. He was wearing a tattered, powder-blue zip-up sweater and dirty black corduroy pants that looked like they were either covered in splotches of paint or condiments. It was hard to tell from Mestoph's vantage, but it almost looked like the man was sniffing the air. He had an overwhelming resemblance to a weasel, which made Mestoph uncomfortable for reasons he couldn't explain.

The Weasel pulled a pack of cigarettes from inside his sweater and took out a half cigarette. Whether he had saved it or found it was unclear, but it reinforced Mestoph's impression that this was an unsavory man. Everything about him seemed dirty. The Weasel took a few puffs from the cigarette, licked his fingers, and extinguished it, putting the remains, now about a quarter of a cigarette, back into the pack. He looked around again and then walked over to the closet door and inspected it. Mestoph hadn't noticed any kind of counter-intrusion measures or anything that would've have given away the fact that the door had been used. He wasn't sure what The Weasel was looking at, but the man was clearly examining something. The Weasel finally opened the door and stepped in, letting it close behind him.

Once again Mestoph didn't have a lot of time to make a major decision. He could jump in the tube and take off, but this would give away the fact that someone had been there. The tube would be gone when he came out, and when no one ever came back in the tube, The Weasel would be able to figure it out. If he stayed and hid until The Weasel left, he ran the increasing risk of being found out. It was a lose-lose scenario, but Mestoph figured that taking the tube bought him the most time. As he was trying to quietly work his way out from his hiding place, The Weasel exited the filing closet.

Mestoph froze.

Again The Weasel just stood there, this time facing Mestoph. The man really did look like a weasel; he had dark, sunken eyes with a small but sharp nose, a patchy mustache that looked more like whiskers, and odd sideburns that seemed to turn and grow toward his mouth about halfway down his face. He was also definitely sniffing the air. Mestoph didn't wear any cologne, but depending on how sensitive this man's senses were, he might be able to tell that Mestoph had showered earlier that morning, or even detect the fear-laden sweat that was now pouring.

The Weasel made a quick, random looking sweep of the room with his small, black eyes and then started walking. Instead of returning to the capsule or pulling Mestoph from his half-assed hiding place, he walked to the opposite end of the station and pushed on one of the white wall tiles. A door opened silently, causing the wind to pick back up. The Weasel cocked his head to the side and then turned, sniffing the air again. His eyes darted around but never landed on Mestoph, and after a few seconds he turned back and walked out of the door, which quickly closed behind him.

Mestoph waited several minutes in the shadows for The Weasel to come back, but he never did. Finally feeling safe, he stepped out and walked over to the wall where the man had disappeared. None of the tiles looked different from any others, but he began pushing randomly in the general area where he thought The Weasel had pushed. It took several tries, but he found a tile that gave way with a little pressure. The door opened into a random hallway somewhere in the Administration area of Hell Industries HQ, far above where he was now, judging by walls that were the most putrid color of green imaginable. That particular color of green had to be the horrendous love child of Avocado and Baby Shit, and managed to be worse than either one could possibly be alone. It was only found in Admin.

The doorway was obviously a portal. He stepped through, looked around for any sign of The Weasel, and breathed a deep sigh of relief. He had done it. He dropped the tube containing the Omen into a mail slot and went home. He needed another beer.

Chapter 5

No good deed...

Mestoph flipped his cell phone closed and stuck it in his pocket with a smile. He was riding on a high of success in his cat-burglary and the hope that coming soon would be a true vacation. With both an Omen and a Prophecy, he and Leviticus held real, awesome power in their hands. It was tempting to go crazy with it, but their plans would never work if they got power hungry. It was the simplicity that gave it a chance of actually succeeding. Success was a thought he hadn't considered up until this point, and it frightened and excited him. They had passed the point of no return. The plan must go forward.

Mestoph was ruminating on various retirement possibilities as he strolled into his apartment, so he was caught completely by surprise when a baseball bat slammed into his back and knocked him forward onto the arm of his vintage couch. He dropped to the floor and had just enough time to roll over and see The Weasel smiling down at him, half a cigarette hanging from his lips, and then the baseball bat hit a glancing blow on his head, just enough to knock him unconscious.

Stephanie was walking down the dream path again, but her Grams was nowhere to be seen. She had never been here before without her grandmother, and it felt much more foreboding and dangerous now. A strong wind seemed to blow straight up the narrow, tree-lined path. It whipped branches at her face as if the forest were fighting her off—or warning her.

Clouds swam across the night sky and engulfed the moon, letting only the dimmest hint of moonlight through to light her way. She thought of turning back, but there wasn't anything back there, any more than there was anything in front of her. It was a dream, after all. She continued down the path, stumbling here and there over the roots that grew out of the hard-packed dirt.

A full-on storm was now brewing; the winds gusted and lightning arced in the distance. Flailing tree limbs grabbed at Stephanie's nightgown as the rain began to fall, plastering the fabric against her skin. She felt the tiny hairs on her arm, wet as they were, stand on end and then a jagged bolt of lightning ripped through the sky in front of her and struck a tree only a few feet away. She stopped, afraid to go forward, but also afraid to go back. As if answering her fears, she saw a bright flash and heard the thunder at nearly the same time, coming from behind her. Her dreams had never taken on this intense feeling of danger, and she didn't know what to do.

And then she felt that cold, prickling fear crawling up her spine, the same sensation she had felt the last time she was here.

She could sense a presence behind her, could hear the flapping of wings and the soft coldness of breath on her neck. She couldn't move despite her frantic attempts to escape. She was paralyzed to the point that she couldn't even scream. There was another lightning strike, this one a safe distance away, but it backlit something small on the path in front of her. She could have sworn it was a dog.

"Let her go!" boomed a deep voice.

Stephanie couldn't see the creature behind her, but she sensed confusion or at least a shift in its attention. At last she was able to move and, hedging her bets on the devil she didn't know, ran toward the other voice. She began to regret the decision when she saw two small white orbs glowing at the height she imagined the dog's eyes would be, and then she heard barking. Tiny, yappy dog barking.

"Alright, this is just getting ridiculous," she shouted above the noise of wind, thunder, barking, and flapping.

It was at that point that the glowing orbs grew in size and then shot out like lightning, zig-zagging toward her. Stephanie froze as the bolts passed on both sides of her, just above her shoulders. She heard the crackle as an arc of electricity passed within inches of her face, and then a brilliant white-blue explosion of light blinded her. All sound was drowned out by the kind of high-pitched whining roar that she had always associated with dinosaurs and lizard monsters in cheesy sci-fi movies. Cheesy or not, as the roar died out so did the cold, creepy feeling. She braved a glance behind her and saw nothing but trail and trees. She turned back around, and right in front of her was a small Scottish terrier.

"Sir Regi?" she asked.

Mestoph came to in a pool of what he hoped was his own drool. It was warm and wet, so it could've been blood. He tried to open his eyes, but the second he did his head was filled with intense pain. He let out an uncontrollable moan. Moments later, he was forced to roll over as someone grabbed him by what he realized was a chain linked to a pair of handcuffs. As he landed, his head flopped backwards, hitting something hard despite the fact that he was on something soft, and sending a whole new wave of pain flooding into his head.

His vision slowly came into focus, though the haze seemed to throb with his pulse, and he realized he was still in his house, lying handcuffed on his vintage couch. The Weasel was standing over him, smiling with what looked like the same cigarette hanging precariously out of his mouth. He leaned in and Mestoph flinched, expecting a headbutt, but The Weasel stopped inches from his face and inhaled deeply through his nose. He was taking a large whiff of Mestoph's scent like a hound dog.

"I thought that was you I smelled down there," he said with a self-satisfied smile on his face.

The ridiculousness of a human tracking him by smell aside, Mestoph couldn't imagine how The Weasel would have known his smell to begin with since their paths had never knowingly crossed before. It mattered not since the man had tracked him down regardless. The thought barely had time to sink in before The Weasel gave him a backhanded slap, a hand full of cheap, gaudy rings making nicks and cuts on the Demons cheek and lips. Mestoph leaned over and spit out a mouthful of blood, but wouldn't give the Weasel the satisfaction of whining.

"Shouldn't you make your demands before beating me up?" Mestoph asked.

The Weasel gave a quick-take of mock revelation, said "So *that's* how you do it," and then gave Mestoph another backhand. "Oops, there I go…getting it backwards again."

Mestoph spit out more blood and forced a smile. His lip was cut in several places, and the effort was repaid with intense pain. "If you're not going to make any demands, what do you want?"

The Weasel made to backhand him again, but stopped with his hand pulled back. He stroked his muttonchops, smiling at Mestoph's flinching.

"What *do* I want with a useless, disappointing never-was

of a Demon?" he asked in mock contemplation. "Why don't you start by telling me what you were doing down there in the Hall of Records?"

"I was doing some last minute taxes," said Mestoph with a smile that was met with a quick openhanded slap from the opposite direction as the others. The Weasel's unusually long fingers left long, stinging marks around Mestoph's ear and eye, as well as the rest of the left side of his face. It brought involuntary tears to his eyes, but he tried to shake them off.

"Listen, Mestopholes. We already know your little fairy friend stole a Prophecy. Add an Omen to that and you two would be holding on to some serious power. All I want to know is *why*. And why a used one? It's useless."

Mestoph arched a brow in genuine surprise. He knew Heaven would figure out they were missing a Prophecy pretty quickly; he didn't realize they would connect him to the crime this fast. Especially since he *just* stole the Omen. So then who was the "we" that the weasely guy beating the crap out of him referred to?

"Who are you?" asked Mestoph.

"My name is Atreyus."

"What the Hell is going on?" shouted Stephanie as she looked down at the little Scotty dog.

"What was that thing?" she asked, just as Sir Regi was about to answer her first question.

"What are you doing here?" She continued the tirade of questions as Sir Regi just stood there waiting for her finish.

"Are you done?" he asked once she was silent for more than a second. When she didn't answer he continued, "That thing was either a Seraphim or a Nephilim. It's hard to tell in the dark. Regardless, it seems to want you dead, which means you're special. To someone, at least. I came to warn you," Sir Regi added, though warning her was the last thing on his mind. "You have unknown friends that can help you."

Sir Regi spun a series of spontaneous lies about being part of a secret order sent to protect her, how she played an important part in some unknown plot, and how he and his friends could keep her safe. After giving away a few honest details, like the fact that Marcus was involved, she agreed to meet her new friends.

What Sir Regi neglected to say was that whether it was a Seraphim or a Nephilim determined whether she was important to someone in Heaven or Hell, respectively. Neither strayed far from their inner circle unless dictated by God or Satan, or if the balance of Good and Evil were suddenly skewed in one direction or the other. The Seraphim and Nephilim were the highest order of creatures in Heaven or Hell, and they were charged long before the Ancient Agreement to keep the Holy Order in balance. That had largely been marginalized by Freewill International and the Ancient Agreement and they spent most of their time singing the praises of their masters. What interest they could have in an ordinary barista Sir Regi wasn't sure, but he was sure it wasn't coincidence that she played a part in Mestoph and Leviticus's scheme.

The connection clicked in Mestoph's head: Atreyus was known in certain circles to do freelance work for Agents of Heaven Inc. Specifically St. Peter. It was assumed that Lucifer was aware of Atreyus' actions and was sanctioning them on some level, if only by not stopping him. This was enough of a connection for Mestoph to assume that St. Peter was on Leviticus' tail, and, as a result, now his. Mestoph had heard what he needed and taken enough of a beating for one day. As Atreyus went on talking about some great plan—Mestoph honestly wasn't listening—he popped a cufflink out of his sleeve. Having done this more than once—it was one of the reasons he made sure to always wear cufflinks—he quickly and quietly unlocked the cuffs behind his back.

Mestoph started to laugh, wearing a large smile that showed off a mouthful of teeth. This stopped Atreyus' seemingly rehearsed speech. He looked over at Mestoph, still lying on the couch but now with a ridiculous grin. "And just what the Hell is so damned funny?" he asked.

"You think yourself some great villain, but you hit like a fucking pussy. You hit like my accountant," said Mestoph, though his accountant had been a champion Nazi boxer, so that wasn't exactly the insult it seemed.

Atreyus looked at Mestoph for a moment and then sighed, shaking his head as he walked over.

"Some people just have no respect for a good monologue," Atreyus said, more to himself than to Mestoph. He reared back to give his captive a proper swing, but as he reached the apex of his backswing, Mestoph jumped up and decked Atreyus with a two-fisted hammer swing.

The Weasel's surprise and off-center balance, combined with the hefty punch, sent Atreyus sprawling to the floor. Mestoph ran over and punched him again, and although it was awkwardly delivered, the Demon not being used to boxing someone lying on the ground, it had the desired effect and knocked Atreyus out cold.

Mestoph quickly removed the other cuff from his wrist and put handcuffed Atreyus to the frame of his sleeper sofa in the corner of the living room. He didn't want Atreyus destroying his favorite couch, plus the sleeper sofa was considerably sturdier and heavier. Mestoph looked at the floor and saw the baseball bat Atreyus had used to knock him. He realized that he'd been beaten with his own bat. He looked back at Atreyus, who still appeared to be unconscious, and nudged him with the bat. No response. Mestoph went to the fridge and grabbed one of his precious beers, the only cold drink in the place, popped the top, and poured it over Atreyus' head.

The Weasel jerked awake and sputtered as beer went in his eyes and mouth. Mestoph gave him a few moments to look around and take his bearings, and then swung heartily at his head. Blood sprayed the wall to his left, and Atreyus screamed. His scream faltered for a moment as both Atreyus and Mestoph noticed that his long jaw now hung awkwardly to one side. The pain of his shattered, dislocated jaw hit him, and his scream rang out again with renewed anguish. A second swing took the jaw off, and Atreyus passed out, mid-scream, almost before the jaw hit the ground.

Mestoph took one last swing with all the power that his pure Demon blood granted him. There was a crack that would have sent a stadium to its feet cheering, though the blood and the head flying through the air would have caused the crowd to pause at least momentarily. Atreyus' head slammed into a bookshelf, knocking Mestoph's collection of vintage tin rocket ship toys off, and then fell to the ground with a wet thud. Mestoph, his floor, his couch, and his wall were covered in blood, but Atreyus was dead. The weasely man's soul, headless like his body, floated up. He flipped Mestoph off as he vanished. It would take a while for his soul and body to get recycled—and there was no doubt he'd be returning to Hell—but it would give Mestoph plenty of time to get out and warn Leviticus. This would push their schedule up a bit, but it wasn't an insurmountable obstacle.

Mestoph wiped his bloody hands on Atreyus' sweater

and then rummaged through his pockets, finding a cell phone, and then dashed out of his apartment. He dropped his own phone down a garbage chute as he tried to walk quickly but nonchalantly down the hallway. There was a good chance they were tracking his phone, so he flipped open Atreyus' and dialed an all-too-familiar number.

"They're on to us, Leviticus," Mestoph said into the cell phone as he left his apartment.

Chapter 6

...is without its faults

It was almost one a.m., and Mestoph and Leviticus were standing at the partially opened door of Marcus' apartment. He stared blankly at his visitors, trying to decide if he had heard what he thought he had heard. Luckily, one of them repeated it.

"We need to talk to Sir Regi," said Mestoph.

Unfortunately, it didn't make any more sense to Marcus the second time. He looked down at the little dog at his feet, who was obviously paying close attention to what was going on.

"You want to talk to my dog? My little Scottish terrier dog? Well...by all means. Talk away," Marcus said as he stepped aside. There was a brief pause, and he looked down at Sir Regi. "Do you have anything to say for yourself?"

"Well, you could let them in first," said Sir Regi.

Once Marcus finally accepted the fact that Sir Regi could talk, or at least had stopped staring at him without speaking or blinking, he let Mestoph and Leviticus into his apartment. He sat on the arm of a small leather chair, trying to comprehend all that was going on. Sitting on his old beige couch were two people who claimed to be from the Afterlife, and his best friend and companion of many years (who just happened to be a dog) was standing on top of the coffee table and chatting with them about the end of the world.

"So let me get this straight: there's an impending

catastrophe of an unknown nature that involves all of us and the barista at my usual coffee shop, and we need to go…where now?" asked Marcus.

"We need to go to Truth or Consequences, New Mexico," said Mestoph.

"Truth or Consequences? What the Hell is in Truth or Consequences?" asked Marcus.

This was the part that neither Leviticus nor Mestoph were really sure about. How do you explain to someone— who was only just coming to terms with a talking dog and an ominous, vaguely apocalyptic, and completely fictional conspiracy—that Purgatory exists, is on Earth, and happens to be a tiny, dusty desert town in New Mexico?

"It's where Purgatory is located. Someone there can help us. But we have to get to him before *they* get to us."

In the story Leviticus and Mestoph had told Marcus, "they" were a shadowy fifth column in the Afterlife—in telling their story, they had slyly evaded mentioning a Heaven or Hell and left everything under the nebulously defined *Afterlife*—that was trying to bring about the end of humanity so that they could have Earth all to themselves. Whatever catastrophe was planned was to be the first domino. It was basically just a hodge-podge of bullshit conspiracy theories that they were making up on the fly. Leviticus left most of it to Mestoph since he was much more versed in the art of lying.

Marcus was quiet for a few moments. His initial hope that this had all just been a very vivid, unexplainable dream had long since evaporated, and he was now trying to decide if he had just gone crazy in the middle of the night. Since he desperately wanted to be sane, he decided to just go with it and see what happened. Though he needed one last thing.

"Prove you're from the Afterlife," he said.

Leviticus and Mestoph looked at each other and smiled.

"Follow me," Mestoph said as he walked to the door outside.

Mestoph led them all, including Sir Regi, to a small patch of grass outside Marcus' apartment and told them all to hold hands. Sir Regi hopped up into Marcus' arms, and then the three men clasped hands.

There was a pop and a puff of smoke, and suddenly Marcus found himself not in his apartment but in a small, dimly lit room with brushed steel walls. It took a moment for his eyes to adjust to the low light, but as they did he noticed that the only exit was a giant and insanely complicated safe door—and they seemed to be on the wrong side. There was a glass panel across the entirety of the mechanism and behind it were hundreds, if not thousands, of gears, all polished to a shine even with the meager light.

They were inside a safe; Marcus was sure of it. Mestoph and Leviticus were just standing there, both with their arms folded across their chests. Mestoph motioned behind Marcus. When he turned around, he saw a large display case that contained several regal looking crowns made of gold and jewels with little crosses pattée and four fleurs-de-lis atop them. There was an old wooden throne sitting against the back wall, with a number of ceremonial swords mounted on racks to either side of it.

"Are these...you know?"

"The Crown Jewels of the United Kingdom of Great Britain and Northern Ireland? Yes, these are those," said Leviticus.

Marcus' eyes widened as he took a second sweep of the room. They had just teleported thousands of miles from his apartment to the Tower of London. He also considered the fact that this was the first time he had ever left his home town. At least now he could say he was a world traveler.

"Can I touch them?" Marcus asked.

Leviticus and Mestoph looked at each other and shrugged. Mestoph walked over to the display case, waved his hands like a magician, and then tapped the top twice. He motioned to Marcus to have at it. Marcus reached for the case with trembling hands, pausing a moment to give one last look for approval from Mestoph and Leviticus, and then lifted the glass off the display. He set it down gingerly and then delicately picked up the Imperial State Crown.

"Go ahead, put it on. Grab a scepter while you're at it. Then we've got to run. We've got a lot to do tonight," said Leviticus.

While Marcus was picking out a scepter to match the crown, Sir Regi, who had been remarkably quiet, ambled over to Mestoph and Leviticus and hopped up on the arm of King Edwards's coronation chair.

"These aren't the *real* Crown Jewels, are they?" he whispered.

"Hell no," said Mestoph quietly. "These are props for a heist movie that a college student is working on. We're like, ten miles down the road."

They all stood outside Stephanie's window: Mestoph, Leviticus, Marcus, and Sir Regi. Sir Regi had told Stephanie in her dream to expect them at any moment, but he didn't realize it would be only a few short hours later. He had also told Mestoph and Leviticus about the Nephilim, and they in turn had told him about Atreyus and St. Peter. Marcus had still been in a bit of a confused funk during this part of their talk, so they decided to keep it vague for him as well as Stephanie. But they couldn't just shine over the fact that they needed to leave—tonight. Killing Atreyus only bought them an hour or two, which was up by now. Regardless of whether Atreyus ever got free, neither Mestoph nor Leviticus were convinced that St. Peter would wait for confirmation to make a move.

Stephanie looked out from her bedroom window and saw Marcus, who was wearing an ornate crown and holding onto a bejeweled scepter, and Sir Regi. With them were a black man with long dreads and a trench coat and an olive-skinned man with a long, flowing white robe. The sprinklers were going off around them, and they were backlit by the streetlamp. They looked like a rather pathetic, motley group of super heroes—or criminals.

She vaguely remembered seeing the two mystery men once or twice at the coffee shop over the last few days. She rubbed the sleep from her eyes and unlocked the door to let them in. She wasn't entirely sure why she was being so trusting but figured it was probably because she knew Marcus was harmless. She assumed anyone with him would be as well.

She started a pot of coffee and glanced at the clock on the front of the pot. It read 2:33 a.m. Even in the middle of the night—or the morning—it was still just like being at work. Here she was, making coffee for a group of people she hardly knew. In fact, it seemed to her that the one she knew best of the group was the dog. Everyone seemed to be waiting for the coffee, so they remained silent until Stephanie laid out several empty cups and a pot and let them take care of themselves. She stared at Marcus, who was still wearing the crown and had the scepter sitting in his lap. Now that she saw it closer, she noticed that it was incredibly detailed. The gold and jewels on both looked real.

She nodded at the scepter and asked, "What's with the regal get-up?"

Marcus looked at the scepter and then at Mestoph and

Leviticus. They either didn't pick up on the non-verbal communication or didn't care.

"They're part of the Crown Jewels," he said, shrugging.

Stephanie arched a brow, but Marcus didn't offer any further explanation.

"So you show up in the middle of the night with two residents of the Afterlife, a talking dog, and the Crown Jewels and expect me to take your word and runaway to some shithole town in New Mexico?"

When they left thirty minutes later, Marcus was no longer wearing his royal vestments. He had felt guilty about stealing from the Queen. Stephanie, however, was carrying a small gold orb with a jeweled band down the center and a bejeweled cross at its top. She also had a small travel bag with her.

"So if you can just pop us here and there and everywhere, why are we outside?" she asked as they stood in her front yard in the pre-dawn darkness.

"The popping here and there causes a quick decompression and then re-compression of the immediate area, along with a fair amount of smoke. It's been known to cause small buildings to...well..." Leviticus paused for a moment.

"They kind of explode," said Mestoph, and the group disappeared into a puff of smoke with a small cork-gun of a pop.

Chapter 7

Once Upon a Town

They stood at the top of a tall hill overlooking the city of Truth or Consequences, New Mexico. A water tower decorated with a typically Southwestern motif of eagle feathers, dream catchers, and Kokopelli in pastel colors stood on the hill with them, watching the sun rise in the east. Down amongst the small, blandly colored houses and the sickly beige dirt roads, it was a calm and still somewhat cool morning. Up on the hill, there seemed to be a permanent gusting of wind that sent hot air into everyone's nostrils and was already whipping up a small swirl of sand around them.

They weren't up there to enjoy the view; they were trying to find a Nazi. Not just any Nazi, though—*the* Nazi.

"You could have told me that your forgery artist and hacker extraordinaire was Hitler," Leviticus whispered to Mestoph.

Mestoph stopped squinting at the houses down below and stared at Leviticus blankly.

"Would you have gone along with it if I had?"

When Leviticus just sighed, Mestoph smiled. "That's what I thought," he said, and he went back to squinting at the grid of streets below them.

Considering most of Truth or Consequences fit in a two mile by one mile rectangle, comprised of a compact grid of streets, and that the view from the hill gave them sight of most of it, it should have been easy to spot the Nazi house from a couple hundred drably painted houses with nothing more than rocks and cacti for decoration.

"Would it be too simple to just look him up in the phone book?" asked Stephanie. "It's not like there's a bunch of

Adolph Hitlers out there."

Leviticus and Mestoph looked at Stephanie, clueless.

"Don't know about phone books, huh? How long have you guys been dead?" asked Stephanie.

"About two thousand years," said Leviticus.

"I was never alive," said Mestoph. Leviticus looked sharply at him. They had decided not to mention that Mestoph was from Hell, so he needed to be careful of what he said about his history. "And we know about phone books, we just don't really expect someone to list themselves as Adolf Hitler. Not sure if you know this, but he's not exactly a well-liked guy."

"Then why do you think his house is going to look like Nazi Headquarters? Is he supposed to have a cactus in the shape of a swastika?" asked Stephanie.

Mestoph looked like he was about to say something but he stopped, leaving his mouth hanging open. He had finally seen the flaw in his logic, and although he hated being wrong, he didn't really have a comeback. Leviticus started laughing; softly at first, but then it became a loud and obnoxious guffaw that sent a couple of nearby birds flying in retreat. Mestoph shot Leviticus a dirty look.

"Oh come on, Mestoph. You've got to admit she's right," said Leviticus.

He didn't have to admit that she was right. Even if she was. But regardless, he did have to admit that looking for a Nazi from a hilltop wasn't the most efficient way to go about it. He had avoided calling Hitler, even though he had taken Atreyus' phone and dumped his own, for fear of St. Peter getting wise. Out of alternatives, Mestoph finally gave in and dialed up the Fuhrer. Fifteen minutes later, they were walking up a broken sidewalk to a small, pale green ranch house. It was just one drab house amongst dozens, with only its choice of (drab) color separating it from the others. Like all the houses in the area, it had accumulated a thick coat of fine sandy dirt on the walls and windows. The lawn was mostly desert rocks and pea gravel except for a single large boulder next to an extremely stout poplar tree. There were also a few cacti planted throughout the yard. Leviticus tapped Mestoph on the shoulder and pointed to a corner of the rock-strewn lawn at one in particular. When he had spotted what Leviticus was pointing at, he laughed triumphantly and then tapped Stephanie on the shoulder in turn and pointed. Marcus and Sir Regi looked over as well and saw a cactus in the shape of a swastika.

"Maybe he converted to Buddhism," said Sir Regi. Marcus just shrugged.

"So just how does someone like, oh...say, Hitler go to Purgatory and not Hell?" asked Stephanie.

Neither Mestoph nor Leviticus really wanted to go into detail about the whole balance of good, evil, and neutrality, or how there's no cosmic law against criminal masterminding or war crimes. For the same reason, he hadn't been credited for all the medical breakthroughs, especially in the field of psychology, that had happened through the torture and experimentation by Dr. Mengele and others. That left an egomaniacal failed artist with little to speak for or against him. Instead of explaining any of this, Leviticus just said, "The universe is a very mysterious and fucked up place."

Mestoph knocked on the door, and it jerked open. A surprisingly short man with a shaggy bowl cut, still sporting the trademark inch-wide mustache, popped his head out

"Get the Hell in here!" he said in an odd blend of an American and German accent that sounded an awful lot like Mel Brooks impersonating Hitler.

There was a look of pleading urgency on his face as Mestoph ushered the others into the house. Hitler slammed the heavy door behind them, securing the dozen locks with practiced swiftness. He peered through an off-center peephole that was much lower than the standard.

"Assassins knock on the door, expecting people to look through a peephole, and then shoot them because they know where their mark's head will be." Hitler said matter-of-factly.

Everyone nodded or muttered in agreement.

"Oh yeah, of course," said Sir Regi.

Hitler checked the peephole one more time and then led everyone into another room, locking that door behind them as well. The room was sparsely furnished, containing only a single chair and a table. The room was in the center of the house, and its chalky white walls had no windows. Except for the dim, bare bulb in a fixture on the ceiling there were no lamps. The only decoration was a well trampled and ugly as Hell Turkish rug that was a mishmash of garishly contrasting colors. Hitler kicked it aside to reveal a nearly seamless door in the floor. It had no knobs or keypads, but when he laid his hand flush against the surface, there was a loud clanking noise and then a hiss as the door slid sideways. The hole in the floor was inky dark for a moment, but then clinical fluorescent lights flickered to life down below and revealed a long set of diamond plate steel stairs. Hitler motioned the rest to follow him down what was easily a hundred feet below the surface of Truth or Consequences.

Once at the bottom, the long stairwell opened up to a large, open space of what could only be described as a concrete vault. It looked like it had been built as a fallout shelter in the 1950s and, considering its depth, the apparent thickness of the concrete walls, and what looked like a self-contained ventilation system, it could probably have survived everything but a direct hit. Scattered throughout the open space were several large metal desks covered in computers, routers, switches, and a chaotic mess of network cables running to and from devices and then out through a hole drilled in one wall.

In stark contrast to the high=tech equipment strewn all over the place, there was one clean and orderly corner with a large easel and shelves of paints, brushes, canvas stretchers, and all sorts of art supplies. There were jars ranging from tiny baby food jars to large mason jars full of a variety of plants, minerals, and even a few semi-precious stones for making a rainbow of colors. Sitting on an otherwise empty desk near the easel was a newly sealed Omen and calligraphy set with the pen still sitting in a well of India ink.

Mestoph pointed over to the desk and asked, "Is that ours?"

Hitler nodded as he walked over and picked the scroll. "Signed, sealed," he said as he handed the scroll over to Mestoph, "...and delivered."

Mestoph looked at the scroll in his hands and smiled. It had been a spent Omen when he had stolen it, but now it was rolled and sealed with a blob of wax bearing the Sigil of Lucifer. Mestoph absentmindedly picked at the wax seal with a long fingernail, which sent Hitler running over to snatch the Omen from his hands. He gave a caustic look of disapproval and inspected the seal carefully. Once satisfied that Mestoph had not damaged it, he took a wooden scroll case from a drawer and carefully slid the omen inside.

"For all intents and purposes," said Hitler, "this is an Omen-in-waiting. It's inactive until the seal is broken. Once broken, though, it can't be undone."

Hitler ran his fingers along the wooden case possessively as Mestoph put his hand out to take the Omen. Hitler handed it to Leviticus instead. The Angel took the case hesitantly, looking at Mestoph as he did. Mestoph just shrugged, and Leviticus stuck it in his sash opposite the Prophecy.

"And now my payment." said Hitler, much more confident than a few moments before.

Mestoph reached into his pocket, pulled out a flash drive, and handed it over.

"All the solo albums of all the Spice Girls, as requested," said Mestoph.

Hitler grabbed the thumb drive with a greedy smile and then ushered everyone back to the stairs leading up to the surface.

"Why the Spice Girls?" asked Stephanie.

"Ever heard of psychological warfare? This is what they use. If I listen to it enough times, I'm hoping to become immune," explained Hitler.

"You've got everything you need down here, so why not download it yourself?" asked Stephanie.

"Haven't you ever heard of the RIAA? Those bastards are brutal!"

Stephanie looked to Marcus, who just shrugged.

"Alright, guys. You don't have to leave, but you can't stay down here. It's against regulations," Hitler said as he corralled everyone, but he looked straight at Stephanie.

"Regulations?" she asked.

"Yes. The last time I was in a bunker with a woman, I ended up committing 'suicide'," said Hitler, making air quotes as they were walking up the stairs. "So now I don't let them stay down here. Or much of anyone else, so don't feel too slighted.

"No worries," said Mestoph, "We've got a pretty busy schedule ahead of us."

Once the group had exited the door in the floor, Hitler sealed it shut again with the touch of his hand. It closed with a slight sucking noise and then deep, loud clank as the locks engaged. Hitler took a quick look out of the offset peephole and then slid the array of chains and bolts on the heavy front door. He opened it slightly and peeked out again.

Satisfied the coast was clear, he opened the door to let—

or, more accurately, force— everyone out. As he was waving them out, they heard a distant pop, and then Hitler spun and fell down on the floor face first. He was bleeding and moaning, which meant he was still alive. Mestoph and Leviticus came to their senses first, both having been under gunfire before. Mestoph pulled Hitler, who screamed as the Demon grabbed him under the right shoulder painfully close to the bullet wound. As soon as Mestoph had Hitler out of the doorway, Leviticus slammed the door shut and latched the first bolt he could reach. He then grabbed Hitler under the other shoulder and pulled him back into the central room, yelling for Marcus and Stephanie to get away from the windows and doors.

Leviticus checked for an exit wound but found none. Hitler was bleeding a great deal, and the risk of sending the unaccounted for bullet further through his body was outweighed by the need to flip him over to see if they could stop the bleeding. He hesitated a moment, wondering why he cared about whether or not Hitler lived or died. Again. In his moment of hesitation, Mestoph grabbed Hitler roughly and flipped him over.

"Alright, Mein Fuhrer. You got any weapons in this paranoia death trap?" asked Mestoph.

Hitler couldn't seem to muster the strength or focus to speak, but he pointed to the door in the floor. Mestoph sighed and then grabbed Hitler's good shoulder. He looked at Leviticus and then nodded toward Hitler. Leviticus tried to grab the injured shoulder without causing more pain. He realized that it was impossible, so he just grabbed where it was easiest for him and tried his best to ignore Hitler's cries.

They dragged his body to the door in the floor, and then once again Mestoph brusquely flipped Hitler over like he was a doll, grabbed his hand, and pushed it against the surface of the door near where they had seen him touch it before. The door hissed open. At the same time, they heard another muffled pop and the shattering of glass.

"Sorry! Just wanted to see if I could find out where the shooter is," said Sir Regi, jumping back from the window in the front room.

"Outside," said Mestoph as he took off down the stairs.

Marcus and Stephanie sat on their haunches in a corner in the sparse room, trying to stay out of the way but ready to run if necessary. Stephanie looked upset, but Marcus, who was holding her hand, looked remarkably unshaken. That, or he was trying to play it strong for Stephanie's sake. Sir Regi ran over and curled up near Marcus. He looked as scared as Stephanie. Considering how close he had just come to getting shot, it was understandable.

Leviticus followed Mestoph into the bunker, where they looked around for suitable places to stash weapons. Mestoph was checking the large number of crates and steamer trunks, all of which ended up containing art or ancient artifacts. He assumed that they were all real—and, for the most part, he was correct. His search turned up nothing immediately useful.

Leviticus was going through the many desks and storage cabinets. The desk drawers contained countless folders filled with what looked like classified information from various governments, and the cabinets were full of art supplies. At last, the Angel and Demon both reached the area at the back of the bunker, where they found a long console table with a display case full of World War II weapons. There was a set of German Luger P08s, a British Sten submachine gun with a suppressor, and a German baton-style hand grenade. There were also several boxes of 9mm ammo and extra empty clips sitting in a crate underneath the table. The crate was stenciled with the Nazi Reichsalder, an eagle holding an oak wreath and a swastika.

Mestoph grabbed a stray hard drive from one of the

computer desks and chunked it at the glass case, which shattered with a pleasing crack and tinkling of shards on the hard concrete floor. Mestoph brushed aside the glass with his leather sleeve and grabbed the Sten, while Leviticus grabbed both Lugers. They both looked at the grenade and then back at each other. Leviticus shook his head no as Mestoph looked at him with a big grin.

"No," said Leviticus emphatically.

Mestoph gave a disappointed smirky-frown and then shrugged. They both grabbed a handful of ammo from the crate and then took off for the stairs. As Mestoph crested the threshold of the floor-door, there was another pop and cracking of glass.

"Goddammit Sir Regi, get away from the window," shouted Mestoph.

Instead, he saw Marcus propping up Hitler's body against the window with the curtain pulled to the side. Marcus was struggling to hold the limp body up, but managed to hold him while Sir Regi pulled on his limp arm by biting onto his shirt sleeve and tugging to the side, which caused Hitler to sway left and right like a marionette. The shot hit Hitler square in the chest without a grunt. He was undoubtedly dead.

"The shooter is behind the shed in the backyard across the street." said Stephanie, who was peeking out of the smallest possible corner of the opposite window.

Now that they had succeeded in their mission Marcus let Hitler's body fall, hoping the shooter would think he had hit his mark and stay in the same place. He and Stephanie both dropped low and hurried into the room with the floor-door. Mestoph and Leviticus exchanged a surprised yet pleased look. The humans had used an ingenious if grisly approach to draw out the shooter, and it had actually worked.

Leviticus offered Marcus one of the Lugers, but the man

declined.

"Fine, then you two are on ammo duty," Leviticus said, and both he and Mestoph tossed the ammo and extra clips at their feet.

Marcus and Stephanie obediently took up the clips and began loading them. Leviticus noticed that Stephanie was much calmer than she had been earlier. He figured she was probably in shock. Mestoph began looking around the rest of the house, searching for another way out. There wasn't much more of the house to discover. Beyond the entry way and the room with the floor-door, there was only a kitchen that looked like it hadn't been used since the house was built and a small bathroom with a walk-in shower. There was a tiny window in the kitchen over the sink, but no other windows besides than the ones that were currently watched by the unknown sniper. The front door was both the best and worst option they had.

Mestoph and Leviticus conferred with each other and agreed that their best chance was to draw fire away from the door while everyone escaped. They agreed to meet up later at a hot springs spa called Las Palomas and teleport out. Since Mestoph had the machine gun, it was decided that he would burst out of the door, spraying and praying, while everyone else ran. They quickly went over the plan with Marcus, Stephanie, and Sir Regi.

"Why can't we just teleport out of here?" asked Stephanie

"Did you forget about the whole house blowing up thing?" asked Mestoph.

"So do it in the basement. It's got walls at least a foot thick, and it's underground." "The more confined the space, the bigger the explosion. Plus we don't want to attract any unnecessary attention," explained Leviticus, trying to cut off Mestoph's short fuse before his demonic tendencies kicked in.

"Because a gun fight isn't going to draw any attention?"

Stephanie handed Mestoph the three extra clips she had loaded for him. Mestoph stood at the door, poised to pop out. He took one last deep breath and then counted out loud. On three, he burst out the door and opened fire, concentrating it on the small shed Stephanie had pointed out earlier.

The gun chewed through the thirty rounds in the magazine in less than four seconds. As Mestoph hit the release and slammed another clip into the Sten, Leviticus and the others ran out the door. Leviticus ran ahead with one of his Lugers held close to his chest so that no one could grab it but he could still aim and fire easily. As they rounded the corner, Mestoph began firing again. There hadn't been any movement by the shed, but he continued shooting at it anyway. The sound of the thin aluminum being punctured was louder than the actual gunfire, and it made for a fast but rhythmic drum roll.

Leviticus and the others subconsciously ran to the rhythm of the machine gun drum line as they rounded the corner of the house and ran right into Atreyus. He had been waiting for someone to come round the back of the house, but he had been distracted by the rhythmic firing. Leviticus and the closely held Luger slammed into Atreyus, and the Angel pulled the trigger.

Atreyus looked down at the flowering of blood on his chest and then stared at Leviticus, confused. The expression on Leviticus' face closely mirrored Atreyus' look of shock. He hadn't intended to pull the trigger, but it had happened nonetheless. He knew immediately that he had killed Atreyus, even before the weasel-faced man began to fall, because he had felt a sucking sensation deep inside him. It was the feeling of having his angelic powers taken away from him. It happened any time one side took the life of someone on the other side, and one had to go through an official debriefing to get those powers back. Leviticus would no longer be able to teleport. This would put a bit of a kink in their plans.

Marcus and Stephanie rounded the corner less than a second after the gun went off. They were just in time to see Atreyus fall. Stephanie gave a slight startled shriek but quickly reigned in her panic and clasped her hands to her mouth. Marcus tried to check for a pulse, but he jumped back when Atreyus' soul lifted from his body.

"You do know that I'll fucking kill you when I get back, right?" said Atreyus to the group as a whole, and then he disappeared.

Marcus looked to the others nervously, but Leviticus was preoccupied and Stephanie just shrugged. Without hesitating any further, Marcus pulled the sling of the MP4 off the lifeless body and threw the gun over his shoulder. He slid the clip out to take a quick ammo check and then tossed the gun so that it hung at his back. Stephanie gave Marcus a curious look as he deftly handled the weapon.

"What? I play a lot of video games," said Marcus. He put a comforting hand on Leviticus' shoulder.

"There'll be plenty of time to think about it later," said Sir Regi as he ambled up beside the body to sniff at it. "We've got to keep moving. St. Peter won't be far behind."

Leviticus took one last look down at Atreyus' lifeless body, at the bloom of blood on his chest, and then at Sir Regi. The little Scotty nodded, letting Leviticus know he understood, and the Angel nodded back.

Chapter 8

The Best Laid Plans of Angels and

Demons...

Leviticus and his group were just leaving the Las Palomas office and heading to their rooms when Mestoph careened around the resort's fence. He slid to a halt—or tried to—but unfortunately Sir Regi hadn't seen him coming and managed, in the way only dogs can, to get precisely under his feet, sending the Demon rolling on the ground. Mestoph laughed and panted in exhaustion as he came to a stop on his back. He looked up at Leviticus with a pleased smile. It dropped as he saw the look in the Angel's eyes. Something had gone wrong.

Mestoph did a head count. When he had verified that everyone had made it through the ordeal alive, he pulled himself up off the ground and looked to Leviticus.

"What gives?"

Leviticus didn't answer immediately, so Sir Regi, who had managed to avoid getting tangled up in Mestoph's fall despite actually causing it, spoke up. "Atreyus got in the way."

It took a few moments for Mestoph to work out the obvious result. If they had made it through a bout with Atreyus, that could only mean the Demon was dead again. It was another moment before the implications of that sunk in.

"Ohhhh," he said.

He looked at Marcus and Stephanie. They were obviously waiting for someone to let them in on the secret, but at least they were waiting quietly. They waited until everyone had squeezed into one of the rooms, and then finally Marcus spoke up.

"There are things going on that you haven't been honest and upfront about," Marcus said.

Stephanie, who was standing should-to-shoulder with him, nodded in agreement. It was obvious that they had at the very least broached the subject with each other while the others were preoccupied with shooting and running.

"I took you guys at your word because Sir Regi trusted you," said Stephanie. "And I trusted him because he had saved my life. At least my dream life. But since then it's just been too much to swallow. People from the Afterlife, teleporting, getting shot at. Adolf fucking Hitler? I mean, really? Hitler? I get that you say there's some apocalyptic conspiracy going on and that creature in my dream is proof someone is after me, but why are we in Purgatory— which by the way, I totally believe in after seeing this dead little town— making deals with Hitler for some mystery scroll? And now, when we should be popping the fuck out of here, why are we holing up in a couple of dingy resort motel rooms?"

Leviticus sighed and Mestoph put up a halting hand, more to tell him not to let it all out than to say he would take care of this. Mestoph cleared his throat and looked down, trying to make it look like what he was about to reveal he did so with a fair amount of reluctance.

"The man shooting at us and the man Leviticus was forced to kill are known to us. They are demons. From Hell," Mestoph paused to let that sink in. "Which means, obviously, we are Angels."

He paused again, expecting that to be a bigger revelation than it turned out to be. Neither Marcus nor Stephanie seemed terribly surprised.

"We're up against a rogue band of demons that are ignoring the Ancient Agreement between Heaven and Hell to let things take their own course. The End is inevitable, but they're trying to speed it up and wipe out mankind long before your time is up," said Mestoph

Marcus and Stephanie both looked at Leviticus for confirmation. He nodded his agreement.

"If that's true, what does that have to do with us?" asked Marcus. He looked at Stephanie, and she surprised him by taking his hand.

"We don't really know. The demons seem to think you're important, and we don't know why," said Mestoph.

Leviticus interjected suddenly, "Come on Mestoph. Let's be honest with them."

Mestoph gave him a threatening look and started to say something, but Leviticus held up his hand and stared back sternly. Mestoph shook his head and cursed under his breath. He knew Leviticus was not going to back down.

"It's believed by those of us at the upper echelons that as the Apocalypse draws near, as it does now, that a line of Protectors will be born that will protect humanity from outside meddling. At no other time than the End Days is the future more susceptible to tampering. From expediting The End to forcing mankind to draw and cross lines they were never meant to know about. Based on recent movements and intelligence from Hell, we think that line of Protectors starts with you two," said Leviticus

The look of honesty and sincerity in Leviticus eyes consoled and frightened everyone in the room for drastically different reasons. Mestoph tried his best to fight the overwhelming urge to laugh. He had never known Leviticus to be capable of such convincing and well-crafted bullshit. He was truly impressed. Even Sir Regi was swayed by his story, looking at them both with a hint of betrayal, thinking that they had lied to him about the nature and danger of their mission.

"The problem we face now is that we are bound by rules

that cannot be broken. When I shot that demon, I lost my Angelic abilities. That means I can't teleport any longer, either on my own or with Mestoph's help," said Leviticus. He looked to Mestoph to see what his response would be. St. Peter was on their trail, and they didn't have the luxury to waste days waiting around for Leviticus to catch up by plane or whatever it took to get to the national reserves of northeastern Peru, which is where their next leg of the plan would take them. It was remote enough that whatever disaster they created would cause negligible collateral damage, and it had minimal presence by Heaven, Hell, or Freewill International. There were the minor tribal deities, but Mestoph seriously doubted either God or Satan would really complain about taking out some annoying demigod.

Mestoph looked back at Leviticus, weighing all the possibilities and repercussions as quickly as he could. At last he said, "We'll have to do it here."

"Are you sure?" asked Leviticus.

"Do what here?" asked Sir Regi.

Mestoph did his best to explain the situation, using as much truth as possible without revealing anything damaging. He explained that the scroll they got from Hitler was a Counter-Omen. Leviticus interrupted to give them the basics on Omens and Prophecies. Mestoph jumped in with some rules he had made up on the fly, stating that Omens and Prophecies can contradict but never negate one another. When they contradict it comes down to the will of the people involved to do what they deem best. He told Marcus and Stephanie that there were already Omens and Prophecies regarding the two of them, so the Demons were doing what they could to get their Omen to win out over the Prophecy. The Counter-Omen they got from Hitler could potentially negate the previous Omen, but would definitely create a conflict between Heaven and Hell. They had hoped to transport Marcus and Stephanie somewhere more remote where they could operate without dragging the rest of humanity into the battle. Unfortunately recent events had made this impossible. Mestoph couldn't leave Leviticus to fend for himself. In the days to come they would need everyone they could get to keep them safe.

"So we'll have to activate the Counter-Omen here and see what happens." said Mestoph.

Chapter 9

...Oft Go Awry

They all sat around the small motel room in a rough circle. Marcus and Stephanie were sitting against the headboard on one of the twin beds, still holding hands, while Sir Regi had curled up at Marcus' feet. Leviticus took the Omen from his sash, handed it to Mestoph, and then sat on the corner of the other bed.

Mestoph stood in the middle of the room and looked down at the scroll. This was a pivotal moment in his life. He was about to change the course of history and set things on an irreversible path. His only hesitation came from doing it in such a populated area, relatively speaking. The deserts of Africa were much more conducive to keeping collateral damage to a minimum when summoning down the wrath of Heaven and Hell, but he took solace in the fact that *most* of the people who would be caught in the middle of this had died once already. Without any more hesitation he dug his thumbnail into the great wax Seal of Satan and pried it away from the parchment. He felt a welling up of power in him and looked around to see if the others could feel it, but they just looked on expectantly. He finally pried the seal all the way off, feeling the tension in the scroll, both physical and spiritual, immediately release. And then there was nothing.

The fragments of the wax seal fell to the floor and the power Mestoph had felt building up immediately fizzled out. He looked around. Was that really it? No thunder? No lightning? Not even a light gust of wind? He walked over to the window and pulled the curtains back to look outside hoping to see a sky of blood and ash, trees aflame, and hear the agonized screams of people running around in chaos.

Instead the cloudless sky was clear blue, the sun shining down merrily.

"What the fuck!" Mestoph shouted.

Leviticus sighed with disappointment while Sir Regi, Marcus, and Stephanie looked at each other with confusion. They weren't really sure what they had been expecting, but Mestoph and Leviticus clearly had expected something and it hadn't happened. Mestoph unrolled the Omen and read through it quickly, trying to understand what had happened.

"Are you sure the Omen is right? Maybe Hitler screwed it up?" Leviticus asked, trying to be helpful.

"Of course it's fucking right," said Mestoph as he threw the Omen at Leviticus.

Leviticus picked up the scroll off the bed and unrolled it. Leviticus arched his brow and began reading slowly; using his finger to make sure he caught every word. Finally he looked up and asked, "Who the Hell is Persephone?"

Mestoph, who had plopped into a chair in the corner and was staring dejectedly at the floor, looked up blankly at Leviticus. He shook his head, not really comprehending the point of the question.

Leviticus looked around, not wanting to read the Omen aloud since it didn't really jive with the story they had fed the others. Instead, he held it up in front of Mestoph and pointed to the relevant word. Mestoph read it and then asked, "Who the fuck is Persephone?"

"The daughter of Demeter and unwilling bride of Hades," answered Stephanie.

"Who?" asked Mestoph.

"Persephone," answered Stephanie.

"Well unless you're a distant relative, we are royally fucked," said Mestoph as he rolled his eyes.

110

The wind was picking up drastically, and the man was desperately searching for a place to stay the night and weather the storm. It was dark, and his lantern was fluttering in the stiff gusts. He didn't have much oil left. As it was, it only offered a meager amount of light, more for comfort than for navigating the rocky fields they had been walking through for the last few days. He looked down at the lamb that had been following him. Despite her thick fleece, the weather was getting to her.

She looked up at the shepherd and bleated. He looked down, concerned, and then picked her up and carried her close to him. "Don't worry. It's just a typical early spring storm; it's the last holdout of winter. They blow out as quickly as they blow in," said the shepherd.

The lamb didn't seem too comforted as she kept looking around nervously. She had begun to shake, but the shepherd couldn't tell if it was from the sudden cold or from fear. He stroked the lamb's soft fleece and began singing an old song in a harsh, Germanic sounding language. His voice warbled and lilted as he sang what sounded like a child's bedtime song full of warmth and sweetness.

The shepherd continued to walk through the field, carrying the lamb in one arm like a football and holding the lantern low but in front of him in the other. A bolt of lightning arced in the distance, backlighting what looked like a dilapidated barn. It had been the only thing remotely resembling shelter that they had seen since sunset so he altered his course and set off toward it. The wind picked up even more, thick rain drops began to fall and lightning shot down in jagged branches more and more frequently. He wasn't sure they could make it much further, so the barn was their only hope for the night.

"Don't worry, Persephone, we're going to be alright," said the shepherd.

"So now what?" asked Sir Regi.

He looked at Leviticus and Mestoph, waiting for an answer. He was beginning to doubt their story about Marcus and Stephanie siring a line of Protectors, but they were still the ones with the plan. Now that he thought about it, he wondered why they hadn't explained about the Protectors to begin with. It was a lot less risky than talking about a plan to get kicked out of Heaven or Hell and using him as an intentional traitor to the cause. No, the more he thought about it, the more the original plan made more sense. Only it hadn't worked; at least not as they had intended.

Finally Mestoph made a decision. "We wait. I felt definite power in the Omen. It worked; it just didn't work the way we expected it to. Something has got to be happening somewhere. We just need to find out where."

Everyone started talking at once. How would they find *something* happening *somewhere* when they had no idea what or any clue where? How long could they hide out and expect to stay hidden? Were they really just going to sit around this motel room until they found what they were looking for, or got desperate, or got killed?

Sir Regi was the first to provide anything productive to the argument.

"How 'bout a sports bar? They have tons of TVs and we can turn them all to different news channels and wait for something to stand out. Something new and violent. Maybe we'll get lucky and a giant pentagram will appear in the sky over Greece or Rome and then we'll have our sign."

They argued a little more, but ultimately decided to take at least a part of Sir Regi's plan and put it into motion. For the time being they were safe at the dusty little resort, so it seemed foolish to waste a good hiding place. Not to mention that neither Leviticus nor Mestoph could remember having ever seen a sports bar during their various trips to Truth or Consequences. Instead they raided a consignment shop down the road and picked up a stolen shopping cart full of old TVs that people had dumped over the years on the sidewalk in front of the shop.

With Marcus' help, they found all the cables, splitters, decoder boxes in nearby rooms, and hooked up a total of six TVs. They had one turned to the local news channel, another turned to CNN, a third hooked to Fox News, a fourth to the PBS station out of Albuquerque where they could get BBC World News and Deutsche Well, a fifth was tuned to Al Jazeera even though it seemed to piss off anyone who watched, and then for shits and giggles, and because *Storm Stories* gave them a break from yelling at Glenn Beck, they had The Weather Channel on the final one. And then the waiting began.

It started out as kind of a novelty: hanging out in the rooms, taking turns watching TV, and soaking in the hot springs. They ordered pizza and Chinese food at first, but no one had really brought a lot of money with them because they hadn't expected to need it. Mestoph and Leviticus were flat broke. However, as hours turned into days, the smallness and closeness of having four people and a dog, who still insisted on being let out to take care of business, began to take its toll.

Then there was the monotony of the news and weather. The day's issues were repeated ad nauseam every half hour, yet spun in drastically different directions depending on the channel. What seemed like a straightforward issue could be turned for or against any cause if you said it loud and often enough. And the weather struggled to be interesting even on bad days. No one cared about record highs in the west, droughts in the south, a cold snap in Australia, or severe thunder storms in Iceland. The first-hand accounts of major storms of the last thirty years could all be summed up quite easily:

"I never saw it coming."

"It sounded like a freight train."

"I slept right through it."

It seemed like no matter the freak of nature—whether it was an F5 tornado in Kansas, a mud slide in Peru, or an earthquake in New Zealand—the survivors always said the same things.

Nerves were beginning to fray and patience was quickly running out, so they all began taking turns going out to get food. They let Stephanie go first since she was the only normal person in the group and possessed a debit card to get money out of the ATM at a ridiculously inflated service charge because it was some no-name locals-only bank. They quickly found that there were very few places in T or C that had anything resembling a normal schedule. They were running on recommendations from the clerk at the motel office and the nearby gas station; however, none of them could seem to agree on when anything was open. One restaurant that came highly recommended was only open on Tuesday, Thursday, and Saturday. Another was only open Friday, Saturday, and for breakfast on Sunday. Others were only open on weekdays or weekends.

Being that it was Wednesday and almost nothing was open, they ended up eating burgers from a local joint called Big A Burger. No one could give a reasonable explanation for the name, not even the employees. The cashier said it was a polite way of saying "big ass burger." The cook said the A was short for the original owner's name, Al. Why Al needed to be shortened he couldn't explain. A customer, one of the few veterans to a town who seemed to have absolutely no natives, said that the place used to just be called "A Burger" before they opened a smaller satellite drive-through on the other side of town. The drive through became known as Little A, while the original place became Big A. The two teenaged employees laughed and completely dismissed this version of the etymology. Regardless, the food seemed to hit the spot and was a nice change from the bland, greasy pizza served up by the pie shop near the motel.

When Stephanie returned to the motel, Mestoph and Leviticus were in the midst of a heated debate over whether or not abortion was a sin, a topic courtesy of the news. Mestoph seemed to believe that murder was murder, regardless of whether it was something a day old or a hundred years old. He argued that if abortion was OK, then the logical extrapolation was that it should be OK to kill the kid up until it was eighteen. This set Leviticus off, and he was in the process of explaining how that kind of arbitrary extrapolation was what started wars. At the sight of food they both quickly gave up their arguments and jumped to snatch bags out of her arms, digging through them and tossing aside what wasn't theirs.

Stephanie looked at Marcus and he just smiled and shrugged. They both waited for the frenzy to die down. During dinner they had gotten in the habit of turning down all the TVs, though they never turned them off. Even late at night, someone would be up and giving them all at least a cursory glance.

They all sat around the small circular table in the kitchenette of one of the rooms—whose room was whose had long since become a pointless differentiation. Despite the fact that they had only been together for a little less than a week, they had bonded into a sort of dysfunctional family, and dinner at least had a semi-formal ritual of sitting at the cramped table and discussing things like they all imagined a normal family did. Mostly it consisted of asking Mestoph and Leviticus questions about the afterlife. To Marcus and Stephanie, they seemed to have markedly different perspectives, though they never outright contradicted each other. They assumed it had to do with the different lines of work in the Angels were in. Leviticus was rather straightforward about his menial administrative work while, Mestoph was more vague about exactly what his job entailed. It seemed to be more along the lines of Heaven's equivalent to the CIA. Stephanie even suspected that Mestoph had actually spent a bit of time in Hell on his assignments.

Seemingly contradictory views and lifestyles hadn't gotten in the way of their friendship. If nothing else, it seemed they got along better because of their differences. The constant updates about Iceland on the Weather Channel had prompted a story about Thor trying to get both God and Satan to go in with him and the other Norse gods on some sort of cell phone deal.

"You mean Thor and the others are real?" asked Marcus.

"Yeah, most of the gods of old are, or at least were. The Norse are particularly stubborn. The Egyptian gods were pretty good sports about falling out of favor and retired voluntarily. I know things in Heaven were pretty tense at that time. We were prepared for war," said Leviticus.

"War?" asked Stephanie, shocked.

"Oh yeah," said Mestoph, "There have been quite a few wars between the gods over the millennia. The Romans, or more accurately the Greeks, were especially troublesome. But they were fighting a war on multiple fronts and weren't remotely unified. Hades, easily the strongest and most organized, was focused solely on battling Satan for control of

116

the Underworld. They were struggling to remain relevant while dozens of tribal, family, and newcomer gods skirmished on various fronts. There was in-fighting, double crossing, back stabbing, and sellouts. And then they all had to fight God and even Satan when he got bored with the battle against Hades. War is a way of life for gods. Where do you think you guys got it from?"

Marcus and Stephanie just shrugged.

"So what happened with the cell phones?" asked Marcus.

"Oh, everyone told Thor it was a stupid idea and that it'd never work, and even if it did no one would want to always have a phone with them everywhere they went. It appears that God and Satan were both wrong about that," said Leviticus.

Dinner went on with other random bits of afterlife trivia or sharing the rare interesting things they had seen on one of the news channels. When they were all finished, Sir Regi proceeded to clean up after everyone, eating the leftover fries and bits of hamburger that no one else wanted. After he had licked every bit of cheese off the burger wrappers, which he dubbed cheese paper, he curled up on one of the beds, cleaned himself thoroughly, and then went to sleep.

Since Stephanie got to go out that day, it was her turn to pull the late shift of TV watching. She decided to get an early nap before a long night of regurgitated news and infomercials. She quickly fell asleep and found herself on the familiar path in the woods, which she hadn't seen since the nightmare almost a week ago. It was a bright, briskly cool day with more blue in the sky than clouds. It was a drastic change from the dry heat of the Truth or Consequences. She was dressed for the cool weather in an off-white wool pea coat and a light scarf wrapped loosely around her neck. The light wind tousled the end of the scarf playfully.

She wasn't used to seeing this place during the day, but

then again she rarely slept in the middle of the afternoon either. Also unusual was the fact that her grandmother wasn't there waiting for her. She wondered if she had a life of her own during the day, visiting dead family members and talking about the good old days with friends that passed on before her. She also wondered if Grams would come back after what happened the last time.

Without a guide, she decided to explore the dreamscape on her own. Everything seemed peaceful in the daylight, and Stephanie wasn't at all afraid. The roots and twigs that had grabbed at her in the nightmare now seemed nothing more than nature taking its natural course. Hopping from limb to limb were small winter starlings that seemed to look on with great interest, following her down the path in a slowly growing entourage. After fifteen or twenty minutes, she arrived at the graveyard her grandmother had shown her. Unlike the last dream, she didn't see her name on any of the headstones. She wondered if that was some prophetic power only her grandmother had, or if things had changed since then.

The graveyard was the furthest she had ever come in her dreams, and with nothing pressing or predatory lurking, she decided to venture even further. The path beyond the graveyard seemed much like what she had already traveled, though the branches hung lower and the worn footpath was a bit less worn. She wondered if other people used this place when she wasn't there.

Stephanie was lost in idle thought as she walked when she suddenly stopped. She thought she heard what sounded like someone clearing their throat behind her. She felt the sucking feeling she knew heralded one of those winged creatures, but she didn't feel the same overwhelming fear and danger. She turned slowly and saw that she had somehow walked past an older gentleman sitting at a small cafe table just off the trail.

Shimmering into existence behind him were two winged creatures. Although it had been dark the last time she had seen one, she knew one of them to be a Nephilim from its inky blackness. The other one—a Seraphim she presumed—was blindingly white. There was a subtle sound beyond or mixed in with the Seraphim's soft but frantic flapping of wings that sounded almost like chanting. It was like a church choir singing "Holy, holy" repeatedly, but infinitely changing tone and overlapping impossibly. No noise save the insane flapping came from the Nephilim.

The man stood in the bygone way that a gentleman used to rise when a lady entered the room. He was broad shouldered and seemed to have an intense animal strength that he downplayed with a benevolent facade. He politely motioned to a chair opposite him as he moved to pull it out for her. She felt an overwhelming urge to comply with his friendly gesture—so she did. He slid the chair in for her as she sat at the table and then took his place opposite her.

"Let me introduce myself, if I may," he said in an evenly paced tone. "I am St. Peter."

Stephanie tensed up at the mention of his name. This was the man chasing them, not to mention shooting at them. He seemed to know the power of his name and left an appropriate pause while she absorbed the full meaning of it.

"What do you want?" she asked.

St. Peter smiled, his face suddenly taking on a gorilla-like quality she hadn't noticed before.

"I wanted to let you know what you're really getting into. I can't honestly believe that you would involve yourself with the likes of Mestoph and Leviticus willingly. I don't think you understand the danger you put yourself in by associating with them," he said.

Stephanie looked intently at St. Peter. He didn't hesitate

locking eyes with her; he was a man used to being in charge. In response to her attempted stare down, St. Peter rolled his shoulders, the thick muscles hidden behind the white suit he was wearing pushing at the seams He seemed to be saying to her that there was no way she could psych him out. He had been doing this for far too long to feel threatened by some little mortal girl.

"I know exactly what kind of danger I'm in. Being shot at by you and your goon made that abundantly clear," said Stephanie.

St. Peter chuckled. "I'll be honest, I didn't know there was anyone other than Mestoph and Leviticus in there until you all poured out in a blaze of glory. And it wasn't until these guys got involved," he said motioning to the two winged creatures behind him with something that Stephanie could have sworn was uneasiness, "that I even knew who you were. I'm still not sure who the guy with the dog is."

St. Peter paused to let Stephanie smile at his admitted ignorance. "Don't worry, I will find out who he is. And once I have all the pieces, I'll have you," he continued. "But you could save all the pain and heartache and just tell me where you are now."

Stephanie surprised everyone, including herself, when she bolted from her seat, kicking the table at St. Peter in the process. The glancing blow from the table sent him sprawling. The Nephilim and Seraphim just floated to the side gracefully, avoiding the table and St. Peter.

Stephanie ran into the woods. The two creatures turned and followed her. They weren't fast, but they seemed to be able to avoid the trees and branches with an effortless grace. Stephanie had to run as fast as she could while avoiding the many obstacles the woods presented her.

Although it had been no later than noon when she had started her walk, it seemed as if the sun was beginning to set faster and faster the further from the trail she got. That and the suffocating closeness of the dense woods made it seem to get dark unusually quickly. She could hear the flapping and choir chanting still in the distance. It seemed that she had gained something of a lead on the creatures, but she couldn't bet on them ever getting tired while she was already beginning to feel her strength waning.

She began looking for a place where she could potentially hold off the Seraphim and Nephilim and survive until someone came to save her or she woke up. Sir Regi had defeated, or at least sent the Nephilim back to where it had come from, but she didn't know if they were vulnerable to physical attacks or if you had to be a laser-shooting dream dog.

As the light faded, she noticed a soft green glow in the distance. She changed her course and headed toward it. There was no way of knowing what it was, but if St. Peter and the Seraphim were behind her, then she figured it couldn't get any worse than them. She steered around a large thicket of briars and jumped over a low log, landing in an unnatural clearing in the woods.

The clearing looked as if a perfect sphere of fire had evaporated everything in its way. The result was a charred sphere in the middle of dense, old growth forest. The sphere dug several feet into the ground, creating a perfect, glass-smooth crater. The globe of destruction extended twenty feet above Stephanie's head. Despite all the burnt wood, there wasn't even a hint of smoke, just the smell of the exposed earth, which she noticed seemed to be completely untouched by weather. It was either very fresh, or perfectly and permanently preserved. The green glow seemed to be coming from everywhere and nowhere at once.

After she had taken in the oddity of scene, she noticed that there were some objects at the bottom of the crater that clearly didn't belong there: random pieces of riot gear, a gas mask, and a futuristic looking rifle. She was startled from her cursory inspection by the sound of flapping and chanting, which had suddenly become loud and close. She jumped into the crater and grabbed the mask and futuristic rifle. She tugged the mask on and spun around as first the Seraphim approached the crater. It came to a quick but smooth stop at the edge and stood there, seeming to hesitate.

Stephanie did not hesitate. She pulled the trigger. A green globe of light, much bigger than the barrel it had come from, shot out of the rifle and traveled toward the Seraphim. It all seemed to happen in slow motion, so slowly she was sure the Seraphim would strafe to the side and easily avoid the globe. The Seraphim did try, but it took the globe full in the chest.

The Seraphim flew backwards like it had been hit by a cartoon cannon ball. Unlike a cartoon, the globe was burning the Seraphim, feathers singing in green crackles of sparks. She could now see all six of its wings moving slowly and clearly. She also noticed that her vantage point was shifting, as if she was moving up. She looked down, and her feet were no longer on the ground. She *was* floating upwards. It was all happening so slowly, but her mind raced in real time. She looked up and saw the source of green light above her. There was a rift in the air—paper thin, maybe even one-dimensional, so that when she had stood at the precipice of the crater she must have been seeing it edge on, which would have made it practically invisible.

As she drew closer to the rift, which she had no way of avoiding, time seemed to speed up. The Seraphim was burning up faster. The chanting had slowed to an ultra-low warble of notes that blurred together but was underlined by soft whispers that sounded like they were reciting scripture. The Seraphim continued to fly backwards, now a ball of green sparks and feathers, hurtling toward the Nephilim. She saw the Nephilim wink out moments before she did.

For just a moment, Stephanie winked back into existence inside what had been a small glassed in room, though most of the glass lay shattered on the ground. There were busted monitors all across one wall, and the body of a security guard was sprawled out on the floor. Just as she had taken in her surroundings, she felt herself being sucked backwards and the green glow of the rip in time began to grow and fluctuate wildly. As she drew near the rip and time sped up again, there was a soft bloom of what she thought looked like a supernova, but it vanished before it reached its peak.

When she popped back into existence again, she was back on the dream path in an eerily familiar scene. Standing across the clearing from Stephanie was another Stephanie. She suddenly recalled this moment from over a week ago. Standing behind the other Stephanie—though she considered at this point in her history *she* was now Other-Stephanie and was looking at Past-Stephanie—was a Nephilim.

Future-Present-Other-Stephanie, the one with the rifle, pulled the trigger and another green globe of energy sprang forth from the barrel. It ripped through the Nephilim's neck, almost severing it. Black feathers and blacker blood shot from the wound, and the Nephilim roared out in rage. Past-Stephanie disappeared with a shimmer, and then the Nephilim's body fell to the ground. It smoked and sizzled as it collapsed into a pile of ashes and black feathers.

Stephanie woke up. She was back in the hotel room.

"St. Peter just visited me." she said to no one in particular; though it was Sir Regi who jumped up first.

Chapter 10

A cold day in...

Although dawn had come, it was only marginally brighter than it had been during the night. The shepherd had barely slept, and although the lamb had, it was hardly what could be called a restful sleep. The storm had only intensified in the night, and it had gotten surprisingly cold for this time of year. The shepherd had tried to start a fire with some of the wood that had once been essential to the structural integrity of the shabby barn they were hiding in, but it was rotten and damp and produced more smoke than flame. It only provided psychological comfort, and even that was marginal.

The shepherd pulled out the last of his meager food from a small sack he had tied to his belt and divided the rest of the hard bread and cheese he had taken from his home nearly a week ago. When Persephone had told him they were in danger, she had given him little time to pack. She had told him that "he" was after them and they had to run. She had told him years before that their love was forbidden, but that didn't stop either one of them, and now they were supposedly paying the price.

He looked down at the lamb and sighed. He didn't look forward to a day of walking through the wind and rain through the wilderness, but she had insisted that they stay on foot as it would be harder for "him" to track them if they stayed off the normal paths. The shepherd sighed one more time before he shook Persephone awake. It would be a very long day.

Mestoph listened intently as Stephanie went over every detail of her dream for the second time. He and Leviticus were mostly interested in St. Peter. Sir Regi seemed much more interested in the Nephilim and Seraphim. Marcus was silent throughout the whole interrogation, but even Mestoph could see the concern in his eyes—and that Stephanie was comforted by his concern.

"And you're sure you didn't say anything before running off?" Mestoph asked once again.

"No! I asked St. Peter what he wanted; he said that I had no idea what I'd gotten myself into. I'm starting to think he was right."

"So you didn't tell him anything about us?"

"I didn't give away your plan, if that's what you're really concerned about," she said, crossing her arms over her chest.

"Look, I'm sorry to bruise your fragile little ego, but if you said—"

"That's enough!" said Marcus in that tone that fathers used when they're fed up with their kids' bickering.

Everyone looked over at him. He had stood up to speak, though whether it was for emphasis or because he was about to rescue Stephanie from Mestoph's barrage of questions was up in the air. Stephanie got up and walked into the adjoining room. Marcus followed her. Sir Regi looked to Mestoph and Leviticus and they shook their heads. Sir Regi made a soft, chirpy bark and then curled back up on the bed, casting constant glances at the door to the other room. After several minutes, he closed his eyes and settled in for a nap.

Mestoph and Leviticus looked at each other briefly. They didn't quite smile. Things were progressing nicely on that front, at least. Unfortunately, things were less than perfect with the other half of their plan. Almost a week of being cramped into two small rooms with nothing but TV and each other to keep themselves sane, and nothing to show for it. They had started taking turns visiting the hot spring baths, which were the whole reason most others stayed at these rather sad excuses for resorts, but the tension and strain that had melted away in 106 degree mineral water would quickly mount again minutes after returning to their rooms. If St. Peter didn't find them first, Mestoph and Leviticus weren't sure how much longer they would last before they did themselves in.

Mestoph stared at the televisions. Then, suddenly, something caught his eye. Sir Regi jerked awake as Mestoph jumped up, shouting.

"You've got to be fucking kidding me," said Mestoph.

Leviticus turned to look at the screen, and a big smile spread across his face. Sir Regi looked up at them, and then at the weather report. A storm swirled over Iceland. It had brought near record rains and low temperatures, but until now they hadn't paid it any attention. Now it was definitely a sign. The storm had mutated into a slowly revolving pentagram, hovering over one of the mountains in the mainland. The oddest thing was how absolutely no one was mentioning its rather peculiar and ominous shape.

"Alright, kids," said Leviticus, "get your shit together. We're heading to Iceland first thing in the morning."

Knowing where you have to go and getting there are completely different things. Aside from the fact that there was no such thing as a direct flight to Iceland from New Mexico, they also had to figure out how to get tickets for four people and a dog without leaving a trail for St. Peter to follow. Using Stephanie's credit card in Truth or

Consequences wasn't really a big deal because St. Peter already knew where they were. But now they needed to get to Iceland and find what they were looking for without giving up their hand.

They needed St. Peter to assume they were remaining there for as long as possible. The trip would require driving to Albuquerque, getting a flight first to Chicago, then to London, and then finally to Reykjavik. Each stop represented a potential security risk as both Heaven and Hell could have spies and lookouts anywhere.

"What if St. Peter watches The Weather Channel?" asked Sir Regi while everyone was sitting around the kitchen table brainstorming.

"Huh?" asked Leviticus.

"You're all assuming St. Peter hasn't figured everything out already. Why else would we have hunkered down for a week except that we were waiting for something? And if we're waiting for something, then he has to be wondering what it is. Just because the guy with the perfect weatherman haircut doesn't recognize a pentagram when he sees one sure as Hell doesn't mean St. Peter won't," said Sir Regi.

Everyone looked at the little dog, dumbfounded.

"So basically what you're saying is that we don't have to move in secrecy, we just have to get there before he does?" asked Marcus. Sir Regi just nodded.

The next morning they were all sitting on an airplane somewhere over the Atlantic Ocean. Stephanie had maxed out one credit card and pushed the limit on her emergency card for five last minute tickets to Iceland. All told, it cost nearly $20,000. Of course the airline had insisted Sir Regi had to have his own ticket, even after they had spent the entire drive from Truth or Consequences to Albuquerque trying to convince Sir Regi to travel in a small dog carrier they had picked up at the Salvation Army store near the motel. After he had finally acquiesced, and after many assurances from the ticket seller that he could ride as carry on under one of their seats, the stewardess refused to let him on without purchasing another ticket for a little dog. Sir Regi was quite happy to sit in the seat next to Marcus and Stephanie, but Stephanie was thinking about how long it was going to take her to pay off their little trip.

The flight to Chicago and even the long and arduous flight to London had been uneventful to the point of being torturous. Mestoph had thought he had seen a fellow demon at Heathrow, but it didn't really matter how many people knew where they were going because they had to get to Iceland as fast as possible regardless. Their plan, the true plan that Mestoph and Leviticus were following, relied on them being in control of whatever disaster was to befall the people of there. All they had to do was get there first in one piece with the Omen, Marcus, and Stephanie, and then they would have all the bargaining power.

The fact that the Omen wasn't actually about Marcus and Stephanie didn't matter as long as everyone believed it did. And since even Marcus and Stephanie believed it, it was as good as true.

Because they had booked their flight last minute, they were spread all across the coach class of the 747 they were flying on to Reykjavik. Marcus, Stephanie, and Sir Regi had managed to get seats together, but Mestoph and Leviticus were separated from each other and the rest of the group by several rows. They had hoped to get some time alone to talk about what to do about Persephone, as she was a loose end in their plan. Why was she in Iceland? The Greek gods didn't have much sway in Iceland—it was Norse territory, after all—so the presence of a Greek goddess, even a relatively minor one, was puzzling.

Neither God nor Satan had really had a lot to do with

the Greek gods; they remained mostly a curiosity for tourists visiting Rome and Greece and the small sects of people who still believed in their power. Furthermore, the way the Omen was worded would insinuate that Persephone was in Iceland not with her husband Hades, but with some illicit lover. They would at least have to put up the illusion of hunting Persephone down for the sake of Marcus and Stephanie, but they would have to consider searching for her in earnest to ensure they held all the cards. If it became known that Persephone was the actual target of the Omen, they had no idea how or if they could keep the upper hand.

After the flight from Chicago to London, this little hop was like a drive to the store. However, it became a rather bumpy drive as they approached the southern coast of Iceland and hit the outer reaches of the giant storm. The captain came on the intercom and warned passengers that they would be in for some heavy turbulence, but that it was nothing to be alarmed about. After being jostled around for a few minutes, both Leviticus and Mestoph gave up the dreams of a nap. Mestoph looked back to where Marcus and Stephanie sat. Stephanie laid her head on Marcus' shoulder, and the two of them were holding hands, paying little attention to the turbulence. It was nice to see someone at least was getting what he wanted. It was too bad that Mestoph and Leviticus were probably going to ruin both their lives before this was all done.

"You guys traveling together?" asked a man behind Mestoph. The voice spoke in English heavily tinted with an African accent. The Demon had thought the seat had been occupied by an old German woman.

Mestoph turned around to find a very dark-skinned black man in the seat behind him; not Demon dark, but pretty close. He was wearing a solid black shirt with a priest's collar tucked around his neck, which made Mestoph cringe a little.

"Uh, yeah," said Mestoph uncomfortably. "Why?"

"You keep checking on them, so I was just curious. Guess you couldn't get seats together. Last minute trip?"

"Something like that," said Mestoph.

The priest turned to look out his window briefly and then turned back to Mestoph, giving him a broad smile full of brilliantly white teeth, "Sorry I bothered you," said the priest as he sat back in his seat and closed his eyes.

"Yeah, me too," said Mestoph under his breath as he turned back around.

Mestoph looked out the window as the plane flew over the coast and into the mainland. He hadn't realized it, but he had been tensed up. Now he sighed with relief. They had made it to Iceland and had victory in their sights. He was about to close the visor when something bright on the horizon caught his attention. For the briefest of moments, he thought it was the sun rising, but he was on the northern side of the plane and it was the wrong time of the day. Now that he looked at it, it was also far too small to be the sun. He titled his head in doglike confusion as he realized it was getting bigger. He knew what it was, but his mind refused to click.

He just looked at the missile—no, maybe it was just a Rocket Propelled Grenade. Its slightly erratic path seemed to jostle with the same turbulence as the plane, which is when he finally acknowledged that there was definitely an RPG flying straight at the airplane.

"Well, shit," he muttered to himself as he realized the RPG was about to shoot his dreams out of the sky along with the airplane.

There was no time to do anything meaningful about the RPG speeding toward them, so he simply crossed his arms and slumped back in his seat with his bottom lip jutted out, completing a picture that any parent would recognize as pouting. At first it just felt like more turbulence, albeit slightly more intense, but then the explosion ripped off the wing, which in turn ripped a hole in the side of the airplane the size of a small car.

It didn't quite happen like in the movies. There was no sudden vacuum that sucked everyone out of the cabin, but the hole the wing had ripped away was ragged and the drag continued to rip it wider. The passengers stared straight at the front of the cabin, screaming in terror. The only time they quieted was when one of them braved a look at the hole, the view instantly silencing them for a moment—but only for a moment.

Mestoph picked himself up off the floor and looked around. He was facing the back of the plane. There was a giant windy hole in the wall to his right. He could see the ground a few thousand feet below and wondered if the pilot was trying to land in the tundra, or if they were going down against their will. He figured it was probably a little bit of both. Leviticus was getting to his feet after a brief struggle with the seat belt and slid out of the aisle to run over to Mestoph. He could see that Leviticus was saying something, but he couldn't hear anything but a muffled rushing sound. Leviticus was next to him now and trying to get Mestoph to lean on him, finally pointing down to Mestoph's leg. Mestoph followed the direction of Leviticus' finger, and saw several small pocket-knife sized shards of metal sticking out of his left thigh.

"Mother fucker," he thought.

Part of the floor underneath the seats of row 45 suddenly crumbled away. The bolts in the seat legs rattled around without any anchor and began vibrating out of their channels. The passenger nearest the stretching hole tried to shy away, but the seatbelt kept him strapped in tight. He fumbled the seatbelt loose and then began climbing over the other passengers in his row like they were household furniture and he was playing the old childhood game where the floor is made of lava.

He looked like he was going to make it, and then he was gone. The two passengers still strapped to their seats looked surprised, as if they had been witness to true magic. They tore at their seatbelts, but then, with metaphorical lightning striking twice, they too were gone. They took the whole row of seats with them, leaving behind an ever larger hole. Then the plane flew into the storm that surrounded most of Iceland, and the ride quickly got rougher. Amidst flashes of lightning—this time the real stuff—rain whipped around the hole and turbulence got drastically worse.

Leviticus helped Mestoph move closer toward the back of the plane, near Marcus and Stephanie, who looked remarkably calm. Not like they were in shock—it was obvious they were aware of what was happening—but it was the kind of calm of those who knew freaking out wasn't going to do any good. Sir Regi had hopped into Marcus' lap, shaking in that mildly convulsive way that only dogs could. Marcus and Stephanie held tightly on to each other's hands.

Leviticus sat Mestoph down in Sir Regi's vacated chair so he could take a look at the Demon's leg. The shards weren't much bigger than fingers, but if they were fingers they were stuck about two knuckles deep into his leg. With his Demonic metabolism, Mestoph wouldn't stay on the injured list for too long, but Leviticus pulled the shards out and tried to bandage them using the pillowcase of the crappy airline pillow the cranky stewardess, air hostess, sky bitch...whatever she was, had given everyone on the flight. Leviticus was really just trying to preoccupy himself and Mestoph as the plane continued to shake and drop.

After the disappearance of the row of seats near the hole in the plane, everyone had moved out of fear of falling or being sucked out into the void. Most had crowded back into the tail section of the plane, where Mestoph, Leviticus, and the rest of the gang were. They all faced forward to the front of the plane, most in an awkward, shocked silence. No one really knew what they were waiting for: to die, to crash, to land, or even to wake up from a dream and find that everything was really just fine. A few people had slowly begun to get used to the sound of roaring wind and herky-jerky shaking of the plane and were actually beginning to have somewhat calm and casual conversations. Others began to cry, some began to pray, and several did both.

The perception of calm was broken as the plane dipped suddenly and things seemed to bend unnaturally. It was as if the horizon shifted upwards. Everyone had a straight view of row after row of seats that scaled off into the distance in an easily perceptible pattern, and then that pattern just...changed. The straight line suddenly bent upwards, and then to the left and to the right. Everyone sensed it long before they understood it, and then when they understood it they panicked. The plane was falling apart and there was a jagged, imaginary line being drawn from the gaping hole on the left clear across the cabin to the other side. On their side of the imaginary line everything was normal, but on the other it was chaos.

Then that imaginary line quickly became very real as the ugly blue carpet ripped and revealed split sheets of metal and fraying wires. The gaping hole was now spreading quickly, like an opening mouth, and another row of seats jerked loose and tumbled out into the air. The screams and crying that managed to overwhelm the sound of rushing air and rending metal.

Mestoph looked at Leviticus and smiled awkwardly. "You might want to try that praying stuff about now," he said. Leviticus tried to return the smile, but he couldn't manage to stop gritting his teeth.

As far as he could recall, Leviticus had never been truly afraid before. He had been born in Heaven and had never known the kind of danger and fear that most humans would experience during their time on Earth. Mestoph had been in dangerous situations in his work, and had on occasion been in serious jeopardy, so the fear wasn't quite as overwhelming to him. Leviticus found it crippling and was reasonably sure that if he could teleport, he would have been long gone by now. It made him curious, though, and he turned to Mestoph again.

"You know you can leave at any point. I won't hold it against you."

This time Mestoph's smile was genuine as he patted Leviticus on the back. He didn't have to say anything. They could both very well die—maybe not permanently, but it would be painful and it would ruin all their plans. Mestoph's face told Leviticus that there wasn't a chance that he was going to leave him behind.

Marcus turned to Stephanie, still holding her hand, and said. "I just want you to know that I've been in love with you ever since I first saw you at the coffee shop."

"I know," she said, and leaned in to kiss him.

It was bad timing that they chose to have their first kiss at the exact moment that the plane finally tore in half with an ear-splitting shriek of metal on metal. The roaring wind became absolutely deafening. The forward two-thirds of the plane twisted away and began to climb in altitude for a brief moment as it lost a large portion of its weight and drag. The engines on the left wing continued to propel the plane onward, or more accurately upward considering the angle of the body. The twisting created more shear than the wing could handle; it ripped away and the nose plummeted down toward the ground.

Being in the tail of the plane, it was difficult to know exactly what kind of aerial acrobatics it did, but it felt like a ball tossed in the air that had hit the apex of its parabola and was beginning its natural descent back toward the earth. There was the slight feeling of free fall that made a tingling sensation in the stomach, but for the most part it seemed rather calm. Mestoph double checked that his seatbelt was secured and then motioned Leviticus to do the same. He tried not to think about where its former occupant might be and instead checked Marcus and Stephanie, who were leaning in awkwardly close to each other like one had a secret for the other. Then Mestoph grabbed Sir Regi and held on to him tightly, nearly squeezing the air out of him. He was surprisingly calm, considering that they were clearly falling to their death.

That calm remained for a long time, right until they hit the ground. Then it all went to Hell.

Gravity is a real bitch, and inertia is its obnoxiously loud and misbehaving child. Simply put, those passengers who weren't strapped in died viciously. When the tail section hit the ground, those who were standing or sitting unrestrained flew outward in all manner of ways. Some twisted and contorted as they flew through the air and landed hard in the dirt. Others catapulted out and then hit the gnarled rocks of ancient lava flows that littered the landscape, caught along jagged edges of the plane, or hit the seats in front of them and just crumpled.

Having your seatbelt on wasn't a guarantee that you survived either. Some were just too fragile to weather the sudden stop; others fell victim to all the various flying debris whether it was people, luggage, or seats that ripped away. Even at a cursory first glance it was obvious that more people didn't make it than did.

Even the uninjured were going to leave this with lifelong

damage as they were all given front row seats to the fate of those in the forward section of the plane. The tail had landed and come to a stop moments before the nose section of the plan hit the ground, and most were strapped in with no way of turning away from the horror of it all. The nose had evidently broken into two smaller sections when the left wing ripped away. The cockpit nose-dived directly into the ground and crumpled like an aluminum can a kid had stomped on. It rippled and compressed further and further until it was nothing but a flattened accordion of steel. The second half came in at a slightly more subtle angle and skidded violently through the rocky, sparsely wooded Icelandic coast, pulverizing the occasional tree or scrubby bush into a spray of splinters and leaves. It left a relatively short but very deep gouge into the black earth as it slid to a halt. There were some survivors, though not many were moving.

A few seconds later the wing that had torn away flipped downward and pierced the cabin almost squarely in the center. The blades of the engine were still spinning, though it didn't sound like it was actually running, and they turned the inside of the cabin into confetti. It was all very definitive and final.

It wasn't until the whole scene had played out—from violent beginning to violent ending—that anyone in the tail section of the plane pulled out of their shock enough to take account of what was happening to and around them. The first sound outside of the crash that seemed to register to anyone was the whimpering of a dog. Mestoph looked down and realized that he still had a death grip on Sir Regi and was actually hurting him. He loosened his hold and the dog calmed down, looked around, and then sighed. Sir Regi didn't seem any worse for wear after it was all said and done. None of them were really in too bad of shape. The only injury Mestoph had sustained was before they had fallen, Leviticus had a few cuts on his face from fallen debris, and Marcus and Stephanie didn't seem to have a scratch on them.

"Mother fucker," thought Mestoph with considerably more optimistic enthusiasm than the last time. He started to laugh.

A mile away along the Icelandic coast, Atreyus jumped back into his SUV and gave a sigh of satisfaction. It had been a good thirty years since he had last shot an RPG. He was afraid that his aim was going to be a bit off, but he had done a pretty good job of knocking the plane out of the sky. He knew that he hadn't killed either Mestoph or Leviticus because he hadn't felt his powers leave, but it would just be a matter of finishing the job now.

He sped down a rocky trail that passed for a road in the remote areas of the coast, following the flagging airplane. He watched with excitement as it tore itself to pieces on its descent. His trail and the path of the plane merged, and he was now directly behind the plummeting aircraft. Between trying to keep the SUV under control at a high speed and keep tabs on the plane, he didn't pay much attention to the wing being ripped off the plane.

If Atreyus had had an out-of-body experience at this moment, he would have seen the wing spinning through the air like a tomahawk. A two-ton tomahawk spinning at a couple hundred miles an hour directly toward his SUV. Atreyus was not having an out-of-body-experience, however, so he did not realize he was about to die yet again until the wing landed on top of him.

"Shit," said Atreyus as the SUV crumpled in a mess of aircraft and automobile debris and then burst into flames.

The next hour passed by in a fog. It was a slow process to check all the passengers still in their seats to see if they were alive. The dead were pulled out of the wreckage and laid out on the ground in rows of ten. People walked up and down the rows of bodies trying to find those that were missing. Some of the more forward-thinking passengers were searching for wallets, passports, or anything to identify the fallen. There were some who couldn't bring themselves to handle the dead and weren't of any use with the injured living, so they were set to the task of going through the luggage strewn around the immediate site of the crash looking for items that would help them survive in the long and short-term. Slowly Mestoph and Leviticus found themselves taking charge of the situation, since they seemed to be more or less unfazed by the loss of life and were capable of thinking critically and strategically.

No one ventured too close to the wreckage of the forward section of the plane. There were no cries for help, and they were more than busy enough with those immediately around their own wreck. It had become an unspoken taboo; they were the ones who had died and no one spoke about them. Being on the edge of the enormous storm was also creating its own difficulties. The rain wasn't torrential, but it was heavy and constant, and the remains of the tail section of the plane made a leaky, unreliable shelter at best. Mestoph and Leviticus had given Marcus and Stephanie the job of finding supplies to use to either reinforce the tail section or make a better shelter. Once everyone had been given a job, Mestoph pulled Leviticus aside; they needed to talk about what had really happened.

"An RPG? Are you sure?" asked Leviticus.

"I've sold enough of them to know the business end of one when I see it," said Mestoph.

There was no doubt in his mind that they had been shot out of the sky. The question was whether it was coincidence or if St. Peter had absolutely lost his fucking mind and was willing to kill a hundred innocent humans just to thwart two wayward Astral beings. They agreed that St. Peter was a fuck-head and completely capable of it, especially considering the shootout in T or C. They also had to consider the inevitable fact that whoever had shot them down, whether it was St. Peter himself, mercenaries he had hired, or some militant rebel group, would come to at least check their handiwork if not finish the job.

"We have to get the Hell out of here. Now," said Mestoph.

"We can't just leave these people here to die."

"Sure we can. It's our job to leave them to their own devices."

"Oh, *now* you want to do your job? Well it's too late for that. I'm staying, and you know damn well Marcus and Stephanie will too," said Leviticus.

"Fine," said Mestoph, shaking his head in dismay. "But we're gonna need some weapons."

Where they were going to find weapons at a plane crash in the middle of the uninhabited south coast of Iceland was anyone's guess.

Chapter 11

...friendly Iceland

They had been walking all morning and they were cold, miserable, and weary. The shepherd was exhausted from carrying Persephone across the countryside in increasingly worse conditions for over a week. Luckily they hadn't run into any snow, as spring didn't necessarily mean the end of winter weather in Iceland. His clothes, which had become more and more ill-suited as the weather got colder and colder, were soaked and filthy. Persephone's soft wool was matted and caked with mud, and she shivered constantly.

She had woken him up in the middle of the night over a week ago, bleating like she was being eaten by wolves, and banging on his front door. He hadn't recognized her at first, but when she spoke to him the voice was unmistakable. All he could get out of her was that "he" had found her and they had to run. He wasn't entirely sure who "he" was or where they were going, but Persephone insisted with such an intense fear that he couldn't tell her no. He could never tell her no. He was in love with a lamb. Now they were heading toward the only people that might take them in.

They walked through a field and came up to a small, muddy country road. Out of habit the shepherd looked both ways before he stepped onto it. Safety first, after all. Despite the wind and rain, visibility was good enough that he see the coast was clear in either direction. It was quite a surprise, therefore, when an SUV with a couple of pickup trucks trailing behind seemed to appear out of nowhere going incredibly fast. It didn't look like they were going to stop.

St. Peter was complaining with much gusto about the lack of enthusiasm and intelligence the average henchman had these days. Though he was driving, he was only paying marginal attention to where they were going. They were in the middle of bum-fuck-nowhere Iceland where there was nothing but sheep and inbred farmers.

"What I want to know is why it takes so much *fucking* effort to get good henchmen?" asked St. Peter.

He was unleashing this well-trodden tirade on the only passenger in the SUV, a long-time lackey named Wheezy whom he had recruited straight out of Hell over a hundred years ago.

Wheezy was a tall, lanky man with a patchy beard and beady eyes, whose tanned and weathered skin constantly looked dirty even though he was a meticulous neat freak. He had been a guerilla fighter for the Dutch farmers during the First Boer War in South Africa in the late 1800's. Now he was a low-level Shadow in the employ of Hell Industries, so technically he was one of Satan's boys, but St. Peter paid him well and let him do things that he would never get to do as a Shadow. Hell Industries thought he was too stupid to do important work. The truth was that Wheezy was actually pretty smart, but he had been tortured so many times before and after his mortal death that he no longer had a tongue, and his vocal chords were either completely severed or severely damaged.

"It's not like I'm asking for a whole lot. I just want average intelligence and unwavering loyalty. I can get the loyalty, but then they're too dumb to know the difference between following orders to the letter and following the spirit of those orders. On the other hand, if they show a modicum of common sense, I can't get them to do shit."

The demon shot a quick look at St. Peter and sighed.

"You don't have to say something for me to know what you're thinking. You think if they're smart enough to know better than to follow me blindly. So what's your excuse? Just smart enough to know you're not smart enough to do it all by yourself?"

Wheezy gave a concessionary shrug. He might be ignorant, but he wasn't stupid; St. Peter decided he would have to keep an eye on him.

"Don't think that just because you can't talk that I don't know what you really—"

Wheezy rarely made any noise unless it was necessary, and was completely incapable of forming words, so St. Peter didn't automatically recognized the meaning behind Wheezy's haunting wet, raspy, whispered yell. It was more the spit flying than the noise that really got his attention. He still wasn't sure what he was trying to get across until he followed Wheezy's outstretched hand that was pointing out in front of the SUV to something standing in the middle of the road. St. Peter hit the brakes and fish-tailed in the thick mud, sliding directly toward the soon-to-be-hood-ornaments in the road. With less than a foot to spare, the large SUV slid to a halt. The other trucks in the convoy swerved to avoid St. Peter's vehicle, barely avoiding a pile-up.

St. Peter and Wheezy were staring at a wet farmer in tattered and muddy clothes that couldn't possibly have kept him warm even if it weren't raining. He was holding a soaking wet lamb in his arms. St. Peter imagined it had to smell like a sweaty jock strap. The stunned shepherd stared back with a blank expression. After a moment he looked down at the lamb said something to it, paused, said something else, and then shrugged. To St. Peter and Wheezy it looked like the shepherd was consulting with the lamb. They looked at each other, wondering if they were both seeing the same thing, and then looked back as the shepherd continued to cross the road and walked off in the direction of the mountains.

"God damn it, I hate this country," said St. Peter as he hit the gas again. The SUV threw up mud behind it and then roared off. The pick-up trucks, which were full of an assortment of large Nordic brutes in modernized armor with axes and war hammers, along with short, skinny Africans in military uniforms with AKs and an RPG, followed.

It had taken all day, but the survivors had sorted through the bodies and reinforced the tail section of the plane with scavenged aluminum struts. Mestoph and Leviticus were quietly salvaging anything that could be used as a weapon. They had recovered two handguns, one that Sir Regi had rooted around and found on the body of a sky marshal that had died in the crash, and another that Mestoph had found in the cockpit when he sneaked off to the forbidden wreckage as the light was fading. Leviticus had crafted rudimentary but perfectly usable axes and machetes from sharp and jagged pieces of metal. Some of the passengers had apparently been adventurers, or just very well prepared and paranoid, and had flashlights, lanterns, a few headlamps, and even a pair of sinister looking ice axes in their luggage. The lights would come in handy and provide some much needed comfort, and the pair of axes could end up being useful if embedded into some mercenary asshole's skull. Food had been recovered from the galley in the rear of the plane, consisting mostly of sandwiches and boxes of noodles with vegetables. Nobody had much of an appetite.

Easily the greatest comfort came from the large campfire that Marcus and Stephanie had built at the edge of the refitted plane cabin with more wood from trees that had been torn up and split in the crash. It was only partially shielded from the weather, so they had made it big as much for warmth and safety as to survive the rain. There was something calming

143

and familiar about a campfire and most of the survivors, of which there were now only twenty-three, crowded around its calming glow.

There had been more survivors immediately after the crash, but injuries seen and unseen had claimed about a dozen more. One man had slipped away shortly after dark and killed himself, slitting his wrists with a jagged razor of aircraft aluminum. Sir Regi noticed him leaving and had followed him, but had been unable to convince him not to do it. He secretly feared that seeing a talking dog might have made it worse. Sir Regi quietly returned to let Mestoph and Leviticus know, and they buried him in a simple rock cairn beyond one of the surrounding hills. Morale was going to be low enough come morning, when it would dawn on people that no one had come to rescue them in the night; a suicide definitely wasn't what they needed looming over them.

The fact that there hadn't been any planes or helicopters looking for the wreckage hadn't surprised Mestoph and Leviticus, and when Stephanie had mentioned it in a whisper to Marcus, he had just nodded. Mestoph had been unable to find the black box, which was actually bright orange, in the cockpit. Its absence confirmed his suspicions that this was no accident.

"We're not going to be rescued, are we?" asked Marcus quietly, though it was much more statement than question. Mestoph shook his head.

"We need to organize first thing in the morning, before dissent amongst the ranks can entrench itself. We're going to have to leave the wreckage behind and make it to the nearest town," said Leviticus.

Mestoph and Leviticus had decided to tell them the truth about the wreck, or at least their version of the truth. They told them that they thought the wreck was intentional. That they didn't know how, but that someone high up had made it happen. They didn't think the survivors were likely to believe a story about a conspiracy of shadow Angels and Demons, so they would have to tell them something they could believe. While the five of them, counting Sir Regi, would know the "truth", they would tell the survivors it had been an RPG that brought them down. There was an odd sense of irony to telling complete strangers the truth and those close to them a complete fabrication, but Mestoph and Leviticus each had their own reasoning behind it.

Mestoph thought an RPG attack made the mysterious fifth column group that Leviticus had invented sound too human, and he wanted their invented assailants to remain other-worldly. He was afraid that if Marcus and Stephanie thought humans were already involved it was too late and that there was already no hope of survival. Leviticus on the other hand thought it made them look far too vulnerable when some guy with an RPG could take them all out. The truth was they were both right in a way – they were far too vulnerable, and the only thing that allowed Marcus and Stephanie to continue trusting their fellow humans was the fact that it was still an Us vs. Them scenario.

The sun hadn't even fully risen, and already there was whisperings amongst developing cliques about how they should have, at the very least, heard a plane or helicopter flying over, if not spotlights trying to find them. They also had a surprising ally that had come to them just as the sun rose.

Mestoph recognized him as the priest that had been sitting behind him just before the crash. He couldn't help but feel uneasy. Mestoph had fought alongside African rebels in the early 60s when Muammar al-Gaddafi staged his coup to take control of Libya, he had fought with the Saracens against the Crusaders at Tyre, Jerusalem, and Cyprus, and he had seen the full wrath of Satan himself directed squarely at him—and yet he feared nothing quite so much as a Catholic priest. He blamed *The Exorcist*.

"I'm Father Mike," said the priest in what Mestoph was now fairly certain was the accent of a British-educated Kenyan. He extended his hand in a friendly gesture that made Mestoph hesitate. The priest, whose collar was smudged black with dirt and red with blood, noticed the awkwardness and smiled. "Forgive my forwardness; I feared your friend might be Shia from his complexion, so thought it safer to shake your hand instead. I meant no offense."

Leviticus slipped into the conversation and quickly shook the priest's still awkwardly extended hand. "Please ignore my socially inept friend's heirophobia," he said, giving Mestoph a look of disdain.

The priest looked at him—Leviticus couldn't tell if it was amusement or suspicion that he saw on his face—and smiled again. "Wrong on both accounts, I suppose," said the priest.

Leviticus shrugged. "I'm about as Christian as they come—short of being the savior himself."

Any suspicion or hesitation disappeared from the priest's expression, which in turn made Mestoph relax—though only a little. Father Mike, who explained that his name was actually Makena, told them that he seen something strange right before the plane went down. "I was one row behind you," he said, nodding at Mestoph. "I wondered if you had seen the same thing. It was a rocket-propelled grenade, I'm sure of it."

Leviticus and Mestoph gave each other a meaningful look, as much to be sure they were both on the same page as for the theatrical effect it would have.

"You have a lot of experience with RPGs?" asked Mestoph.

The priest shrugged. "I've seen my share of fighting. I wasn't always a priest."

And with that, Leviticus nodded to Mestoph and they let Father Mike into the inner circle.

Less than an hour later, Mestoph, Leviticus, Marcus, Stephanie, Sir Regi, and now Father Mike stood before the assembled survivors, who were huddled together in the remains of the cabin. They told everyone what they had seen and that they didn't think they were safe staying at the crash site. The survivors were skeptical. Several voiced the opinion that it would be better to wait there for a rescue. Leviticus squirmed uncomfortably as he felt the crowd beginning to turn; it was at least partially his fault that they were in this mess, and he'd be damned—pardon his language—if he'd let more innocents suffer. Not even Mestoph could leave them to fend for themselves. Not to mention that they would likely lose Marcus and Stephanie's faith if they did.

Mestoph revealed that he had been to the cockpit and hadn't found any sign of the black box. That swayed more than a few people. One man had the reasonable point that Mestoph wasn't an aviator so he might have missed it. Mestoph conceded this but offered to go along with anyone who wanted to look again. This quieted a few of the non-believers. The single point that held the most sway, however, was Father Mike's story about having seen what he thought was an RPG. Several of the survivors admitted to having seen something come at them from the ground. When Leviticus planted the fear that whoever had shot them down would come and finish them off, there were only one or two vocal critics of the plan, and even they seemed uncertain of their own argument. In the end it was a unanimous vote.

The biggest logistical problem was the injured. Of the

twenty-three survivors, six of them weren't fully mobile. For those who couldn't move at all, they would have to fashion together some sort of litter and then work out shifts for everyone to carry or pull them along. Those who were hobbling and limping would be splinted as best as possible and would just have to try not to further injure themselves during the march.

The march itself was the next problem that had to be solved. Most of the survivors weren't Icelandic, so there was a serious lack of geographical knowledge. Father Mike again proved to be invaluable since he was in Iceland to do mission work in the rural and farm areas of the island country. He easily had the best practical knowledge of the lay of the land.

Father Mike worked with Mestoph and Leviticus to draw up a map of the coast. As best as they could figure, they were somewhere between Klaustur and Skaftafell National Park, which meant they could go twenty miles approximately west and maybe hit Klaustur, or walk ten or fifteen miles just about any direction but southeast and hit Route 1. Father Mike thought they were closest to the National Park, which meant they were farther from anything resembling civilization.

While Mestoph and Leviticus worked with Father Mike to plan their escape, Marcus and Stephanie—and, in his own way, Sir Regi—worked with the survivors to get everything in marching order. To make the litters, they had pried the emergency exit door off. The emergency slide burst out of the door and inflated as Marcus absentmindedly pulled the emergency lever. Sir Regi let out a startled bark and one of the other passengers, a young woman in her early twenties, let out a shriek followed by nervous laughter.

They slit the inflated sides of the slide to deflate it and then cut it into long strips that would make up the base of the litter. They then supported it with two long narrow struts from the insides of the plane. They wrapped the jagged ends of metal in strips of cloth from the clothes found in the salvaged luggage. The supports and vinyl from the slide were lashed together with some climbing rope from the suitcase with the ice axes, and when they ran out of that some electrical wiring from inside the plane. Sir Regi brought most of the wire, rooting through the small crawlspaces and digging through the debris to find as much as possible. The result was a crude but serviceable way to pull or carry those who couldn't walk.

As they searched through the suitcases, Marcus and Stephanie learned more than they ever wanted to know about their fellow passengers. In an age of internet porn there was a surprising number of nudie mags tucked underneath clothes. More alarming was the sheer volume of dildos, vibrators, and – not to leave the men out - pocket pussies. It seemed that good old one-handed masturbation, good for guys and girls, wasn't enough these days. There were rubber, silicon, and uncannily skin-like genitalia of a startling degree of accuracy, or inaccuracy in the case of large foot and a half long jiggly cocks with variable speed vibrators.

To a man like Marcus, who had never set foot in a sex shop, the sheer variety of fake phalluses was astounding. There were ones shaped like animals, dolphins and rabbits in particular. There were ones with a complicated array of rotating "pleasure beads" inside. There were ones where the head, and only the head, rotated and squirmed like a flailing fish. The other startling thing was that no one seemed to travel with only one dildo, but almost always a pair, and in some cases there were small travel boxes dedicated solely to their owner's toys. One box had half a dozen dildos, French ticklers, condoms, lube, and a burned DVD he was fairly certain was full of porn. When he looked up at Stephanie, wanting to share his surprise with someone else, she just shrugged. Marcus suddenly imagined a similar black and chrome travel box tucked underneath her bed back at her house. As if reading his mind, she nodded. Marcus shook his head in dismay, and felt a sudden inadequacy in his boring, vanilla sexual habits. She put her hand on his shoulder and whispered to him, "Don't worry, nobody stays innocent forever." Marcus felt a blossom of excitement and fear inside him.

It had taken the better part of the day to get everything together between scavenging for provisions, trying to prepare the injured for transport, and the back and forth debating about where they should go. In the end they decided to head in the general direction Father Mike believed Klaustur was, but agreed to follow Rt. 1 west toward Reykjavik if they hit it first. They also decided that they had burned enough of the day that it would be pointless to leave now. By the time everyone was assembled and motivated to move out in the miserable weather, they would be lucky to get an hour out before it started getting too dark to safely navigate the rocky and uneven terrain of the seemingly endless lava fields.

Leviticus and Mestoph were the only ones who thought an hour of travel was better than nothing. Resigned to another night at the crash site, they arranged to keep watch in pairs. Marcus and his dog would take first watch, Stephanie and Mestoph, who wasn't comfortable spending too much time with the priest, would take second watch, and Leviticus and Father Mike would keep watch until sunrise. Mestoph gave Marcus and Stephanie a private, impromptu weapons lesson, showing them the safety, what to do if it jammed, and the quickest way to change a clip. He gave Marcus the 9mm that he had found in the cockpit.

Sir Regi suggested that they at least try to arm some of the other passengers in the guise of utilitarianism by making rough hatchets and machetes from jagged metal and support beams, wrapped together with the leftover wires that weren't used for the makeshift stretchers. Now they passed them out under the pretense that the makeshift weapons could be used for gathering wood for fires and clearing brush as they traveled the next morning.

First watch with Marcus and Sir Regi was uneventful, and they gratefully returned to the dry spot Marcus called a bed and the pile of clothes he would be using as a pillow. He tapped Stephanie on the shoulder and she sat up instantly; he was fairly certain she hadn't been asleep. Marcus handed her the gun and she awkwardly stuck it in the waistband of her pants. Marcus walked over to the small fire where Mestoph and Leviticus were huddled together, deep in conversation. They hushed as Marcus walked over; he didn't take it as an insult since he was sure there was plenty of things mortals like him weren't meant to know about. Mestoph nodded to Marcus and then got up to take his watch, leaving him with Leviticus. Marcus didn't stay to talk.

Mestoph found Stephanie sitting on a row of seats at the edge of the fuselage. The weather was starting to clear up a bit, the ominous storm moving further inland, and in the random gaps of clouds they could see stars peeking through. They sat there for close to half an hour before she spoke. "You're not really an Angel are you?"

Mestoph looked at her intently for a moment, a look that went briefly from amusement to a complete lack of surprise. He wasn't so much shocked that she had doubts; he couldn't hide his true nature forever. He was surprised that she was so sure and so unafraid. He smiled ruefully and nodded.

"So what are an Angel and...a Demon?" At Mestoph's nod, she continued, "What are an Angel and a Demon doing running around together and trying to stop the end of the world? I mean, I can see why an Angel might, but not a Demon. And not an Angel and a Demon working together."

Mestoph looked up at the clouds, which parted again briefly to show a sliver of moon. He hadn't planned on having this talk, at least not yet. He had hoped maybe it could be avoided completely. Stephanie was too smart to be blown off, so Mestoph decided to go as close to the truth as he dared.

"Me and Leviticus have been friends for a very long time. I'm not going to lie and say that I haven't done some things you'd flinch at; it comes with the territory. However, Leviticus and I meet in the middle when it comes to our views of our jobs. I'd be lying if I said either of us weren't both anxiously awaiting The End. Ultimately, that's what both sides are working toward. However, you—humans, that is— deserve a chance to do it your own way. That whole free will thing. It's a pretty amazing thing, but it's really all you have going for you. Without it you're just playthings for God and Satan to push around the chessboard in their unending cock-measuring contest. Someone is out to take that one and only thing of yours away by jumpstarting The End. Seeing Leviticus as good and me as evil is far more simplistic and inaccurate than the truth. It may surprise you to find out that some really good people end up in Hell while some really shitty people end up in Heaven. It has absolutely nothing to do with a lack of faith or devotion respectively. There's not a lot in life that's fair, but if we can do something to keep free will alive as long as possible, it behooves us all to do our part."

Mestoph was surprised to find that he actually believed what he was saying. Not all of it was true and some of the facts were omitted, but the sentiment was there. He actually did care about what happened to humans—at least to these humans.

"I won't tell Marcus," was all Stephanie said in response.

Mestoph looked at her expectantly for several minutes,

but she didn't look at him again. They continued their watch in silence. It wasn't an uncomfortable silence; it was just a lack of talking. He finally spoke up, the curiosity close to killing him.

"Are you OK with...you know...me being a Demon?"

Stephanie looked over at him and smiled slightly. "Yeah, I'm OK. It explains a lot. And to be honest, it makes me feel better knowing you're...you know...a Demon."

Mestoph cocked an eyebrow, his curiosity piqued instead of sated. "Better?"

"Yes, better. Because I know when the Nephilim, Seraphim, St. Peter, or who knows what else finally finds me...us...you won't hesitate to kill them."

The bright beam of a pair of headlights broke over a distant hill, revealing the jagged outlines of lava rocks. Five more pairs of headlights followed. They all pulled up side-by-side on the crest of the hill, pointing toward the cockpit section of the wreck. Mestoph drew his gun and tapped Stephanie on the knee, motioning for her to wake up Leviticus and Marcus.

Whoever had shot them down had finally found them.

Chapter 12

The Taint of Taint

The second RPG hit the forward section of the wreckage squarely through one of the cockpit windows and exploded inside. What was left of the front half of the plane shattered in a ball of flame and debris that rained down on the survivors, startling those still sleeping upright and awake. Mestoph returned with a three round burst from his .40 and saw a silhouette fall down in front of the headlights. Moments later, it silhouette stood back up and began to reload the launcher.

Mestoph took aim again, knowing he wouldn't get another shot before yet another RPG was spiraling its way directly at him. This time he took a moment to breath in, hold it, and then let it back out. He squeezed the trigger, getting off a single round.

The shooter fell backwards as the grenade launched, sending it upward in an almost imperceptible arc. It shot up like a flare, and everyone stared up at it, entranced. Then it ran out of propulsion, and since it hadn't hit anything to trigger detonation, it began to fall. The second half of its trajectory was shrouded by darkness, but it became apparent what had happened when the vehicle furthest from the wreck exploded.

The second explosion jerked everyone out of their trance, and people began screaming and running. Survivors were grabbing their axes and machetes or running for cover behind wreckage and lava mounds. It made for a disorganized front, but would also make them harder to pick off all at once. On the other side, the attackers were screaming, too. There wasn't enough light to tell if it was because they were dying or injured or just startled at having their own vehicle blown up. Mestoph thought he could hear the cursing of a dying demon, its guttural language ringing out above the others, but in the chaos he wasn't sure.

Leviticus, Marcus, and Stephanie soon joined Mestoph behind the row of seats. It wasn't much in the way of protective cover, but it kept them out of sight. Mestoph was filling them in on the scant details of the events so far when gunfire finally broke out. They ducked instinctively, but the guns weren't aimed at them. Again Mestoph heard the sound of a demon, muffled and gravelly but distinct, maybe even sounding slightly wet and raspy, and then one of the vehicles backed up and sped off away from the crash, leaving four sets of headlights and one mangled wreck of a burning truck.

It became apparent that all the gunfire was coming from one half of the group and aimed exclusively at the other half. The scene then played out solely through the silhouettes and shadows created by the headlights. It looked like the group taking fire was armed with nothing but swords, axes, and war hammers. Not the makeshift type the survivors had, nor the weird fantasy weapons that geeks with too much money bought, but large, chunky, utilitarian looking accoutrements of war—albeit war in the Dark Ages.

The barbarians seemed to be winning. A few of the anachronistic assailants fell to gunfire, but sparks of ricocheting bullets leaped off what could only be armor as they charged forward, laying the gunners to waste. The skirmish only lasted a few minutes, and then the gunfire ceased completely. Not sure how to take this awkward turn of events, Mestoph and the others stayed hunched behind the seats with their weapons at the ready.

"Aim for the head," said Mestoph.

"You mean, like zombies?" asked Sir Regi.

"Yes," said Mestoph with all seriousness.

There was absolute silence for what felt like an eternity, and then there was a loud, deep "Halooo?" from the trucks.

"Is anyone out there?" asked a deep voice in Germanic-tinged English.

Everyone looked to Mestoph with questions in their eyes. He shrugged, making a bewildered face in response. He had no idea if this was a trap to lure them out or some sort of mob remorse. He didn't have to think too long about it, though, because a hulking figure of a man emerged in front of the trucks waving what was most likely a white flag. In the dark the color was moot.

"I think they want to…what…parley?" said Sir Regi, making it as much a question as a statement. "Ask for terms," said the dog.

"Name your terms," shouted Mestoph. There was a brief moment of silence and then they heard some sort of discussion taking place in the distance. It was either too low to understand or they weren't speaking English. Mestoph squinted and turned his ear, trying to make it out.

"It's Icelandic or maybe Old Norse, I think," said Sir Regi, his superior doggy hearing paying off. "Please God, don't let them be Neo Vikings."

It looked like everyone was about to ask what Neo Vikings were, but there was finally a response from the barbarians. "No terms. Unconditional surrender," shouted the Nordic negotiator.

"Who's surrendering? Us or you?" shouted Mestoph.

The barbarian looked as if he turned to those behind him and shrugged. "We surrender," he shouted back.

"Why?" asked Mestoph. The others looked at him in surprise.

"Who cares!" said Stephanie.

"Well, mostly 'cause we'd rather not kill you. If that's ok with you."

"We accept!" shouted Stephanie, not willing to risk having Mestoph ruin everything with his inane questions. There was murmuring from the other survivors, some of whom had drawn near to where Mestoph and the others were taking cover.

The barbarian threw the flag down and walked toward the survivors with his hands up in the international "I come in peace" gesture. The light from various fires lit the barbarian's features; what could only be described as a Neo Viking stood tall before them. The man stood just shy of seven feet with blonde hair pulled back into a ponytail with a leather thong and a long mustache and beard braided and capped with copper beads. The Viking was wearing tactical cargo pants and a skin-tight endurance shirt, but he had armor made of iron plates the size of playing cards draped on top of it.

Although the barbarian had dropped his battle axe, he still had various weapons from various eras strapped to him. Tucked into sheathes at both hips were two large Celtic sgian-dubh, angled so they could easily be cross-drawn. Clipped to the many pockets of his cargo pants were medium-sized tactical folding knives and a multi-tool. He even had a small push-dagger, shaped like a bear claw, hanging from a chain around his neck.

"I am unarmed," he said, gesturing toward the empty leather sheath on his back that should have held his battle axe. Mestoph raised an eyebrow, but he signaled for everyone to lower their weapons. Leviticus swung the ice axe so that it stuck into one of the cushioned arms of the row of seats in front of him. The barbarian grinned, which made Mestoph feel like they had fallen for some trick, but the hand that he held out toward Mestoph was empty and open.

"Komdu sæll," said the large man, still grinning enormously.

Mestoph reluctantly grasped the man's hand. The barbarian clasped it eagerly and then pulled him in for an uncomfortable bear hug, patting him roughly on his back.

"We were afraid you were all dead," said the large man, seemingly on the verge of tears. "They never said anything about survivors. Please...please, forgive us." He finally released Mestoph and yelled something in Icelandic to the rest of the group, to which they shouted enthusiastically in response.

The Neo Vikings rushed toward them. Many of the survivors shouted in excitement, and equally as many shouted in fear because they thought they were being attacked. Luckily the other Neo Vikings had been sensible enough to put their weapons away before charging headlong toward skittish survivors. In the midst of the celebration, there was a high-pitched scream in the darkness. Coming swiftly into the light was a short African rebel whom Mestoph recognized as the leader of one of the guerilla groups he had dealt with in his failed coup in Kenya. The rebel was running full tilt toward him with a grenade raised in one of his hands. The screaming rebel and the look of surprised confusion on Mestoph's face got the attention of the enormous Viking leader, and he sprang into action.

Without pausing, he grabbed Leviticus' ice axe from the arm of the seat, turned, and threw it with the speed and force of a Major League pitcher. The axe spun toward the rebel and stuck with a resounding thud into his forehead, causing him to do a back flip onto the ground. The grenade flew upward into the air, and everyone's mouth dropped open as they watched it rise. At the peak of its ascent it exploded in a flowering of flame and a concussion that knocked several people to the ground.

And then there was nothing but silence; the war was now officially over. After the panic subsided, the survivors universally greeted the barbarians with hugs and tears. The leader of the group introduced himself as Magnus Magnuson. He was not only their leader, but the frontman of a Neo Viking death metal band known as Odin's Taint. They were a rather motley crew of behemoths chiseled of ice and stone, none under six feet tall, who lived as modern Vikings by day and melted faces off by night with dark, insidious metal of the most ferocious variety.

Magnus explained they had been approached about a job by a distant acquaintance of their drummer, who called himself Fenrir, after they had played at a dive bar in Reykjavik the night before. Being that Odin's Taint wasn't exactly playing in sold out stadiums they could really use the money and signed up. Fenrir's acquaintance said there was an unmanned stealth drone belonging to the U.S. government that had crashed, and they were offering top pay to scavenge what they could from the wreckage: specifically hard drives, cameras, and any serial numbers, badges, or insignias that could point to the U.S.

They were told that it would be unguarded; they were just there for the literal heavy lifting. The Americans didn't want the Icelandic government to know they were flying drones over their country, and since the crash had apparently gone unnoticed, it should be safe to go in under cover of darkness, grab what they needed, and be out by dawn. When they arrived at the prearranged meeting place and met their contact and his boss, whom Magnus described in detail and was undeniably St. Peter, it seemed they had enlisted a few others to help with the job. The employer revealed that he had learned that it wasn't a simple, small unmanned drone after all but an experimental intelligence plane.

The Vikings still thought everything was going well until they arrived at the scene and it became immediately obvious that things didn't quite jibe with what they had been told.

One rocket propelled grenade and twenty-three screaming survivors later, Odin's Taint realized they had been lied to, and being the Neo Vikings they were, they had no qualms fighting those who would try to take advantage of them—and who would, in all likelihood, have tried to kill them too when the job was through.

Their story told, there was immense relief on everyone's faces, Vikings and survivors alike, but there was an ever growing unease that Mestoph and the others were trying very hard to keep to themselves. Between the attack in Truth or Consequences, the plane being shot down, and now the story Magnus the Neo Viking had told them, it was undeniable that St. Peter would go to any extreme necessary. This was clearly not the last time they would come to heads with him, and it probably wasn't the last time it would involve excessive force.

Odin's Taint was more than just a metal band. It was a commune of about twenty-five Neo Vikings that lived the life of a modern barbarian. While they did have many modern conveniences like internet, geothermal heating, electricity, and motor vehicles, they also tried to live off the land as much as possible. They were hunters, gatherers, farmers, traders, grifters, and of course rockers. The band itself had four members: lead singer and guitar Magnus, bass player Fenrir, rhythm guitarist Skjorn, and drummer Johnny Machine Gun.

Although Magnus Magnuson was likely the large singer's real name, Mestoph had serious doubts about the authenticity of the others. Fenrir was a ferocious wolf beast that would eventually eat Odin, at least according to Norse mythology. Mestoph did make note of a chain around Fenrir's neck with a small sword pendant hanging from it. He wondered if it was supposed to represent the magical chain that bound the mythological Fenrir until the day of Ragnarok. The man did have rusty, fox red hair that was more a shaggy mane than flowing locks, a sharp, predatory nose, and an aggressive grin, so the name at least fit.

Skjorn was the tallest of all the members of the group, towering easily above seven feet. He had long, straight black hair that hung loosely half way down his back. What little skin wasn't etched in deep grooves of woad-inked tattoos was pasty white, almost sickly. He was lean but muscular, with hard cords of muscle running the length of his unnaturally long arms.

Johnny Machine Gun was the odd man out. He was of average height and lanky, with a gaunt face and jittery demeanor like he lived off of cocaine and fast food. He looked like a Chihuahua crossed with a rat, which as far as Sir Regi was concerned was the same thing. His uncomfortably tight black jeans and tattered black denim jacket covered in strategic rips, safety pins, and Misfits, Black Flag, and Sex Pistols patches sealed the deal that he was the black lamb of this barbaric herd. He hardly looked like he could hold, let alone swing the large battle hammer he was reluctantly dragging behind him.

Skjorn, on the other hand, blithely tossed it over his shoulders, smiling down at Johnny as he did. Johnny gave a mousy and sarcastic "aren't you fucking special" grin in return. Johnny Machine Gun briefly flashed open his denim jacket to reveal a vest-like harness that held a dozen throwing knives, which were coated matte black with only the finely sharpened edges glinting in the light of the campfire. It was then that Mestoph also noticed leather bracers on his forearms, mostly hidden by the jacket, which he was fairly certain held daggers as well.

Dawn was only a few hours away, so no one even

pretended to try to get back to sleep. Most of the barbarians from Odin's Taint spent the time preparing the funeral pyres for their four brothers who had died in combat. In rummaging for something to prime the fires, as most of the timber was too green to burn very well by itself, Skjorn uncovered the plane's drink cart, which was packed full of mini-bottles of Icelandic vodka and Kentucky whiskey. The whiskey they set aside for the fires, but the vodka they passed around and saluted their comrades with a hearty "Skol!"

Magnus sat down with Mestoph and Leviticus, having marked them as the leaders of the survivors. He looked at Marcus and Stephanie, ignoring Sir Regi completely, and only seemed at ease when Leviticus gave a nod that meant they were in the inner circle as well.

"Is there any reason you can think of why someone would send a hit squad to take you out?" asked Magnus.

Mestoph and Leviticus kept steady poker faces, but both Stephanie and Marcus glanced briefly at them. Magnus did not fail to notice this and smiled. It was a mirthless smile. It was an understanding of secrets.

"They were after you," he said quietly, not making it a question.

Mestoph looked to Leviticus, who in turn reluctantly nodded at Magnus. Their little quest for some R&R had killed approximately a hundred passengers and four Neo Vikings, and who knew what else it had cost. If Mestoph and Leviticus had possessed a better understanding of the value of a human life—and if they weren't justifying it all by placing the blame squarely on St. Peter—they would have backed out of the plan long ago. But if they had a real understanding of what it meant to be human, which neither of them had ever been, they might not have set out in the first place.

"Why?" asked Magnus.

There wasn't an answer they could give him that didn't

betray far too much. Yet only something approaching the truth, or at least revealing their true nature, would really satisfy. Marcus was about to open his mouth and explain how they were witnesses to a heinous act by the head of a ruthless crime syndicate, which probably wouldn't have worked, when Sir Regi stole his thunder.

"They were protecting me," said the Scottie as he hopped up on Magnus' leg.

"Odin's beard!" shouted Magnus as he jumped up, sending Sir Regi scrabbling for traction. Sir Regi sat back on his hind legs in a very formal pose and shouted in an unusually deep and commanding voice, a voice Stephanie recognized from her dream, "Sit down human! I am an emissary of the Vanir and you will do as I command."

Magnus stood there, mouth completely agape, obediently sat. Sir Regi, now looking regal and dignified, waited for everyone to compose themselves. "I have been here in Midgard, your human world, as a spy for the Vanir, and I have a message of the utmost importance for Odin. The filthy monotheists, whom you ignorantly served in an attempt to wipe us out, will stop at nothing to ensure that message is never delivered."

"That changes everything," said Magnus, awed.

"No shit," said Mestoph, annoyed.

Chapter 13

Don't kill the messenger...please.

Magnus had gone off to talk to the other members of Odin's Taint about this new twist of events. The second he was out of earshot, both Mestoph and Leviticus turned to Sir Regi. "What the Hell was that?" they asked in unison. Sir Regi shrugged, or what passed for it in a small dog.

"*That* was me ensuring we have body guards for the remainder of this trip. Otherwise we were going to have to ride with them all the way to Reykjavik, figure a way to disappear before the officials got involved, and then trek back out this way. In case you haven't noticed, the storm is moving inland. And in case you didn't notice, St. Peter hired a bunch of barbaric goons to kill us and anyone else associated with us. His failure will be obvious by the time we leave here, and he's not just going to give up. We need protection, transportation, and guides. I just got us all three rolled into one. Religiously devout bodyguard-chauffeur-guides."

Mestoph and Leviticus each looked like they were about to broach an argument, but the words fell just short of being spoken. It probably wouldn't have been convincing, anyway. Marcus finally spoke up, "Who are the Vanir?"

"Norse gods, separate from Odin and the rest, but gods none the less. I think they're supposed to be dead or in hiding. Something like that," answered Stephanie.

"Actually, they're not dead. There was a war between the Vanir and the major Norse gods called the Aesir. As part of an eventual peace treaty the two groups exchanged members and the Vanir taught the Aesir to use magic, which hitherto they had no knowledge of. Now the Vanir are essentially a subgroup of the Aesir. Not necessarily equals, but not subordinates either," explained Sir Regi.

"Thank you, Britannica," said Mestoph.

Stephanie raised a brow in mild surprise. "You say that like they're...oh..." she said as she realized the truth, the raised brow dropping in dismay.

"Oh, what?" asked Marcus.

"They are real, aren't they?" asked Stephanie.

The three of them that weren't human just shrugged and nodded, like it was no big deal to them. The truth was, to them, the Norse gods *were* no big deal. They were more annoying than useful or relevant.

Iceland might have been the land of the midnight sun during summer, but in late spring it was the land of the nine a.m. sunrise. Rise it finally did, and with it so did the funeral pyres. Being hearty people and used to heavy drinking, the cart of mini-bottles had done little to dull the faculties or the sentiments of the barbarians. They burned their brothers in the early light with little fanfare. The rock mounds and scrubby wood of each pyre had been fashioned in the shape of a crude boat. There were small effigies of scrub brush and twigs that looked faintly feminine and were presumably meant to represent the Valkyries that were to lead the dead on their journey to the afterlife. The barbarians were silent and observed the rite with little show of emotion. Though they had fallen in battle and would be well on their way to Valhalla, they were still sad to see their friends and comrades go.

Once the service was over, the barbarians gathered more rocks and finished building cairns from the raised daises that had served as the base for the pyres. It was quickly done, and then the barbarians made to prepare the survivors for departure. They gave only fifteen minutes to gather up anything the survivors wanted to take, and then they were pulling out. Magnus was very clever about keeping Mestoph and Leviticus' little group separate, giving them tasks and using them as coordinators. One of the vehicles they had arrived in was a mangled wreck, but they still had two large SUVs, two trucks, and one old army Range Rover. They assigned the survivors to various vehicles and arranged for drivers; Mestoph, Leviticus, Marcus, Stephanie, and Sir Regi would be riding in the Range Rover with Magnus and Fenrir.

Although all of Odin's Taint had wanted to help escort Sir Regi to the Vanir, they had reluctantly agreed to split up and traveled light. When the fifteen minutes were up, only a few of the survivors were still digging through belongings—whether they were looking for sentimental items or looting was anyone's guess—everyone jumped in their assigned vehicles and got ready to head out. Everyone, that is, except for Father Mike; he was leaning against the Range Rover with his arms folded across his chest.

"You guys are up to something," said Father Mike as the other vehicles pulled off, leaving them no choice but to take him along despite the limited room.

"Obviously, so are you," said Leviticus.

Father Mike smiled. "I come to Iceland to do mission work with the pagans, and God drops Vikings in my lap. I'm thinking that's no coincidence, so I'm sticking with you guys."

"Technically, God shot you out of the sky and then sent Vikings to kill you. Maybe *that's* no coincidence," said Sir Regi, who seemed to have totally forgotten he was a talking dog.

"You all aren't from around here, are you?" Father Mike asked, gesturing to the world around them. "And I don't just mean Iceland."

"No, we're not," said Stephanie with a finality that broached no further discussion— something only a woman seemed to be capable of doing—and got in the Range Rover.

The shepherd and the lamb came to the edge of a deep chasm made of sleek, glassy obsidian. Warm steam rose up from it, making it impossible to see how deep it went. These kinds of vents gashed Iceland here and there from one end of the island to the other and were as commonplace—and possibly more so in certain areas—as houses. The shepherd stood perilously close to the edge, trying to absorb as much warmth as he could. It had been over a week since he had been anything resembling warm, and he had to fight the urge to simply jump in.

Persephone stirred and jerked in his arms. The shepherd put her down a few feet from the edge and then stood back, waiting for further instructions. Instead, there was a brilliant flash and then, standing where the lamb had been, there was the Persephone he knew and loved.

She was curled in the same position the lamb had been in, and it took her a minute to stretch to her full height. She stretched her arms, rolling her shoulders back at the same time, and then gave her head a quick twist to the left and then the right as if she were giving herself her own chiropractic adjustment. The shepherd watched with both admiration and lust. Her skin was the palest of whites, and in the steam from the vent she sometimes seemed to disappear; only her long, curly black hair kept her from floating away. She was lean but had the build of a woman who was not averse to physical exertion—or perhaps even the occasional battle. Lean muscles rippled and coiled as she stretched, emphasizing her strength and beauty.

That's not to say she looked like a boy with breasts. On the contrary, she had just the right amount of curves for her slight frame, and her face was that of a goddess. Literally. She had classic Greek features, but not like an ancient statue; no, hers was the beauty of dreams. Her eyes were the deep blue of the arctic seas, with stormy flecks of violet that hinted at her mischievous side. She was everything a goddess should be, and more than any man should ever want, and the shepherd suddenly felt inadequate.

When she was done with her contortions, she stood and smiled at him. It was a smile of both love and sadness. He had gone through Hades for her without the slightest explanation. Now the man that stood before her hardly looked like the one she had come to know. He was haggard and sickly. He was pale and covered in mud. His clothing was soaked and torn and despite his best efforts not to, he shivered uncontrollably. It was only then that she realized her nakedness, and with a soft whisper a black gown seemed to shed from her skin to cover her. It did nothing to dampen her sexuality.

She walked over to the shepherd and caressed his face, paying no attention to the grime and mud that clung there. With another whisper his muddy rags fell to the ground and were replaced by a thick woolen sweater and heavy cotton pants. The rain streaked down them like they would a duck's well-oiled back and ran into puddles on the ground. The shepherd felt true warmth, inside and out, for the first time since they had left.

"We're here," said Persephone softly.

The softness disappeared suddenly and she turned toward the chasm, shouting with an authority the shepherd had never heard before.

"Heimdall! Show yourself," she commanded.

Her voice echoed, and then there was silence. A swift wind picked up and sent the steam swirling into sinister spirals. The earth shook from somewhere deep, and then there was the sound of stone grinding on stone. Finally a figure appeared. It rode on a piece of multi-colored stone up through the steam. The stone was various shades of gray, black, dark brown, and green, with a single band of shiny red all sandwiched together like Paleolithic plywood. It was what one could imagine the droll and dour Vikings of a thousand years ago might have called a rainbow.

Standing at the helm of that extending stone bridge was a tall and bulky man in iron and leather armor burnished and etched by years of battle followed by years of disuse. Standing out starkly against the darkly weathered armor was skin so white it was far beyond pale, like alabaster. Long hair billowed behind him, and a braided beard reached to mid-chest, so white it could've been spider silk. This was Heimdall—the White God.

As Bifrost, the stone bridge that linked Asgard with Midgard, moved closer, the god squinted his eyes and both the shepherd and Persephone felt they were being scrutinized in a way they had never been before. The god shifted uncomfortably and touched an intricately detailed horn strung at his side. His thumb rubbed over what looked like an etching of a jester and a wolf, as if remembering or dreading something. Then he shook off the emotion or memory, literally shaking his head, and put his hand on the hilt of his sword.

"Persephone," said Heimdall as the bridge came to a stop directly in front of her. He spoke in tones far older and more Germanic than even the shepherd's Icelandic accent. "Where is your master? I hear him not, and see not his baleful visage."

Persephone sighed. "I fear he is not far behind, and I beg asylum for my companion and I."

There was a long pause as Heimdall appeared to be contemplating the possibility. Again his hand went to the horn at his side. Finally he laughed, more to himself, like someone who couldn't believe what he was about to say.

"That decision is not mine to make, but if you wish to plead your case to the Allfather, then I grant you both passage to Asgard."

Heimdall sighed and lead them across the bridge. As Bifrost bridge pulled back into the steam and out of sight, there was a flash of lightning and a loud crack of thunder and up from the ground rose a man of slight build and angular features. He was olive skinned with solid black, almond-shaped eyes. There was no hair at all on his head; not on top, on his chin, or even above his eyes. He had long, slender fingers, which he had a habit of tapping randomly against each other as he was thinking. He wore a long, black robe that was tailored closely to his physique but flared out and pooled at his feet like ink.

The man walked toward the edge of the chasm and knelt down to put one of his long-fingered hands just a hair off the ground. He smiled and the edges of his thin, harsh mouth curled up. He pinched up a bit of dirt and sniffed it, then sprinkled it into the wind. The smile turned into a full grin, revealing two rows of pearly and perfectly aligned teeth.

"Persephone," he said in a slithery whisper, drawing out the S so much that his tongue poked out briefly from his mouth, as if he were tasting the air.

They had been driving for almost an hour in complete silence. Magnus had asked where they were heading, and all Sir Regi had said was "inland." Since then there had been glances between Magnus and Fenrir, Marcus and Stephanie, Leviticus and Mestoph, and between Father Mike and everyone else. No one would meet his eyes, though they all had their own reasons for avoiding talking to him. Only Sir Regi seemed oblivious or impervious to the awkward staring cliques that had formed around him.

Mestoph and Leviticus weren't just staring intently at each other; they were deep in a hypnomancy argument.

"We've got to get rid of that priest!" said Mestoph.

Leviticus shrugged. He agreed, but as he had been stating over and over for the last half hour, there was no clean and easy way of doing it.

"We could kill him," suggested Mestoph, somewhat sheepishly.

"You're right. We *could*. But we're not. Too many innocent people have already died for this."

Mestoph pinched the bridge of his nose, closed his eyes briefly, and sighed. Somewhere close to a hundred people had died on that flight. Despite the fact that he and Mestoph hadn't been the ones who had fired the rocket, hired the mercenaries, or given the order to take them down at any cost—one which even Leviticus had agreed was hard to believe God *or* Satan would have been able to justify— Leviticus blamed himself. He believed deep in his heart, or whatever he had, that they had died because of him.

"Don't start that again," said Mestoph.

"Start what? Feeling guilty for all the shit we've caused? The plan was to bring things to the *edge* of catastrophe. Our catastrophe has gone AWOL, and another one happened in its place."

Mestoph rolled his eyes and sighed. "Come on. A plane crash is not a catastrophe," he said, but he regretted it even as the words came out, even before he saw the horrified look on Leviticus's face.

It *had* been a catastrophe. Even he had to admit that. It had once been his job, his pleasure even, to arrange catastrophes of just this sort. But spending time around Marcus and Stephanie had given him an insight into the human condition that he had never experienced. Leviticus didn't say anything. There was nothing to say.

"When it comes time to act, we can't have him hanging around. The second he finds out you're and Angel—or, God forbid, that I'm a Demon—it's all over. He's gonna pull some Super Pope powers on us, and then we're toast. It's bad enough that Stephanie knows."

"Stephanie knows what?"

"That I'm a Demon," said Mestoph as if Leviticus should have known exactly what he was talking about, not realizing he hadn't told Leviticus about it before the rebels attacked.

"How the Hell did she find out?"

"I told her."

"Why?" said Leviticus, throwing his hands up in agitation.

"Well, she already knew...mostly. She was OK with it."

"OK? She was OK with it? You tell her you're an elder Demon from deepest pits of Hell who used to revel in the pain and suffering of humans, and she's OK with it?" asked Leviticus, his voice getting higher and higher pitched as his frustration peaked.

"I never reveled! I might have gotten some pleasure out of it on occasion, but I *never* reveled. And I didn't say it like that. She said 'You're not an Angel are you?' and I said 'No' and that was pretty much it."

Leviticus just shook his head in disbelief. Nothing was ever simple when Mestoph was involved. Not that it was simple when he was involved either. To get there they had told so many lies that they could no longer talk openly in front of anyone. Their plan had fallen to shit, and then their shitty plan had fallen to shit. Now they were stuck in Iceland with two humans who thought they were trying to save the world, two Neo Vikings who thought they were trying to save the world for all Viking-kind, and a priest who thought they were the key to him fulfilling his Godly calling. This priest was just one problem too many with one solution too few. He couldn't let Mestoph kill him; it just wasn't right. Although their moral compass had spun far from pointing in the direction of the righteous, killing a priest was too much.

"We'll just have to put up with Father Mike until we find an opportunity to ditch him," said Leviticus.

"Well until then, what are we supposed to do? This Vanir gig is only going to work as long as these barbarians don't realize we have no idea where we're going or what we're looking for. Then I don't think they're going to be quite so friendly."

"Just keep our heads down and make it up as we go along," said Leviticus.

Chapter 14

The Punishment Due

Stephanie wasn't sure when it had happened, but she had managed to fall asleep despite all that had been running through her mind. All those worries and thoughts seeped away as she slipped into deep sleep, and suddenly a fog cleared, literally and figuratively.

As the fog receded, she saw a wide chasm, which separated her from something that she somehow knew was important. The fog seemed to be sucked down into the depths, revealing an impossibly tall mountain on the other side. It rose almost perfectly vertically, with jagged, snarling crags of rock jutting out at random intervals and angles. Somewhere near the top it all became deliberately sheer and a fort was carved out of the peak. It was dark and looked dead, if an enormous lump of carved rock could have ever been alive.

Climbing up the side of the mountain were three...well, they could only described as monsters. Even given the large scale of the mountain, these monsters were unbelievably large. They were mostly humanoid in shape and proportion, though their arms were longer than a normal human's and they happened to be on fire. Beneath the flames they appeared to be made of some charred, petrified wood. The lead monster was having a hard time climbing because it kept obliterating the boulders and crags that it found for hand and footholds.

Standing on the shoulder of the lead beast was a dark figure, protected from the flames by a shimmering globe of energy. He was tall and pale with inky tattoos that writhed beneath the skin of his bald head. The dark figure was screaming something that Stephanie couldn't quite make out. She couldn't tell if it was muffled by the distance or if it was a different language altogether. The tattoos on his scalp seemed to slither down the back of his neck and disappear underneath the long, flowing black robes. Moments later, the tattoos reappeared on his hands and seemed to swarm around his fingertips. He screamed again, his voice amplified unnaturally, and this time clearly speaking another language. Blue light pooled at the end of each hand and grew into brilliantly bright balls of energy that he then threw toward the fortress at the top of the mountain.

The balls of light moved up, seemingly in slow motion, and then slammed into a minaret at the nearest corner of the fort. There was a thunderous crash, and then the stone cracked and the fortification sheared away. It rained down on the man and the flaming giants. The pieces that should have hit him bounced off a shield of blue energy. When pieces hit the lead giant, they merely shattered and fell further below, leaving the giant completely unscathed.

A muscular figure stepped to the edge of the hole and surveyed the situation. In the figure's hand was a large war hammer that looked like it should have been far too heavy to wield. The figure raised the hammer high above him, shouting, and a bolt of lightning shot down and hit it. Then he reared back and tossed the hammer down. It hit one of the secondary giants on the shoulder, and there was a bright light on impact. As the light faded, Stephanie could see one of the giant's arms falling to the ground while the hammer boomeranged around and returned to its owner.

Stephanie watched the unfolding battle from her oddly clear and precise vantage at the edge of the chasm. The giants made steady progress as the dark figure continued to throw balls of energy up and the hammer-wielding figure threw his hammer down. Stephanie didn't notice until there was a slight lull in the fighting that her grandmother was standing just a few paces away. Once Grams had her attention, she pointed over the chasm to a single, impossibly large oak tree that grew out of a crack in the rocks near the base of the mountain.

The tree had a large hollow in its broad trunk, and two pairs of eyes stared out of that crack at Stephanie. With the kind of certainty that only comes in dreams, she knew that one of those pairs of eyes were her own. Then there was a flash so bright that it hurt her head, followed by a rumbling that made her lose her balance, and she began sliding toward the edge of the chasm. As she began to fall, she startled awake, finding herself still in the SUV lying against Marcus, his arm around her protectively. She looked up to see him staring down at her, concern in his eyes.

"You were having a nightmare," he said.

She just nodded; she wasn't sure it was a dream worth explaining. It could have meant anything—or nothing. She leaned in closer to him and tried to relax, though didn't allow herself to go back to sleep.

They drove for another hour or so down what Magnuson called the Sprengisandur highland road before they came to a small village just north of the Vatnsfell Power Station. It was comprised of a gas station, some small houses, and the god-awful stench of something rotting.

"What *is* that?" asked Leviticus.

"Hakarl," said Magnus. "It's fermented shark. Icelandic delicacy. There's a ranch a few miles down the road from here that cures it."

"A few miles? God, I'd hate to live next to them," said Leviticus.

Mestoph looked at everyone, their noses curled and their faces scrunched at the offensive smelled, and shrugged. "I can't smell anything," he said.

"Too much fire and brimstone," said Sir Regi.

176

Stephanie and Leviticus shot Sir Regi a glance that could've killed, to which he just shrugged in an odd doggy fashion. Father Mike was also looking at Sir Regi, but they hoped it was just the residual shock at the revelation of a talking dog. The priest glanced at everyone else as he walked past them to go inside the gas station to check for a bathroom. Leviticus gave the dog a little kick, to which he yelped disproportionately loud, hopped out of the SUV and ambled to the rear with a dejected air about him. Then he pissed on one of the tires.

Magnus and Fenrir went into the gas station to check out their food selection and pay for gas. When they were out of earshot, Marcus, Stephanie, Leviticus, and Mestoph all looked at each other and spoke in near unison.

"We've got to get rid of Father Mike."

"I don't trust him," said Marcus, somewhat defensively.

"No. No. Neither do I," added Mestoph.

"I think he knows more than he's letting on. He wasn't as surprised as he should've been about anything that has happened so far," said Marcus.

The others looked a bit confused, since that wasn't the angle they were thinking. They were more afraid of him finding out too much, not *already* knowing too much. Marcus continued, explaining that throughout the events of the last two days, the Father had been remarkably calm and far too interested in them even before they crashed.

"What do you mean before the crash?" asked Stephanie.

"He changed seats to be directly behind after we took off. He saw the RPG at the same time you did, and while you tried to warn everyone, he just sat there calm as a Hindu cow. He immediately gravitated toward us after the crash. And now he's insinuated himself into our group and is tagging along with us despite not having any logical reason to do so."

"Are you sure? You have to be absolutely sure," said

Mestoph, like he was talking to a child whom he suspected was exaggerating the truth.

"Actually, now that you mention it, I saw him changing seats too," said Sir Regi. "I just thought he wanted a window seat. But Marcus is right; he was cool as a fucking cucumber the whole time. Like he knew he was going to make it."

"I never saw him praying or anything during the crash," said Stephanie.

"Shit," said Mestoph.

"Shit, what?" asked Stephanie.

"He's FI," said Leviticus.

Mestoph nodded in agreement.

"Who's FI?" asked Father Mike, who had snuck up on them from the other side of the SUV. He had a gun with a silencer held in close to his body that was pointed at the group in general. Mestoph made to grab for the .40 he had stashed in the back of his waistband but stopped when Father Mike raised the gun to a steady, two-handed stance and aimed directly at him.

"Uh-uh, my fiery friend," he said. Father Mike moved wide around the group until he was behind Mestoph. "Pull that thing out and then drop it. Then kick it behind you," said Father Mike.

Mestoph looked behind him to see if he could possibly kick Father Mike, or at least kick up a face full of dirt, but the padre had given the Demon a wide berth. Resigned to the fact that now was not the time to act, he slowly pulled the gun from his waistband of his pants and let it fall to the ground. Mestoph had a brief bullshit hope that it would fall, go off, and take out Father Mike with an increasingly implausible series of ricochets that would land the bullet straight between his eyes.

The gun fell with a thud and a clatter but a distinct lack of magic bullet firing. He kicked the gun backwards as hard as he could. The groan from Father Mike told him that he had succeeded in sliding it underneath the SUV. Mestoph was rewarded with a quick, but mostly harmless, smack to the back of the head.

"Smartass," said Father Mike.

He then moved behind Leviticus, sticking the gun roughly into the small of the Angel's back, and then patted him down through his robes but found nothing. He didn't bother searching the others, confident that they would have tried to make a move if they were armed. He nodded to himself and smiled.

"All right everyone, about face and not a word until our Viking friends join us. I'd hate it if you spoiled the surprise for them," said Father Mike.

Everyone looked to Mestoph, who nodded and then slowly turned to face Father Mike and the SUV. Before they fully turned, Stephanie tried to catch Mestoph and Leviticus's attention by discretely pointing at herself and then making her thumb and index finger like a gun, going so far as to pull the imaginary trigger of her imaginary gun. Mestoph's eyes widened briefly and he mouthed "You?" to which Stephanie nodded. She had never given the gun back that Mestoph had given her during her watch and still had it in her coat pocket, which she patted to show him where it was. He quickly mouthed "Wait," and they all turned to face the smiling padre.

"What do you want?" asked Mestoph.

A smile that had previously been warm and reassuring now took a sinister turn as it spread across the Father's face. "I want to know what you two are up to," he said. He waved the gun back and forth at Mestoph and Leviticus, directing the question at them.

"Us? We're just saving humanity," said Leviticus.

Father Mike burst out laughing, though never took his

eyes off his captives.

"You two? No, you've never done anything for anyone but yourselves. And from what I've heard, you're not even very good at that."

Marcus pushed past Mestoph and Leviticus and stood at the front of the group. "They've saved our lives several times, so if you have a problem with them, you have a problem with us."

The smile on Father Mike's face stayed plastered there. "Saved your lives? It's their fault your lives are in danger to begin with. You two," he said, now pointing the gun at Marcus and Stephanie, "don't even know the kind of people you're keeping company with. That one right there," he continued, gesturing at Mestoph, "is a damned—"

A loud, cracking report interrupted Father Mike midsentence, and the smile slowly faded from his face. His pupils widened as he looked down at his chest where blood, human blood, was flowering from a bullet wound. He looked up and saw Stephanie standing with a gun pointed at him, the barrel smoking still. Father Mike coughed, blood coming out in faint specks, and then the cough turned to choking as he fell to the ground.

"Problem solved," said Stephanie as she dropped the gun, shaking visibly. "Now let's get the Hell out of here."

Magnus and Fenrir ran from the gas station, panic on their faces. They ran up to the group but stopped short when they saw the body of Father Mike lying on the ground, twitching and gasping. The two Vikings just stood there, mouths agape.

Father Mike suddenly jerked upright in a loud, explosive cough. A glob of squashed metal flew from his mouth, and the bullet that had just killed him fell to the asphalt. He did one of those kung-fu undulations that sent him springing to his feet. At the same time, he grabbed the gun that Stephanie had dropped so that he now held a weapon in each hand. He pointed one at the main group and the other at the two Vikings. Everyone took an involuntary step back.

"Did you know they could do that?" asked Leviticus.

Mestoph just shrugged.

"Now climb into the car; we're finishing our trip. Stephanie, you're driving. I'm calling shotgun. Any more funny shit and I plug little missy here," said Father Mike as he kept one gun on Stephanie and motioned the others into the SUV with the other.

"Keys?" asked Father Mike.

Magnus reached into his pocket, which made Father Mike give him a stern look of warning, and slowly extended his hand toward the padre. At the last moment, Magnus tossed the keys over Father Mike's head. It didn't have the desired effect. No doubt he had expected the Father to automatically grab at the keys or turn to follow them, but instead he pulled the trigger, shooting Magnus in the shoulder. The Viking screamed in pain.

By now the gunshots had finally gotten the attention of the gas station clerk. The short, pudgy man waddled out of the store with an indignant look and began shouting in Icelandic. Father Mike turned sideways so he could point one of his guns toward the attendant while keeping the other on his hostages. He fired a round. It missed the attendant by several feet, but shattered a window and sent the appropriate message. The clerk dropped, covering his head with his hands, and duck-waddled back inside the store.

"Now come out here and get those fucking keys and hand them to me properly," Father Mike said calmly.

Magnus looked at Father Mike in disbelief for a moment and then looked at the others. They all motioned their heads and mouthed words along the lines that he should do what the crazy bastard told him to. Magnus sighed and climbed back out of the SUV, holding his shoulder and keeping his useless arm close to his chest. It wasn't bleeding as much as he would have expected, but it hurt like Hell nonetheless. He began to reach down with his good arm when Father Mike glanced down and tutted.

Magnus looked up at him, confused.

"The other hand. The *other* hand," said the priest.

Magnus reached down, obediently using the arm in which he had been shot. Leaning over sent pains shooting up and down his arm and into his neck. Despite the intense pain he managed to keep from screaming or crying, but the pain was evident in his face. He handed the keys gently to Father Mike, who took them with equal gentleness.

"Good dog. Now back in the truck," he said.

Magnus walked back to the SUV, clearly angry and in pain, but what struck Mestoph was the way he cowered and wouldn't look anyone else in the eye. He wasn't going to be putting up a fight against Father Mike; the priest might as well have shot him in the head.

"Alright now kids, let's get back on the road. The sooner we leave, the sooner all this will be over. You *don't* want me to have to stop this car to discipline anyone," said Father Mike.

They drove on down the highland road towards the center of the storm. The closer they got, the worse the rain got, which meant the already rudimentary road got worse as well. The failing light made the pentagram at the center of the storm look even more eerie as its darkness seemed to glow in the dark. Stephanie slowed down, squinting through the sheets of rain.

"We won't make it at all if we keep going like this," she said.

"Floor it, missy," said Father Mike, poking her in the ribs with the barrel of the gun.

182

"I think we should stop," said Marcus.

"We'll stop when we get there and not before," said Father Mike.

"No, you don't under—"

Father Mike pressed the other gun against Marcus's forehead.

"I *said* we'll stop when we get there," said Father Mike, a dangerous edge coming into his voice.

Marcus remained calm as the gun dug into his skin, not shaking, sweating, or breathing heavily. Instead he very slowly raised his hand and pointed at the windshield. Up ahead at a slight bend in the road there was a roadblock of three vehicles sitting abreast with their headlights shining in their direction. Stephanie slammed on the brakes. As they slid to a halt, a figure climbed out of the middle vehicle and walked to the front, standing there patiently.

"What do you want me to do?" asked Stephanie.

Father Mike looked out to the roadblock and then back at his little group of hostages. He repeated this process several times.

"Well?" asked Stephanie.

"Give me a minute to think, damn it."

Father Mike briefly lifted the gun he had pointed at Stephanie and took steady aim. She tensed and started to cry. He let the gun fall back to his lap again, but then flexed to aim once more. Before he could make a decision, Stephanie slammed her foot on the gas. It was the moment everyone had been waiting for. Marcus grabbed the wrist of the arm with the gun pointed at him, using both hands to push Father Mike's hand up to the ceiling of the SUV. At the same time Leviticus, who had been sitting directly behind Father Mike, grabbed Father Mike's right arm. The gun went off and shot a hole through the windshield, directly at the middle vehicle of the roadblock. It was hard to tell if the person standing in front of the truck actually took the bullet or just ducked at the sound of gunfire, but either way he dropped to the ground.

"Seatbelts!" Stephanie shouted above the noise of the jostling SUV, gunfire, and struggling passengers. She kept her foot on the gas, intending to ram the roadblock. Another figure climbed out of the truck at the center of the roadblock, hoisting something on his shoulder. The stance and silhouette was all too familiar to all of them—it was another RPG. Leviticus tried to shake the gun out of Father Mike's hand, which caused another shot to go off. The shot was high and wide, but it startled the man with the RPG and he fired slightly prematurely.

The next seconds went by in slow motion. Everyone stopped struggling as the SUV sped toward the roadblock and the RPG flew toward the SUV. Its familiar, erratic trajectory teetered and spiraled slowly across the distance between them. It flew low, getting lower in the painfully slow seconds that passed like honey. Finally the RPG struck just a few feet in front of them. The explosion rocked the SUV and made a deep crater. They had so much speed at that point that instead of careening headfirst into the hole, the SUV slammed into the rim and then flipped. The first spin sent the tail end of the SUV onto the ground, which then catapulted them high into the air.

The SUV soared for a moment, but the front-heaviness caused it to angle down, and they were looking at the ground coming directly at them through the windshield. Staring up at them, confused and terrified, were the two rebels who had been standing in front of the truck, one still holding the empty rocket launcher on his shoulder. The SUV smashed down deep into the earth, causing all the airbags in the vehicle to inflate simultaneously, and flipped over a half turn, top down onto the center truck. At last, it slid back down to the ground, nose first.

Then there was stillness, and silence.

Chapter 15

The City of Your Final Destination

At first, there was the sound of shifting glass shards, creaking metal, and the ticking of the cooling engine. Then other sounds broke through the veil of dulled consciousness, and Stephanie heard raindrops pattering on the chassis of the SUV. There was the sound of someone moving, but her vision was still a bit fuzzy. There was light coming from somewhere outside the vehicle, but inside it was near dark and she was having a hard time focusing.

She tried to move, and it was then that she realized she was hanging upside down, strapped into the driver's seat. Just as that knowledge sunk in, her body jerked and then tumbled to the floor, which was actually the ceiling of the SUV. She tried to sit up but couldn't; she then tried to roll over onto her knees but felt herself being restrained. Then she was pulled free and suddenly she was outside, rain falling on her face and the lights from a truck in her eyes.

The others regained consciousness over the next few minutes and made the same realizations in roughly the same order Stephanie had, but no one came to pull them out. Marcus regained mobility first and struggled out of his seatbelt, falling shoulder first onto the ceiling with a groan and sliding toward the shattered windshield of the SUV. It was hard to tell in the dimness, but he could see the outlines of what looked like Magnus and Fenrir laying in a depression of the roof near the back end of the vehicle. He climbed up and checked both for a pulse. Once he confirmed they were both still alive, he slid back down toward the front of the vehicle. He made similar cursory checks of Mestoph and Leviticus, noticing but cataloging away for now the fact that they had drastically different pulses from each other and from any human heartbeat he had ever felt.

Then he scrambled up toward where Stephanie was—only she wasn't. Even in the dimness, he could see that both front seats were empty and the passenger door was open. It was hard to tell, but it looked like the driver side door was creased and probably jammed.

"Stephanie?" he yelled, but there was no reply.

Panic hit him and he felt his aches and pains dull away to nothing. Before he realized it, he was standing in the rain outside. In front of him, silhouetted in the headlights of the truck, were Father Mike and Stephanie. He was holding a gun to her head.

"That's far enough lover boy," said Father Mike.

Marcus couldn't see it, but he could feel that cold smile beaming out from the man's face. Just the thought of it made him feel sick. He looked around, hoping one of the rebels might have survived, but if they had they were still unconscious or hiding. He saw that Father Mike was only holding one gun and cursed himself for not checking the vehicle before he came out.

"So now what?" asked Marcus.

"We wait for the others. Nothing has changed. We're all going to the center of that storm together," said Father Mike.

Marcus heard noises coming from the SUV and saw the glint off of a pair of eyes peeking out of the driver's side window. He chose then to speak up, hoping someone inside heard him.

"So what happened to the other gun?" asked Marcus, a little louder than necessary.

Father Mike laughed mirthlessly and pulled the second gun from his coat pocket and raised it high, pointing it up at the sky. Even in silhouette there was no denying it was the real thing.

"Nice try. Warning your friends isn't going to do any good. I hold all the cards here," said Father Mike.

He lowered the second gun and aimed it at the SUV, near the rear, and fired off two quick shots. By Marcus's count that was the eighth shot from that gun, though he couldn't remember any being fired from the padre's personal gun. He didn't know exactly what the capacity of the Sky Marshal's .40 was but he had played enough video games to recognize it as a subcompact, probably the Glock 27, and he figured it could only be nine or ten, depending on whether one had been chambered and assuming the clip had been full. If they were lucky and Father Mike wasn't paying attention to his ammo the second gun could quickly be made useless.

"Alright, everyone out," said Father Mike.

Both Mestoph and Leviticus climbed out of the wreckage, Mestoph through a shattered side window and Leviticus from the passenger side. A few moments later Sir Regi dropped out through the busted out rear window, whimpering a bit as he put weight on one of his legs. The dog was covered in blood, but it didn't seem to be his own. All of them were dirty and covered in scratches, and the headlights glinted off of pieces of glass in their hair and falling from the creases of their clothes.

"What about the other two?" asked Father Mike.

"Magnus is out cold. I think he might be in a coma. Between being shot and the wreck his body has been through a lot," said Leviticus.

"And Fenrir?"

Leviticus shook his head somberly. Mestoph spoke up. "You, um, warning shot him in the head."

Father Mike turned and looked at the SUV. Half of his face was lit by headlights, and they could see that his twisted smile was gone. He harrumphed and shrugged his shoulders.

"No matter. I've got who I need. They were dead weight

anyway," he said.

Father Mike moved sideways, keeping Stephanie as a shield in front of him, and pointed at the remains of the roadblock.

"Alright, why don't you guys start checking vehicles and find me one that works. Just start them long enough to see if they run and cut them off. If any of you make like you're going to take off I won't hesitate to shoot her," he said as he pulled Stephanie closer, pressing the gun harder against her temple. She made a strained face but didn't make a noise. Sir Regi growled, and Father Mike pointed the second gun at the dog.

"Listen you little furry bastard. I don't know what your deal is, but I'll take you out just for fun if you don't shut up," he said.

Sir Regi's growl went low and deep into his stomach. Father Mike threw him a warning look and adjusted the gun in his hand to emphasize his point. Sir Regi let out a muffled half-bark as he lowered his head, his tail going down as well.

"Now who's a good boy?"

Marcus, Mestoph, and Leviticus walked past Father Mike, who put the second gun down by his side but not back into his coat, and kept himself turned so that Stephanie stayed facing them. He had almost turned his back to Sir Regi, whose head had suddenly shot to attention and had begun to crouch, but Father Mike saw his error before the dog could do anything. Father Mike backed up a bit until he was near Sir Regi, kicked at him, and motioned toward the others with a nod. The dog hesitated for a moment but finally moved closer to the rest of his comrades, reluctantly going submissive again. By now everyone had pretty much traded places with Father Mike now facing into the headlights of the roadblock vehicles and the flipped SUV at his right only a few feet away.

Something changed in Sir Regi's demeanor, and he began growling and making gruff little chirrups that sounded as much like barks as bullfrog croaks. The Scottie got louder and started bucking forward with each bark in the aggressive stance of a larger dog defying an attempt to invade onto his territory. Father Mike began to lift his gun, and then things got confusing. Sir Regi lurched forward as fast as he could. At the same time, a blur came from the top of the flipped SUV and landed on Father Mike. The gun went off, and there were the simultaneous screams and yelps of two men, a dog, and a woman.

Mestoph, Leviticus, and Marcus ran over but stopped short when they suddenly made sense of what was happening. Stephanie was on her back and propped up by her hands behind her watching the scene along with them. What they saw was Father Mike's vacant eyes staring up, laying on top of a body that had an arm wrapped around the padre's chest. That arm was gripping the handle of a pocket knife shoved deep into his chest somewhere close to where his heart should be. There was also a large chunk of the Father's throat missing. It was hanging from Sir Regi's mouth, who was shaking like a nervous Chihuahua. There was blood all over Father Mike, pouring from the gaping hole in his neck and from around the blade in his chest. The body suddenly lifted and rolled over, revealing Fenrir with a slightly unnerving grin on his face.

"Don't like priests," he said as he picked himself up off the ground, shaking gravel, glass, and dirt off himself.

He walked over and gave Stephanie a hand getting off the ground. When he turned to look at Sir Regi, he seemed genuinely surprised.

"Freyja's tits! You're a vicious little bastard," he said.

Sir Regi finally spit out the mouthful of flesh and then ran over to the back of the flipped SUV and began retching violently. Everyone stood around the body of Father Mike for several minutes, waiting to see if he was going to go undead again. He didn't. They all shrugged, looked at each other, and seemed to breathe easy for the first time since they had left the gas station. Sir Regi came back as Fenrir and Mestoph began pulling the body off to the side of the road. Leviticus kicked around the dirt and rocks that made up the rural highland road to cover up most of the blood. It wasn't that they were trying to hide their crime, if killing in self-defense could really be seen as a crime; it was just that no one wanted to keep seeing the body and the blood lying there. Besides, it was going to be pretty hard to hide a crater and a twisted pile of truck and SUV.

"So now what?" asked Marcus. He held Stephanie tightly against his side. She looked ragged from being held hostage for hours and was clinging on to Marcus.

"We've all been through quite a bit, and it's getting late," said Mestoph as he and Fenrir came back from dragging Father Mike's body away. "I say we try one of these trucks and see if we can't get a little distance before we try to get some rest. We're beat, and Magnus is still unconscious."

"You mean he's really in a coma? I figured after Fenrir had a noticeable lack of being shot in the head that Magnus was just hiding somewhere," said Marcus.

"Yeah, he's not doing so good. Can't believe the padre didn't at least check to see if you two were telling the truth, though," said Fenrir.

Marcus and Fenrir, being the two conscious humans with the most mechanical acumen, tried getting the two trucks on the outsides of the roadblock in working order. Neither would start immediately, and one of them had been damaged enough in the collision that the hood wouldn't open. After some prying and banging, they finally got the hood up on the other truck and found it missing far more than could be cannibalized and fitted from the other vehicles. Both vehicles had been intentionally scuttled prior to the wreck.

Everyone else scoured the wreckage and the sides of the road and only found two bodies. Fenrir identified them as two of the mercenaries they had joined up with to "salvage" the airplane wreckage. These two had been in the truck that had left as soon as fighting broke out, the truck that St. Peter and his demon lackey had presumably been driving.

The haunting light of the storm still shone darkly in the distance and the rains hadn't let up, so the Prophecy and Omen were still active. That meant that even if St. Peter had found Persephone, he hadn't done anything with her yet. The truth was that they didn't know what to do when they found her; the only ones who would were God and Satan. That wasn't a confrontation Mestoph or Leviticus was looking forward to. If the others had known it was looming, they wouldn't either.

There was nothing they could do about any of it now and without a vehicle they were stuck at least for the night. Come morning they would weigh their options as far as what to do with Magnus, how to close the last 50 or so miles to Persephone, and anything else that came up. For now they all piled into the various vehicles for the night. Fenrir crawled into the overturned SUV, not wanting to move Magnus or leave him alone, while Marcus and Stephanie slept in the cab of one of the scuttled trucks and Mestoph and Leviticus climbed into the other. The brush with death and the welling up of emotions between Marcus and Stephanie resulted in the shedding of some of Marcus' innocence that night. No one but Fenrir actually slept easily, but they all eventually gave in to exhaustion.

Hades had created a small bubble of light and shelter near the edge of the chasm. He had also conjured a plush wingback chair and a narrow Victorian end table in the center, and had been sitting smoking a cigar and drinking a glass of Greek wine. The light was the orange color of a fireplace and looked out of place and a bit ominous in the foggy darkness. It wasn't anything near as sinister as the thick beam of cold, dark light that seemed to ooze from the clouds. It shined—which was the only word that seemed to apply despite its oddity—directly onto what he assumed would be Valaskjalf, one of Odin's halls that was supposedly made of pure silver. In that hall was his throne, Hlidskjalf. Hades had no doubt that Odin was sitting on it now, looking over him and trying to figure out what to do with his new bargaining chip.

The two pantheons, the Norse and the Greeks, had never had much to do with each other. They occupied drastically different time periods and were geographically separated even at the height of their respective popularity. That said, they were both waning. Only small groups of people still believed in the old gods, and even fewer actually paid them homage. Hades had long ago lost dominion over the afterlife. God had been rather diplomatic about it, giving all those souls under Hades' watch the option to make a new home in Heaven. Understandably, most of them took the offer. Heaven was the new, cool place to go, and if Hades had been honest with himself, he wouldn't have minded going as well. That, God did not offer. Satan, on the other hand, was his typical boisterous self and claimed he had magnanimously let Hades run his "little shop" while he had been busy, but now he was collecting his debts. Now Hades pretty much ran a small retirement home of faithful Greeks who probably wish they had taken God's offer.

The Norse were no different. They had kept all the fallen warriors who had made it to Valhalla, but their market share was pretty much non-existent these days. So when a fabulous turn of events brought the bride of a god from another pantheon, you had to make the most of it. Despite the fact that Persephone had little love for Hades, he couldn't deny or change the fact that he would never stop feeling the way he did for her. What the Norse didn't understand though, was that he would do *anything* to get her back.

"Hades?" asked a deep, gravelly voice from the darkness beyond Hades' bubble.

The god turned, startled. He had been deep in thought and hadn't heard anything or anyone come up the path.

"Who…is that?" Hades peered at a large, broad-shouldered figure cast in just enough light that he thought he recognized the gorilla shape. "St. Peter? What the Hades are you doing here?"

The figure stepped to the edge of the bubble of light, and St. Peter stood there, limned in the soft glow. It gave menacing shadows to the sharp and angular features of the man's face.

"Mind if I come in?"

A rectangular line began to cut into the bubble protecting Hades, and then it flipped outwards to make a doorway for St. Peter to enter. Then the door closed and sealed shut. Hades conjured up another chair, in which St. Peter obligingly took a seat. He sat silently for a moment, taking in the ambience of the glowing darkness.

"Is that one of your tricks?" asked St. Peter.

Hades looked at him impassively for a few seconds.

"I'll take that as a no."

"I assumed it was always that way. You know how

macabre and depressing those Norse can be," said Hades. He drew out the S's in "those Norse" with a sneer.

"True, but that has more of the flair of someone accustomed to the darker side of things," said St. Peter.

That was something that had annoyed Hades since God and Satan took over. Back in his day Hades had been a revered, respected, and even well-liked god. He was an equal with Zeus and Poseidon. Zeus had reveled in the love of the living, and Hades thrived on the respect and service of those who had crossed the mortal barrier. Meanwhile, a thousand years with nothing but fish and the occasional sailor had made Poseidon a bit bitter. Now? Now everyone assumed that Hades was just the old Greek counterpart of Satan and lumped him in with all that fire and brimstone nonsense. Even those who should know better, like St. Peter, had cast him aside as a proto-Satan.

"Well if that's not yours, then that must mean it's our good friend Satan. And if that's the case, that means there's something up there I want," said St. Peter.

"Well, join the club. My wife is up there, too," said Hades.

"Persephone? Wait a minute…" St. Peter rolled the name over in his head, trying to recall something at the edge of his memory.

"What was that girl's name? Stephanie? Yes, that's it," mused St. Peter. "Persephone. Stephanie. No, it couldn't be that simple. Oh, but it is, isn't it?" He howled with laughter and Hades leaned away, looking at St. Peter as if he had gone feral and would bite him at any moment.

"They fucked up the paper work!" shouted St. Peter through his guttural guffaws. He reached his immense arm over the end table and clasped Hades firmly on the shoulder, despite the other's attempt the squirm away. "My good man, it would seem we're after the same thing. And I think I have a proposition that may interest you."

Chapter 16

Let's Start a Holy War

Although short enough to be ponies, Icelandic horses are broad and stout enough to be any horse's equal in everything but height. They could easily bear the weight of even the massive Magnus. A small herd of them was grazing near the wreckage, outlined in the gold light of sunrise. If they could be ridden, they could quickly close the distance to the mountains by the end of the day since they could cut straight across the highland instead of following the winding volcanic gravel and mud road—more accurately described as the ruts of previous travelers—they had been driving on the night before.

Fenrir was the first to climb out of the Land Rover. The sudden appearance of humans didn't seem to bother the horses in the least. One of them glanced up from a tuft of grass and then went back to munching. Fenrir looked over to the rest of the group with a huge smile on his face. He turned and faced the herd of horses and went into a crouch and calmly, quietly, and slowly stalked up to the horse that had taken notice of him. Fenrir moved with a fluidity that was at once frightening and fascinating. It was no wonder that Father Mike hadn't heard him approach. He was like a wolf stalking prey.

Fenrir, still a good distance away from the horse, suddenly stood upright and lost the predatory edge about him. He looked back at the group, still huddled in the trucks where they'd made camp, with a confused or possibly disappointed look on his face. He looked back to the horses and jumped in place and yelled in a distinctly Icelandic way at the same time. All the horses briefly looked up at him and then calmly went back to what they had been doing.

The horse that Fenrir had been stalking stopped eating and stood facing him and then slowly began walking calmly over, stopping just in front of him. Fenrir, dumbfounded, petted the horse, whose muscles quivered. It whickered contently. Then Fenrir found the rope amidst the slightly tangled mane at the horse's head. They weren't wild after all; at least not completely.

Fenrir returned to the vehicles, leading the horse he had made friends with. It obediently followed him as if this were something he and Fenrir did often. By the time he reached the Land Rover, the others had pulled themselves out of their truck hotels and were trying to warm up. The light had turned from gold to grey as it rose behind the storm, which seemed to be gathering in on itself, becoming more compact though no less fierce.

"They've got crude reigns on them, all of them. They're as docile as a palfrey, and if we can get something to use as padding I don't see why we can't ride them. We can even toss Magnus over one of them, as long as we don't go too fast, which we can't really do if we want to make it all the way to Hofsjökull," said Fenrir.

"Hoffwhat?" asked Stephanie.

Fenrir pointed to the ice-covered mounds of earth where the storm hovered, the dark-light of its center a column of shadow in the gloomy daylight.

"It's a glacier that sits on top of a volcano of the same name," said Magnus with some difficulty as he tried to pull himself out of the side window of the Range Rover. He was sluggish and pale and struggled to get to his feet, but with some help from Marcus he stayed upright. "And I'll not be tossed over the back of a horse like a sack of potatoes," he said.

Fenrir checked him over as much as Magnus would let

him. It looked like the hulking man had tried to change his own dressing and hadn't done too badly, but Fenrir tightened the binding, which made Magnus wince.

"Plus, with my luck you'd pick the shortest horse to toss me over, and I'd hit my head on every rock we passed," said Magnus, trying to force a smile.

Magnus and Fenrir, though not exactly equestrians, were the most familiar with horses, and Stephanie had ridden some as a child; therefore, it was left to them to approach the horses, test their temperament as much as they knew how, and round them up. Meanwhile Marcus, Mestoph, and Leviticus would search the vehicles for anything useful like food and weapons, as well as blankets or anything else that could be used to make impromptu saddles.

The horses were surprisingly easy to handle and seemed as if they actually wanted to be taken control of. Although it probably wasn't necessary, six of the eight horses were corralled near the wreck, with Sir Regi barking behind them like he was a sheep dog, then they were tied off to the tie-down points on one of the truck beds. The other two horses, not wanting to be left out, followed the rest of the herd. Each of them would have a horse of their own, with Sir Regi riding shotgun with Marcus.

The scavenging party was able to pull together a small supply of bottled water, a couple energy and granola bars, and a bag of green flaky leaves that Magnus and Fenrir identified excitedly as roasted sugar kelp. There was also a bottle of some sort of green schnapps called Brennivin.

"Ahh, good ol' Black Death," said Magnuson

"Too bad we don't have any hákarl to go with it," said Fenrir.

"So what is…how-kar-lik?" asked Stephanie, struggling with the Icelandic word.

"Fermented shark meat. Stuff's poisonous fresh, so it's

199

cured until fermented. It's strong, and a bit of a delicacy here, but to you it'd probably taste like piss and vomit. Even we tend to like to chase it with some Black Death, like he's got there, to get rid of the taste," said Magnuson.

Sir Regi gave a curious "hmmm" and Mestoph actually looked like he was interested in trying it. The others hoped they wouldn't have to resort to fermented meats anytime soon. Though with their meager supplies, they would be eating moss and begging for hákarl if it took more than a day to get to the glacier.

As to saddles, they came up woefully short, with only three small blankets and a thick sweater they were reluctant to remove from the dead body of one of the rebels who had been squished by the flipping Range Rover. Magnus and Fenrir had ridden bareback before, although not for more than a few miles, and they were willing to forgo the cushioning. Fenrir tried to get Magnus to reconsider, given his tattered condition, but he firmly refused to give in. That left the other four, not counting Sir Regi, to draw lots for blankets. In the spirit of impartiality, Fenrir grabbed a handful of scrubby grass, counting out four blades, and then cutting each to roughly the same length with his pocket knife and then cutting one in half. Stephanie drew the short straw. Marcus tried to concede his blanket, but she told him that she was the most accustomed, though just barely, to horseback riding, so he would fare much worse over the long run.

They didn't find any weapons other than the two guns they took from Father Mike. There was a mangled rocket launcher, but its safety was suspect, not to mention it was a ridiculously impractical weapon for them to take with them. With the blankets tossed over the backs of the horses, they began the comically awkward process of trying to mount their horses. With no stirrups or pommels to help them, they opted to move each horse alongside the bed of the truck, climb in the back, and then onto the horse.

It was a slow process full of uneasy movements and tenuous balance, but eventually they were all mounted and as stable as could be. Fenrir took point, as much by happenstance as by design. He managed to get his horse to move away from the road and take a more direct approach to the glacier; the others followed suit, with the two riderless horses trailing at the rear. Once the horses seemed to understand where they were heading, they took over navigation as if they had been intending to visit the glacier the entire time. Whether or not Fenrir's horse was the leader of the band of wild horses to begin with, it was the defacto leader now and the others didn't seem to mind.

They set a slow walking pace as they got their "horse legs" and learned a few basic points of horsemanship from the Vikings and Stephanie. After about an hour, both riders and mounts were desperate to speed up, and the short horses broke out into a pleasant trot. They slowed down to a walk every so often for a little rest for both rider and horse, but the horses quickly put themselves back at a trotting pace. They all knew they would eventually have to stop to give the horses a proper rest, and none of them seemed to be looking forward to trying to dismount and mount again without the aid of the truck. For the time being, however, they all tried to enjoy the ride.

It was hard not to be moved by the landscape, despite the circumstances and gloomy weather. The highlands were a harsh and beautiful country, with long stretches of volcanic sand deserts mixed with patches of snow that hadn't yet melted or washed away by the rain. There was virtually no vegetation until they came across random rivulets of water, which Magnus explained were runoff from the glacier. Even then the vegetation was sparse, so they made sure to stop anytime they came near water to take care of the horses.

Being a semi-wild band of horses, they seemed to have some previous experience with this part of the country and managed to find the runoffs with surprising frequency. Around midday the horses led them to the banks of a wide glacial river.

"This is probably as good a place as any to stop. We can use the banks to remount when we're done," said Fenrir. His horse was already drinking from the edge of the river and eyeballing a clump of the relatively plentiful vegetation near the water.

The river looked to be about a hundred feet across, and didn't look like it was very deep. The volcanic sand of the arctic dessert had slowly given way to fist-sized rocks as they approached the river and the bank dipped about ten feet below level at an easily navigable incline. On the other side of the small river, the terrain became steeper, leading up to a small cluster of ice-capped mountains far to the northeast, which Magnus called the Kerlingarfjöll tuyas—a *tuya* being a type of mountain that he claimed were rare, being forming only in areas where volcanoes and glaciers comingled. Directly to the north lay the glacier Hofsjökull, above which the storm continued to grow. The winds picked up dramatically as they approached it.

"I'd guess that once we cross the river, which I would bet is the Þjórsá, we shouldn't be any more than three hours from the edge of the glacial field. Once we get there, I hope you guys have some way of contacting the Vanir," said Magnus.

In the time since Father Mike had taken them hostage, they had forgotten about the cover story Sir Regi had blurted out. It seemed like it had happened ages ago, but the Neo-Vikings clearly hadn't forgotten their holy charge.

"They'll find us," said Sir Regi. It was as good an answer as anything else. Better than the truth, at least for now.

Once everyone had rested up and had a little something to eat—for a little was all they had—they went through the slightly less arduous and embarrassing task of mounting the horses. None of them had ever forded a river on horseback. They crossed it without a problem. The horses handled the water that came up to their knees deftly, not losing a step and hardly slowing down.

They continued on for another two hours and slowly realized that they were no longer heading directly toward the glacier but instead taking a slight angle away from the river that kept them crossing rivulets of water every ten or fifteen minutes. Their trajectory also started taking them toward the western edge of the glacier. Fenrir tried to correct their path several times, but after a few minutes it would be obvious that horses were again veering toward a large icy outcropping of the glacier that rose up like a ramp. He stopped fighting the horses and let them choose the path.

They reached the edge of the outcrop a half hour later. It fanned outwards in a semi-circle with two rows of small, irregularly oblong ponds and puddles dotting the edge of the flow. None of them were more than a few hundred feet wide, but there were easily a hundred of them. The horses walked up between two of the larger bowls of water and then stopped at the edge of a deep chasm that ran the perimeter of the outcropping. The chasm was filled with dense, rising steam. There was no vegetation within a thousand feet, which meant there was no reason for the horses to lead them there—but they had. Fenrir looked back at the others; he seemed to be suppressing a smile.

"End of the line, I suppose," he said.

The others dismounted and looked around. It was a landscape as foreign as if they were on another planet. They were surrounded by dark stone, ice, and a thick and persistent fog that was still slightly warm even as it began to descend after cooling. The warmth of the steam was at odds with the brisk air that seemed to blow gently but unendingly from no discernible direction. The rain had picked up considerably in the last half hour and they were all soaked, but here it seemed to be only a light drizzle that was only slightly more solid than the mist.

"This place feels…old. Like there are old powers at work here," said Magnus as he walked to the edge of the chasm, warming his arms and face. He smiled, feeling slightly rejuvenated.

"Old as the gods themselves," said Fenrir, almost to himself. He then came to attention and turned to the group. "Alright, we're here. Now what?

They shrugged and looked to one another hoping for an answer, even though they knew there wasn't one. Stephanie looked up and saw the center of the storm swirling overhead, so near that the spinning pentagram was visible as it had been on the television. The exact center was a few hundred yards ahead of them. That would put it far on the other side of the chasm, and likely above them as the glacier rose. It was hard to tell what was beyond the steam.

"Well, let's do what any Viking with a passing knowledge of the sagas and mythology would do," said Magnus.

"Kill each other in battle and hope one of us makes it to Valhalla?" asked Sir Regi.

Fenrir looked as if he was contemplating the proposal, but Magnus shook his head in mock disappointment. "No, we call for Bifrost. The bridge that links the lands of mortals to that of the gods."

"Might want to call for Heimdall instead. Don't remember any legends of the bridge being sentient. Or a taxi cab," said Fenrir.

Magnuson nodded, conceding the point, and then the two turned toward the chasm and yelled out Heimdall's name. They both raised their arms, motioning with their hands in internationally recognized Rock Star Sign Language for the others to join in. The others obliged and they yelled out in unison. Sir Regi tried, but anytime he raised his voice it turned into a wordless howling like a dog wailing along with a siren. The howl was clearly involuntary, and he eventually gave up trying. Soon there was the distinct sound of stone grinding on stone, and the call for Heimdall abruptly stopped.

They stood there expectantly, waiting as the grinding sound grew louder and closer, and then a shape began to form in the mist. Gradually, they were able to make out two figures standing on something that was moving, with painful slowness, toward their side of the chasm. One of the figures coalesced into a tall, pale white man with long white hair, while on the right stood a slightly shorter but much more muscular man with a short curly beard who was missing his right hand and part of the arm below the elbow. He was leaning on a tall spear. Heimdall wore the same armor that he had when Persephone had called him, but now it was polished to a shine. The plain sword he had previously worn was replaced with another, this one larger and more ornate. The pommel and cross-guard sported a flame motif much like that of the bridge. The other man wore a massive chest plate that depicted a battlefield with one of the armies being led by a tall one-armed man that looked considerably like the one wearing it. The stump of his right hand had a leather and copper gauntlet strapped to it with a bronze cap on the end bearing a single rune that looked like an arrow pointing upwards. Both gods stared at the waiting group, seeming to look into the souls of each member as they rode through the mists on a wide span of stone.

"Heimdall. Tyr," said Fenrir, nodding to each.

Heimdall reached to a beautiful carved and gold inlaid horn that hung at his side. Tyr touched the stump of his arm to Heimdall's arm, which would have probably been a reassuring gesture were it not for the stump part.

"Not yet, my friend," said Tyr, quietly.

The two figures stepped off the bridge and came in close to the group, looking down at each of them, even Magnus, who was several inches shorter than Heimdall. When they both came to stand in front of Fenrir, their eyes narrowed and mouths clenched.

"You dare show your face here, wolf?" asked Tyr.

Magnus looked confused at their interest in his friend and with his familiarity with what he could only assume were living gods. "I think you might be confused..." began Magnus, but was silenced by a dismissive wave from Heimdall. It wasn't a magical silence; there was just such disdain in the gesture that Magnus didn't see the point in continuing.

"Don't worry, brother. Their bark is worse than their bite. Now my bite, on the other hand..." said Fenrir, flashing a knowing smile.

Tyr lunged at Fenrir, dropping the spear and grabbing at Fenrir's shirt collar with his good hand—his only hand.

"I will kill you and skin you, and then whenever I shit I will clean myself with your pelt," said Tyr, spitting in anger. His muscles rippled in anticipation of a fight.

Fenrir still wore the wolfish smile, "Don't fool yourself. We both know that's not how it happens. I'll die, no doubt. But it won't be by your hands."

"What the Hell is going on?" asked Magnus.

Tyr turned to Magnus, his anger now directed at him. Magnus backed up a step. "You travel in the company of a wolf. *The* wolf. And you bring us to the very brink of our deaths," he said.

Magnus looked at the other members of the group, hoping they might have an idea of what was going on, but they all seemed just as surprised or confused as him. "I've known this man for years. He is a good man, and together we have worshiped you and your brothers," he said.

Tyr stared at him for several seconds, and then looked to Heimdall. Heimdall just shrugged. Tyr shook his head slowly, as if he finally understood, and then turned to Fenrir with some amusement on his face.

"You are your father's son. A trickster in wolf's clothing. Loki be damned, you lot are all the same," said Tyr. He chuckled, but his expression quickly turned sour and he moved faster than should have been possible. The movement startled everyone and they involuntarily jumped back. Tyr reared back with his handless arm and then stump-punched Fenrir in the head. The copper endcap of his gauntlet left an embossed rune imprinted into Fenrir's forehead. And then another. And another. Three arrow-like runes were stamped his forehead in a tight grouping before Heimdall could make a grab at Tyr's arm, already reared back for a fourth hit. Tyr slung off Heimdall's attempt as if he were a weak midget and then began pummeling Fenrir in the chest, taking a step forward with each hit and sending Fenrir back a step closer to the edge of the chasm. When Magnus finally realized what was about to happen, he ran past Heimdal and tried to hold Tyr back as well. Tyr didn't even register the attempt.

After another hit, Fenrir was at the edge of the chasm with his back to the mists with one foot scrabbling to make purchase on the ground. He was held up only by Tyr, who wore a wolfish smile of his own. Tyr pushed Fenrir backwards and turned to walk away. Magnus grabbed desperately at Fenrir, who smiled calmly despite a bloody, mangled face. Magnus caught a hold of something and grabbed onto it with all his strength, pulling backwards to keep from going over the edge himself. In his hand was the sword medallion and part of the thin, silver chain that Fenrir

207

wore.

The wolfish man hung in the air, suspended by the remarkably strong chain and the toe of one shoe that still held traction on the edge of the chasm. Magnus's arm shook with the strain, and his body teetered back and forth as he fought to keep balance. Marcus, the closest to him, ran and grabbed a hold of Magnus to keep him from going headfirst into the chasm.

Tyr saw the look of horror on Heimdall's face and turned to see what was wrong. "You fool!" he shouted.

Fenrir looked up at Magnus's clasped fist and then his eyes followed the chain down. He looked back up at Magnus with a big, warm smile.

"Thank you, brother," he said. Fenrir leaned forward with some effort but then immediately jerked backwards. The chain snapped in Magnus's hand as Fenrir fell backwards in slow motion, the sword pendant falling with him. With the counterbalance of Fenrir's weight gone, Magnuson and Marcus tumbled backwards. Fenrir disappeared into the mist, trailing a maniacal laugh.

Magnus and Marcus picked themselves up off the ground while Tyr rushed to the spear he had dropped earlier. He scooped it up and threw it as he turned, the ridiculously long shaft warbling through the air as it streamed toward Magnus. The Neo-Viking watched, dumbfounded, as the spear flew towards him. A second later, he stumbled and fell to one side, four feet of spear protruding from his chest. The collective jaws of the group hung wide, and then they heard the piercing sound of a horn.

Ragnarok was upon them.

Chapter 17

The One in Which Various Mythological Loose Ends Are Tied

St. Peter and Hades stood in an enormous, dimly lit hall of stone. In the center of the hall were a large inclined stone altar and a pillar that rose a hundred feet with a large eternally burning torch mounted halfway up. Tied to the altar by what looked like intestines or the sinews of something that had lived once upon a time in the distant past was a gaunt and mostly naked man; the Norse god Loki. Wrapped around the column was a snake whose head hung over the top of the altar and dripped poison like a leaky faucet. Sitting next to Loki on a small stone stool was his wife, Sigyn, who was surprisingly homely for the bride of a god. She held a large wooden bowl that was worn around the lip from an untold eternity of use. She used it to capture the poison that dripped from the snake's mouth.

"So how long has this been going on?" asked St. Peter.

Loki looked to his wife, and the two of them seemed to be doing mental calculations. It was a bad sign if it took the two of them that much effort to figure out how long they'd been down there. After several seconds, Sigyn turned to answer.

"At least a millennium. Give or take a century or two," she said, in a voice that was dull and rough with disuse. St. Peter didn't get the impression that the husband and wife had too many conversations.

"You old gods have some of the most ridiculous tortures," said St. Peter.

Loki shrugged; to him it was what it was. Even when

Sigyn's bowl filled up and she had to go off to empty it and the poison dripped down directly on Loki's face, he took it in stride. Granted, his squirming and wrenching caused minor earthquakes each time she left, but once she came back and resumed collecting the poison he didn't seem any worse for wear.

"I knew a fellow once who had his liver torn out by an eagle every day for millennia," said Hades. "But that's what you get for giving the fire of the gods to mankind."

"That sounds awful," said Loki with a smile.

Hades and St. Peter looked at him, both with an eyebrow arched questioningly.

"Well, yeah, this sucks too. But still..." said Loki.

"So what ever happened to ol' Prometheus? I don't remember him being on the list of Titans we hold in the void," said St. Peter.

"Titans?" asked Loki.

"Giants from the dawn of time. They fought the gods and were cast into Tartarus," said Hades.

"We've rebranded it as The Void," interrupted St. Peter. "God's very keen on names he can actually pronounce."

"Oh, you mean the jötunn," said Loki.

"No, the Titans," said St. Peter.

"Jötunn"

"Titans," said St. Peter, getting annoyed.

"They were my jötunn long before they were your Titans," said Loki, pointing at Hades. "...or your prisoners," he said, pointing to St. Peter.

"Yes, yes. We know that. In fact, that's why we're here," said St. Peter.

St. Peter tried to explain as quickly as possible, giving away as little as possible, the situation they were in. They embellished a bit with details that were probably true, but that they didn't know for certain. They told him that his Odin,

Loki's long-time nemesis, had something that they both wanted, and they would go to any lengths to get it. St. Peter told him that they knew he never handed over all the jötunn when the Olympians took them to be their Titans, and that even more went unaccounted when God took over and wanted to be rid of them completely.

Loki listened politely and nodded at pertinent bits. When St. Peter finally finished, he and Hades waited in silence. The silence drew out, and Hades and St. Peter exchanged impatient looks at each other.

"Did you hear me? We're willing to offer you anything within our power for a few jötunn," said St. Peter.

Loki smiled. "Of course I heard you. The only problem is that I don't want anything. I have all I need."

Hades and St. Peter looked around incredulously. They were at the bottom of a chasm with little light, a snake constantly poisoning him, and a kind of ugly wife who didn't say a word unless she was addressed directly.

"You're joking?" asked Hades.

Loki silently shook his head no.

"We could free you?" suggested St. Peter.

"Why would I want that?"

"With our help, you could take control of your pantheon," said Hades.

"That's not in my cards," said Loki.

"But it could be," said St. Peter.

Loki calmly shook his head again.

St. Peter tried a different tactic. "At the very least we could try and spruce this place up a bit. Bring in an interior decorator, some whores, you know? Maybe an umbrella for that snake problem? A TV?"

Loki politely declined each.

"What about…"

Loki shushed Hades, putting a finger to his mouth and

tilting his head to the side.

"Listen here, you—" began St. Peter indignantly.

"Shut up!" Loki was clearly listening for something. They were all silent. Even Sigyn looked unusually attentive. "Do you hear laughing?" he asked with a smile.

"You know what? Fuck you!" said St. Peter.

Hades put his hand on St. Peter's shoulder, "No. I hear it too."

Again they were quiet, and after a few seconds even St. Peter could hear it. It was the sound of resounding, howling, thoroughly satisfied laughter, and it was getting louder by the second. It quickly became apparent that the laughter was coming from above them. They all looked up, even the snake, as the laughter became unbearably loud. And then a body landed squarely on the snake, which twisted, jerked, and then suddenly went limp. Then the body fell off the top of the pillar and flopped to the ground face up. Laying there with an enormous smile, still chuckling even though he was wincing in pain, was Fenrir. He lifted an arm, and dangling from his hand was the thin silver necklace.

"Son!" exclaimed Loki.

St. Peter and Hades gave each other a surprised look. Then the sound of a horn, loud and clear even at this great depth, echoed through the chasm. In response, Loki sat upright, and a look of mischief and glee that had previously been absent seemed to fill the gaunt man.

"About that deal, boys? Let's talk," said Loki.

Everyone was shouting over the sound of Heimdall blowing his damned horn. Marcus and Leviticus were yelling at Tyr, who was in turn yelling back at them. Meanwhile Mestoph was yelling at Heimdall, trying to get him to shut up. Sir Regi started shouting but ended up wailing in tune to the horn, and he looked pissed because he couldn't stop. Stephanie was silently watching it all around her. She looked at Magnus's lifeless body lying in a pool of his own blood, the expression of disbelief still on his face. She looked at the storm above as it darkened, shooting down arcs of lightning into the mist. One arc split a large boulder a couple hundred yards away, the near instant clap of thunder momentarily drowning out the yelling and the horn. She didn't know if it was the stress or the noise, but she was getting a horrible headache. Her head was pounding, and there was a high-pitched whine in her ears.

It wasn't tinnitus, she realized, but an oddly familiar scream. By the time she understood what it was, the Nephilim and Seraphim were swooping down at her. The odd thing was that they didn't really seem to be trying to hurt her, just annoy her. The taunting Nephilim and Seraphim wailed louder and louder in her head, causing her to scream out painfully, "Asylum!" was the only word she could get out before the cacophony in her head became unbearable and then passed out. She collapsed to the ground in a disheveled pile before anyone could catch her.

As soon as Stephanie's body hit the ground, flocks of both Nephilim and Seraphim came down from the clouds and began circling just over head. The Seraphim, circling clockwise above them, spun around a wide arch directly above her, leaving a trail of soft white feathers that dissolved before they reached the ground. The Nephilim spun the opposite direction in a tighter circle, leaving a trail of oily blackness in their wake. Marcus ran over to Stephanie and tried to wake her, but she didn't respond. At least the sound of the horn had stopped, he thought.

"If it's asylum you seek, come now or best your chances out here with your God's buzzards," shouted Heimdall as he hopped on the bridge.

Tyr followed, and the bridge began to slowly retract. Marcus grabbed Stephanie under her arms and carried her like a sack. Mestoph grabbed Sir Regi and stepped onto the bridge, still only inches from the precipice, while Leviticus motioned Marcus to hurry. Marcus began to walk as fast as he could without hurting Stephanie as the buzzards, both black and white, swooped down in two uniform streams. They scraped at Marcus and Stephanie as he ran with her over his shoulder, their claws tearing across Stephanie's back and the back of Marcus's head. Marcus had to endure two waves of strafing runs by the creatures before he got to the bridge. He didn't even think about the gap, now several feet wide, but jumped with all the power that adrenaline and fear could muster. He made a one-footed landing at the edge of the bridge, where Mestoph and Leviticus were waiting to help steady him.

Once Marcus was on the bridge, the swarm of Seraphim and Nephilim bore down on them all. Heimdall tapped a section of rock on the railing and a panel opened, revealing a sort of service hatch. He reached into the opening and began twisting something that made a ratcheting sound, and the bridge began to speed up its return trip. The bridge had been used very little in the last few hundred years, and it groaned in protest. Heimdall closed the service hatch and then stood with arms crossed, seemingly unfazed by the attack.

Tyr conjured another spear from the ether, making a watery sucking sound as he pulled it from nowhere, and then chucked it confidently at a Nephilim. The spear sailed through the air, just as sure as when it had struck Magnus, and the Nephilim flipped backwards in midair as its forward momentum met with the spear's. It plummeted in a spiral into the chasm. Mestoph and Leviticus drew their guns and tried to make well aimed shots, but the creatures moved too erratically and they were too inexperienced at marksmanship to do much damage. After three shots Leviticus was out, having only winged a Seraphim. Mestoph emptied the full clip of his gun and took down another.

Tyr had summoned five more spears and taken down as many creatures in the time it took Mestoph and Leviticus to empty their guns. Although none of them made much of a dent in the creatures numbers, it did seem to serve as a deterrent against their strafing runs. No longer interested in attacking, they returned to spiraling up above in their opposing, concentric circles as the bridge finally entered the mists, making attacks by either party pointless. They couldn't see the flocks above them, but they could still hear the incessant flapping of wings. The sound bounced around in wild and random directions in the misty fog making it sound like they were being surrounded on all sides. The thought of being surrounded finally made Heimdall nervous enough to draw his sword and leer nervously into the emptiness, ready to attack anything that came at him.

The sound of the creatures dulled and the fog began to dissipate, revealing the opposite side of the chasm. The party turned and saw a narrow stretch of grass before them and then a sheer cliff of glassy obsidian rising thousands of feet into the sky. At the top of the cliff, chiseled out of the mountain itself, was a massive fortress. It was carved into a large, main cylinder with smaller towers flying out from it at random intervals on all sides. Each tower, including the central one, was topped with a sharp spire made of highly polished silver. It looked decidedly sinister, like something from an old Saturday morning cartoon. The spinning pentagram of clouds above it and the eerie gleam of the column of blackish light shining down on it didn't help.

215

"What is that?" asked Marcus.

"That is Valaskjalf, also known as the Shelf of the Slain. That is the hall where Odin sits on the great throne Hliðskjálf and watches over everything in all the known worlds," answered Heimdall without even bothering to see what Marcus was pointing at.

The bridge drew within a few yards of the Asgard side of the chasm, and Marcus felt a tapping on his back.

"I think I'm OK now. You can put me down," said Stephanie.

Marcus bent over and gently let Stephanie slide to her feet and then caught her as she wobbled a bit once she was upright. She was paler than usual and something in her eyes told him that OK was not really what she was right now.

"What happened back there?" asked Leviticus when he noticed Stephanie back on her feet.

"She's been doing that Vulcan mind deal with the sky demons and they bite hard," said Mestoph.

"It wasn't by choice, trust me. It was like being brain raped," said Stephanie.

Mestoph started to laugh, but the look of fragile vulnerability on Stephanie's face made him stop. He had never witnessed the Nephilim attack anything in the real world and had only heard of it happening in people's dreams. Their presence meant something big was going to happen that affected both Heaven and Hell, which leant a lot of credence to Heimdall's claim of Ragnarok being upon them. Never having witnessed the end of the world before, he wasn't sure just how serious that was. He wondered if this was The End Leviticus and he had spent their whole lives waiting around for. Leviticus was staring at everything like a kid in a toy factory, buzzing with excitement. If it really was The End of the World, this was going to get very interesting—and maybe a bit bloody.

Finally the bridge reached a stationary platform of jutting bedrock and stopped moving. The grassy strip where the bridge ended was a stark contrast to the gloomy looming obsidian cliff. Although it was a narrow piece of land, scarcely the width of a football field, it stretched on endlessly in either direction and was covered in a carpet of surprisingly thick, lush, and brilliantly green grass dotted with colorful flowers. There were even stands of hearty trees, mostly birch with a few stray aspen, which surrounded a large, two-story cabin nearby. The cabin was made of logs far bigger around than anything that grew there or anywhere else in Iceland. Behind the cabin were several rows of dome-shaped beehives made of coiled grass with colonies of bees swarming back and forth from the fields of flowers to the hives. A well worn path ran from the bridge, made a stop at the cabin, and then ran straight toward the cliff, ending at a cave entrance.

"Where is everyone?" asked Leviticus.

Tyr looked down at the Angel with disdain, snorted, and then walked off down the path that led to the cave. Heimdall looked toward Tyr and then back at the group. He took a deep breath and then sighed.

"Most of the remaining gods have moved up to Valaskjalf with Odin. The others, well, they've moved on. Some went to other religions, some are off being tortured of course, and some just…died. Anyone with an outstanding prophecy is still around, waiting for Ragnarok. We're operating with a skeleton crew these days," said Heimdall.

"So what *does* happen when a god dies?" asked Sir Regi.

Heimdall looked down at the dog curiously. "We die, obviously," he said, a glimmer of whimsy in the slight smile that cracked his otherwise grim face. The smile stuck around as he gestured at the cabin. "Care to come in and rest a bit? I've got some fine honeyed mead that I've just finished."

"I think we should probably go see Odin. You know,

that whole asylum thing," said Mestoph. He almost added something about finding Persephone, but didn't want to tip their hand if it wasn't necessary. They had gotten into Asgard without having to wheel and deal; why screw it up now?

Heimdall's faint smile disappeared at the reminder of the business at hand. "Ah, yes. Of course. We don't get many visitors, and with Ragnarok nigh, I thought one last horn of mead for old time's sake. But no, you're right. I'm sure Odin is wondering what's taking so long as it is," he said as he took one last longing glance at the cabin. Heimdall led them down the path that Tyr had taken. They made their way to the opening in the cliffside, which revealed a spiral staircase. Mestoph looked up at the thousands of feet of sheer cliff and then at the steps.

"No elevator, I take it?"

"It's not as bad as it looks," said Heimdall.

Mestoph shrugged and followed the bulky god as he stooped slightly to avoid hitting his head on the doorway and make his way up the stairs. No one else had to worry about hitting their heads; the tallest of them still had several feet of clearance. They walked up a couple turns and found a window that looked out over the narrow span of land they had just left; it already seemed to be hundreds of feet below them. A few turns later, there was another window that showed them to be about halfway up the cliff. Heimdall's cabin was surprisingly small next to the bridge.

After a few more turns, they exited the spiraling stairway and found themselves in a long curved hall that was open to the air. It ran the entire circumference of the tower they had seen at the top of the cliff. Everything was chiseled from out of the obsidian of the cliff and then polished smooth. A low railing and the occasional support column were the only things that separated the hall from a drop of thousands of feet. Leviticus leaned out over the railing to look down and saw a tiny dot and a tiny line that were the cabin and bridge.

Despite the fact that the cliff couldn't be seen from the human, or Midgard, side of Bifrost, he could see clear to the Icelandic coast. The mists rose high from the chasm that separated the two worlds but didn't come nearly as high up as the cliff did. On the other side he could see the concentric circles of swirling Nephilim and Seraphim, their numbers having grown to thousands of each creature. Stephanie saw the growing swarm and her hands went to the railing for support as she lost the little color she had regained.

"Don't worry. They can't cross with the bridge retracted, and we alone control the bridge," said Heimdall with a reassuring hand on her shoulder.

Whether it was the power of a god or security of such a strong hand, Stephanie visibly calmed down and took a deep breath. Heimdall paid no more attention to the swarm and continued to lead the group through the great hall. They made a complete circle, and then Heimdall opened the same door that they had just come out. Marcus was about to say something when he saw that there weren't any steps inside but a completely new room. The room wasn't very, large considering it was the home of a god, but it was so tall that they couldn't see the ceiling. There were four statues carved out of obsidian spaced evenly around the perimeter of the room; they stood thirty feet tall and looked down at the group as in the center of the room. Each showed Odin in one of his well-known forms.

There was Odin the Traveler, wearing a traveling cloak and a wide-brimmed hat, leaning on a spear as a walking stick. The statue had a patch over one eye. There were two large ravens, one on each of his shoulders, which looked at Odin with great intelligence in their carved eyes.

Another statue showed a muscular and angry looking Odin wearing simple leather armor and riding on the back of an eight-legged horse reared in mid-charge. Both the mane of the horse and Odin's hair were blown back as if frozen in action. Odin's one good eye was large and full of anger as he held a large spear ready to pierce an unseen enemy.

The largest of the statues depicted a nude Odin impaled by a spear stuck into an obsidian ash tree. The carved figure appeared to be pulling the spear deeper into himself, signifying that the sacrifice was self-inflicted. Each of the tree's myriad branches was full of intricately detailed ravens.

The final statue showed a robed Odin sitting in a simple wooden throne, leaning forward with his elbow on his knee in a traditional thinking pose. He looked down on a floor that was a miniature world of hundreds of trees, dozens of rivers, and several little towns. The model world spilled over from the pedestal of the statue and on the floor of the room itself. Stephanie walked over to the last statue and leaned in close; she could even see tiny people, carved in the minutest detail, doing chores around the villages.

In the center of the room was a circular slab of rippled obsidian. A dozen god-sized Vikings held four chains anchored to the slab; the chains ran up into the dizzying heights of the tower. Each link in the chain was as big as a watermelon and made of a dull iron several inches thick. Heimdall stepped onto the slab and motioned the others to hurry. Once everyone was aboard, the chains went taut as the clanking of a large mechanism rumbled and echoed in the tower. The obsidian slab lifted off the ground in a surprisingly smooth motion and rose swiftly up the tower. It took longer to reach the top of the tower by elevator than it had to walk the stairs up the cliff, but only marginally so. Just as smoothly as it had started, the ancient elevator stopped at the top of Odin's great hall.

The penthouse of Valaskjalf was not shaped like a hall at all, but like the top of an enormous, gloomy lighthouse made of obsidian. There were three hundred and sixty degrees of windows and a domed roof that had a large round window in the center of it. Shining directly through the center of the dome was the blackish light of the storm, the spinning pentagram clearly visible. The ring of floor that surrounded the elevator platform was covered in thick furs of a hundred different animals, most of which weren't native to Iceland. There were leopard, zebra, grizzly bear, polar bear, something that was remarkably similar to depictions of wooly mammoths, and a few that the companions couldn't identify.

At one end of the room was a wooden throne exactly like that of the statue in the tower below, and in it sat the very same figure in the flesh. On an obsidian pedestal next to his throne was a severed head that turned and whispered something to Odin. On a plush fur rug near the foot of Odin's throne was a beautiful, dark-haired woman with purple eyes and skin nearly as pale as Heimdall's. She wore a simple flowing robe-like dress of soft white fabric. She was petting one of two large wolves that lay curled around her. Standing behind her was a man in a thick, undyed wool sweater and cargo pants. He was facing away, looking out the window at something or nothing. He didn't turn to acknowledge their appearance. Tyr was pacing back and forth on the other side of the room; he too ignored the group beyond looking at them when they first arrived.

"All-Father," announced Heimdall with ritualistic stiffness, "I bring you visitors from the land of—"

"Now's not the time for theatrics, Heimdall," said Odin in a ragged but warm voice.

The disembodied head began to speak. "The two humans are Marcus and Stephanie. The Angel is Leviticus. The Demon is Mestopholes. And the dog is Prom—"

"Shut up, Mim. I know who they are," said Odin.

Marcus was staring at Mestoph. He hadn't missed the

221

fact that the floating head had called Mestoph a Demon. In fact, now that he heard it, he was fairly certain that Father Mike had been about to say the same thing before Stephanie shot him. He looked to Stephanie and she looked away. She had known too? How? Why would she keep that a secret? They had been following an angel and a demon? What did that mean? Did it mean anything? Of course it did, why else would everyone keep it a secret. Marcus's mind was about to enter a terminal spiral of conspiracy theories, doubts, and betrayals when Odin spoke again and got his attention.

"I find you all guilty and deny the request for asylum," said Odin with casual finality. Heimdall drew his sword and turned to the group. Their eyes went wide in unison as they suddenly understood what a guilty verdict actually meant. Heimdall looked reluctant, but his obedience to Odin was stronger than his own sense of morality and he stepped up to Marcus and raised the sword.

"No need for that Heimdall," said Odin.

Heimdall breathed a sigh of relief and then flashed a "just following orders" smile at Marcus and sheathed the sword.

"Considering the context of the charges, I fear a death sentence is rather pointless. Our end is upon us regardless," said Odin. "Instead, I sentence you all to watch what you have wrought. You will have a front row seat to Ragnarok."

The All Father made a gesture toward a clump of fluffy pelts near the dark-haired beauty, and a pile of plush pillows appeared, one for each of them.

"Sit," said Odin, as much an invitation as a demand.

"What charges do you find us guilty of? God or not, you have no right to sentence us to anything," said Stephanie, a swell of defiance and anger rising up in her. Marcus put a hand on her arm, but she shrugged it off.

"No, he owes us that much," she said.

"You bring about all our deaths, and you ask by what right I sentence you? Did you not bring the wolf Fenrir unerringly to the very precipice of Bifrost? Did not another of your party free the wolf from shackles put upon him at great price?" Odin gestured toward Tyr, who involuntarily rubbed at the capped end of his stump. "You started Ragnarok, something I have spent my entire life trying to forestall, and still you consider yourself innocent? I would kill you twice if I thought it would do any good. I give you asylum in all but name, for you are staying under my roof regardless, and now you show me nothing but indignity? Sit!"

Odin made an angry, sweeping gesture with his hand, and the group felt themselves being dragged against their will to the pillows and roughly tossed to the ground upon them. If they tried to stand they felt a force as if gravity had suddenly doubled and fell to the ground breathing heavily. After a few seconds, the feeling subsided and they were free to move around again. The purple-eyed girl smiled at them and gestured to the wolves.

"We all have our shackles," she said.

Odin stood and walked over to a brass tube that stuck out from the wall, flared at end like that of a trumpet. Odin used the tube to call Freyr and Thor, ordering them to join Heimdall and Tyr. Voices that sounded distant and tinny returned their acknowledgements. While waiting for the others, the Norse gods argued loudly amongst themselves, occasionally consulting with the disembodied head, Mim. First they argued about whether or not to send emissaries to the other pantheons. Odin quickly shot the idea down, but Tyr and Thor both put up a second attempt that the All Father completely ignored. The idea of negotiating with Loki and Fenrir to stall their predestined assault on Asgard was entertained briefly, but again Odin shot it down definitively and the subject was tabled.

They had just begun to discuss their battle plan when a raven flew in through an open window, landed on Odin's shoulder, and spoke into his ear. Moments later a second raven flew through the same window and landed on the other shoulder, likewise speaking directly to Odin. There was absolute silence in the open room, and then Odin sighed. It heavy with the weight of responsibility only a god could know.

"Call forth the Valkyrie," he said. "Loki is free and he marches at the front of an army of Jötunn, joined by St. Peter and Hades," said Odin, looking at Leviticus and Mestoph's group and then at the purple-eyed girl. At the mention of her husband's name, she turned to the man with the wool sweater and gasped.

"Persephone, I presume," said Mestoph.

Fenrir tapped the sword pendant that had once hung from the necklace that had held him prisoner for over a millennium. It turned into a full-sized sword, and he swung it at the entrails wrapped around Loki. The god rose up and pulled the remaining restraints from him as if they were paper streamers. He stretched, stood, and stretched again, causing joints to crack and pop from head to toe. He was not a hulking, muscular figure like some of the other Norse gods, but he had a wiry strength about him that was remarkably similar to Fenrir's build. He stood naked for a moment, enjoying the freedom he had gone so long without.

Despite their attempts at propriety, neither Hades nor St. Peter could help but notice that the trickster god was hung like a porn star. Loki noticed their discomfort and awe, and he smiled as he snapped his fingers and was instantly clothed in a long tunic cinched by a sword belt. Loki put his hand out expectantly toward Fenrir, who handed the sword over. Loki sheathed it and told Fenrir to gather his brother and sister. The wolfish man turned and ran off down the chasm. As he was running, he jumped into the air and swiftly and smoothly transformed into a lean and somewhat mangy wolf with mottled fur of black and charcoal. Fenrir the wolf was at least five feet tall at the shoulders and bounded off at incredible speed.

"Are either of you fireproof?" asked Loki, turning to Hades and St. Peter.

St. Peter shook his head no while Hades nodded yes, though both were hesitant to answer. Loki snapped his fingers, and both St. Peter and Hades were limned in a subtle sparkling blue light. Hades looked down at himself and then to Loki, questioningly.

"Just in case," said Loki.

"Just in case what?" asked Hades.

"Just in case..." said Loki, smiling as he snapped his fingers. All three of them were instantly transported to a realm engulfed in flame, "...you're wrong."

They stood on a pathway of glowing coals that wound its way between blackened trees of flame. Columns of swirling fire shot up from the pathway randomly, sending gusts of hot air swirling around them. Despite Loki's magical protection, it was still uncomfortably warm and the air was stiflingly thick. There was a general burnt smell in the air. It wasn't sulfur, or woodsmoke, or even barbecue, but occasionally faint whiffs of each and then some would distinguish itself to the nose. Loki led the way, taking turns at branches and intersections with the confidence of someone who had traversed the confusing tangle of paths often.

At one intersection they passed through what looked like

an old Norse village that could have been anywhere in Iceland over a thousand years ago were it not for the fact that it was built on a scale about ten times too big, and everything was on fire. Blackened, looming figures that were vaguely human, with skin like charred tree bark, milled about the village. One of the smaller creatures, still ten feet taller than St. Peter, pointed at the group of interlopers and giggled. It said something to a full-sized burnt tree man in a syrupy thick language that seemed to lack vowels or commas. The taller creature smacked the smaller one. It had the uncanny likeness to a human mother scolding a child for making fun of a handicapped person.

"Where the Hell are we?" asked St. Peter.

"Not Hell, nor Hel. This is Muspell. Flameland. Though it lacks a lot of the niceties of your typical amusement park," said Loki in a singsong manner as he made a dramatic pirouette and gestured to the flames around him.

They passed through another giant's village and then came to the edge of a plateau that overlooked a sea of lava. Growing from the plateau was a large gnarled tree whose trunk split in two and then coiled around itself like a snake in an orgy. Wrapped in the tree coils was an enormous Viking longboat that appeared to be made out of some kind of thin shell that, upon closer inspection, turned out to be fingernails and toenails. The longboat was held at an angle so that the mast leaned back and toward them as they approached.

Although both the tree and the boat were on fire, its sail was still intact and was currently being used as a hammock for one of the burnt creatures. It had a large flowing beard of matted and melted stuff that looked more like steel wool than hair. The fire giant was snoring loudly. The sound was deep enough that St. Peter could feel it in his chest, and his ears seemed to vibrate from within. Loki turned to Hades and St. Peter with a mischievous look on his face and put his finger to his lips. He snuck up to the boat, cupped his hands, and let out a shout that was impossibly loud for a man his size. Startled, the creature jerked upright and yelled in surprise, shooting a stream of flames from his mouth.

The shout turned into a stream of what sounded like the same thick-tongued language that St. Peter had heard back in the village. The creature, now on his feet and standing ten times the height of any of them, looked down and saw two tiny humans.

"Who dares," began the creature in a voice that sounded drunk or dumb. Loki charged from behind and somehow, despite his considerably smaller size and strength, caused the creature to tumble. Its hand, nearly as long as St. Peter was tall, missed him and Hades by a foot. The Jötunn rolled over and crushed Loki underneath him, nearly crushing Hades and St. Peter again in the process. The Jötunn was silent for a moment and then bellowed in laughter. Then he shrieked suddenly and jumped to his feet. In a small depression was Loki, his sword poking straight up. The Jötunn raised its foot to squish what had poked him, but stopped when it saw who was lying on the ground.

"Loki," it said thickly. "I should've known."

Loki jumped to his feet and bowed deeply, swinging the sword with a flourish.

"Surtr, it's been too long," he said.

"No, it hasn't," said Surtr sourly.

"Whatever. I come with great news and great offerings. Ragnarok is upon us, and these men are going to get your boat free so we can sail to the shores of Asgard and fuck some shit up," said Loki, saying the last part with vulgar gusto while miming having sex with…something.

"We're going to what?" asked St. Peter.

"If you want help, you've got to help in return. Despite what you may think, you can't possibly get us into Asgard.

Only I can do that. But you *can* get this ship unstuck. Surtr can't do it without destroying it, and I'm not allowed to help," said Loki.

"Why not?" asked Hades.

Loki put a hand on one hip and looked at them both like they were stupid children. "Because it wasn't *prophesized*. In case you haven't noticed, we've got prophecies out the ass. If it weren't for the fact that there's not a prophecy specifically *against* me taking a piss, I probably wouldn't be allowed to."

St. Peter looked to Hades. He had no idea how they were supposed to get an ancient burning boat out of a gnarled, ancient burning tree. Both of which were ten times the normal size. He told Hades he had no powers that would help since most of them didn't work outside of Heaven. Hades didn't seem terribly worried and waved off his concern. Hades studied at the boat for several minutes while Loki and Surtr looked at him expectantly. If Hades felt any pressure, he didn't show it. At last, he lifted a hand and pointed at the ship, which was now surrounded by a protective bubble much like the one he had been resting in when St. Peter found him. Hades lifted his other hand, made it like a gun and shot the tree with his fingers. Blue bolts of energy snapped the coiled tree limbs off just outside the bubble. The limbs toppled over and slid down the outside of the bubble, leaving the ship unscathed. Once the pruning was done, he lifted his hand and the ship rose. He manipulated it around the remaining limbs, slowly turning and lifting it until the ship floated high above the tree.

"Where do you want it?" asked Hades.

A few minutes later, they were standing on the deck of the charred longship made of toe and fingernails as it slowly bobbed up and down in the sea of lava. Like most things in Norse mythology the boat had a name. It was Naglfar, which literally meant "nail ship." Although the ship was nearly as long as a football field, it was uncomfortably close quarters at the moment because it was currently full of about forty Jötnar.

Though there were a dozen ships in the fleet, Naglfar was by far the largest. The others were full of ragged, pale grey humans who looked like they would have committed suicide if they weren't already dead. They were led by Fenrir's sister, Hel, who reigned over the land of the same name. She was only slightly taller than St. Peter, but she was as thin as a person could be and still be recognizably human. Her face was sunken to the point that her eyeballs were held in by skin alone; all muscle had left her body long ago. Her lips and gums were both pulled back so tightly she had a permanent fake smile recognizable in any family photo. Her skin was a mottled patchwork of grey and black that looked like randomly shaped puzzle pieces, and her hair was a brittle and pale grey-green. She wore a tattered robe that was wet and grey that revealed ribs as pronounced as if they were grooves chiseled into her chest.

Swimming playfully in the lava around the ships was Fenrir's brother Jormungand, an enormous serpent. The snake was so large that it could coil around the entire fleet several times. Its scales were the size of surfboards and looked to be made of rusty iron with odd patches of algae. Fenrir stood on his hind legs in half wolf, half human shape at the helm of Naglfar with St. Peter, Hades, and his father Loki. The trickster god stood atop the carved dragon that served as a figurehead, which blew real flames in great gouts in front of them. He had called them all to attention using the same booming voice that he had used to startle Surtr.

"My children, my allies, and my, er, friends. We arrive at the hour of the crowing cocks." To emphasize the point, there were three giant roosters, easily twenty feet tall, standing at the edge of the plateau overlooking the sea. There commenced a racket that could be construed as crowing if one had never heard an actual rooster before. "Ragnarok is upon us and it is our duty to shatter the skies, devour the sun and the moon, and generally *fuck some shit up*," Loki repeated with the same vulgar voice and pantomime he had used earlier, this time to the raucous roars of his friends' approving cheers.

They launched with full sails of fiery wind and the assistance of the Jötnar rowing the giant vessel, with the ships of Hel following suit. Loki snapped his fingers and a bolt of lightning shot from the sky. When the flash had dissipated, there was a black rip in the sky that started at the horizon and went up high into an orange and purple sunset—only there was no sun. He made a grand gesture like sweeping curtains aside, and the rip parted likewise, revealing a gloomy world on the other side. The waters of a wide river rushed in through the rip and into the lava, creating dense steam where the two met. As they sailed toward the portal into Asgard, they passed a single jutting island of rock that was about as big around as a hula-hoop and perfectly flat. Sitting on the rock was a pasty white man playing a lute. Loki waved reverentially as they sailed by. St. Peter looked at Hades and then shook his head. He wasn't sure how much more of this ridiculously random religion he could take

Chapter 18

Battle Royale

Leviticus and Mestoph were in another one of their hypnomancy meetings, only this time they had included everyone else in their little group.

"Yes, I'm a Demon," said Mestoph. "I do bad things for a living. Lying is one of them."

They had gone around in circles for the last ten minutes over what was a very minor detail when it came down to it. No one had any objection to his actions thus far, although only Leviticus knew all of them, but they now questioned his motivations. "They" meaning mostly Marcus. Mestoph now realized that Stephanie had been right to withhold that bit of information. He couldn't help it that he was the spawn of the greatest demon in Hell short of Satan—a detail he was most definitely not sharing with this group. He did the job he was born into, as much because of expectations as the fact that there wasn't an alternative. The only reason his father Mephisto had been allowed to retire was because of his eons of top-notch work and the fact that he had a successor in Mestoph. It didn't matter if the successor was more interested in sipping Mai Tais at a tropical resort.

"What the Hell do Mai Tais have to do with it?" asked Marcus.

Mestoph looked up, startled. He had been lost in thought and didn't realize he had been talking out loud. He really hoped his propensity for fruity cocktails was the only thing he had let slip. He began mumbling something about life being like a Mai Tai, trying to cover his slip, when Stephanie spoke up.

"What does it matter which side of the tracks he comes

from? I'm a barista and you're a computer nerd; what gives us the right to judge him? Maybe being a demon is what allows him to make the hard decisions. He did what had to be done."

Marcus opened his mouth to make a counterpoint, but none came to mind. That was about the time the guilt finally hit Mestoph. The demon looked at Leviticus, but the Angel was staring at the ground. He had been noticeably silent, and Mestoph thought he understood why. Leviticus was still an Angel, and everything they had done was against his nature. Even if it was a nature he tried desperately to shrug off. Leviticus hadn't said anything about it, but this had to have been eating at him from the beginning, the whole using humans for their own gain.

Guilt was a new feeling for Mestoph, and it hit him hard. It was with equal surprise and confusion when he realized he was crying. He wasn't even sure what it was at first; after all, *real* demons don't feel guilt and they certainly didn't cry. He marveled for a moment at the emotions that washed over him. He observed it like a rare animal in captivity; the way the tears formed at the corner of his eyes, and then when they were heavy and full, the tears hurtled down his face and dripped off the edge of his chin into a blooming splotch on his shirt.

"We used you," Mestoph sobbed.

This was met with silence, except for the rushing off blood in Mestoph's head. Leviticus stared wide eyed at him while the humans looked confused. Stephanie looked like she was about to speak, but Marcus held up his hand to keep her silent. He didn't want the moment to fade; he felt he was about to be vindicated in his anti-Demon argument.

"There was never a conspiracy to kill you. We used you to get something we wanted, and things just went horribly, horribly wrong," said Mestoph.

232

Marcus and Stephanie looked at Mestoph and then Leviticus. Leviticus didn't say anything, but he couldn't look either of them in the eye and had a guilty grimace on his face. It was as damning as a confession. Finally, Leviticus sighed and spoke up.

"Mestoph, I think it's time we got some help. It's gone too far now, it's time to end it," he said. "Teleport out of here and summon the cavalry."

Mestoph flashed a car salesmen smile, but it faded to the look of a kid who had been caught with his finger in the cake. "Uh, yeah. I've been meaning to say something about that."

"You can't teleport," said Leviticus. "I should have known it all along."

"Not since Truth or Consequences. I'm pretty sure I winged St. Peter during that shootout at Hitler's."

"Well, now I think we're seriously fucked," said Sir Regi.

The pounding silence returned. Then, like a cat, Stephanie cleared the distance between her and Mestoph and pounced, knocking him backwards. Mestoph lay on his back with Stephanie on his chest, pinning him in a low wrestling mount and pummeling him with her balled-up fists. Mestoph tried to block the blows to his face but didn't put up any more of a defense than that. Leviticus was closest and quickest to react; he ran up behind her to try and pull her off. Without hesitating she punched Leviticus square in the balls.

For those who have never been kicked in the balls, whether you've lived a remarkably sheltered life of non-violence up in Heaven or you lack the appropriate equipment, it's an excruciating and debilitating thing. It doesn't matter if you're a pacifist wimp or a badass mixed martial artists; a swift hit to the cojones will wipe you out. The first time is always the worst, because nothing in life prior to that moment has prepared you for such an intense and sickening pain. It is probably the closest a man can ever come to knowing the pain of child birth. For an Angel who had gone over a thousand years without a cup check or a bean bag to the coin purse, it was a horrific wake up call.

With both Mestoph and Leviticus's concentration broken, everyone was ejected from the hypnomancy bubble. They were returned to a world where they were plastered to the floor by Odin's powers, which made the events inside the bubble manifest oddly in reality. Marcus sat staring, as dumbfounded now as he had been in the bubble. Mestoph was on the floor with blood running from his nose. Leviticus was rolling on his side, gagging and guarding his crotch as he moaned incoherently. Stephanie was still enraged, trying her best to fight Odin's bonds and get to Mestoph again.

"We're going to fucking die, you asshole!" she screamed.

By this point Odin had been joined in the war council by two more gods, Freyr and Thor, as well as three buxom and brawny Valkyries with large pairs of white wings folded behind. All of them turned at the sudden outburst from the group, which had been remarkably quiet until then. The two ravens on Odin's shoulders cawed and scattered to the ledge of the window in the dome. Brynhildr the Valkyrie smiled approvingly at the girl's fire.

"Put some meat on that one and she'd make a fine warrior, don't you think, Kara?" she said to the Valkyrie next to her. Kara just raised her brows in response, clearly not as impressed as Brynhildr. The third Valkyrie, Mist, looked at Stephanie with more than just admiration of her battle prowess.

Odin looked down at the group with the face of a disappointed father, his hair fluttering from an unseen wind that didn't seem to affect anyone else. Mestoph wondered if the god was vain enough that he conjured wind to constantly tousle his hair. He smiled at the thought until Odin forcefully gestured at them, sending them all tumbling and rolling around on the ground toward the wall of windows. Odin clenched the hand into a fist and everyone stuck fast to the ground again, their backs to the windows. He then stuck out his index finger and swiped it once from left to right. Their mouths closed, and they found themselves unable to speak.

"Silence," he commanded.

Odin then sat down and began speaking again to Thor as if nothing had happened. Thor had the look of someone listening intently, though he kept spinning a large, awkward looking hammer in his hand. The legendary Mjolnir, looked like someone had stuck a large, intricately detailed curved anvil on the end of an equally ornate slab of metal for a handle. The base of the handle flared out into another smaller anvil, also curved, giving it an overall circular shape. Whoever had made it seemed to have decided to call it a hammer since it didn't look like anything else. In reality it shared as much in common with a Frisbee as it did a hammer. The shape did look like it would be a great thrown weapon for someone who had the strength to toss it further than his feet— someone like Thor.

Thor stood tall along with the rest of the gods and was rippling with muscles, though his arms seemed far more defined than the rest of his body. He stood bare-chested, wearing only a long loincloth that looked like a kilt without the tartan pattern. He looked like he had oiled himself up just prior to walking in the room. He also kept tossing his long, free flowing red hair behind his shoulders as he talked. It looked like something straight out of a shampoo commercial. Kara gave Thor the "tall, cool drink of water," top-to-bottom look.

Standing in stark contrast next to Thor was Freyr, who was easily the shortest and leanest of the gods present, easily outweighed by Brynhildr and possibly even Kara. Freyr wasn't a weakling by any means; he just didn't seem to spend as much time at the gym as the other gods. His hair was shorter, coming just below his ears, but it was bushier and less carefully coiffed than any of the others. Freyr was also the only god present who wasn't armed with anything; not a fancy, legendary weapon nor even an old butter knife.

The gods and Valkyries resumed their discussion in earnest. Persephone and the shepherd whispered quietly but emphatically to each other, while Stephanie burned Mestoph and Leviticus with hateful looks. The moments dragged by slowly as they all waited for something to happen.

When it finally did, things happened too fast for anyone to take it all in. The only warning, a second before chaos ensued, was when Mim, the head that had been hovering there quietly on the pedestal next to Odin, spoke.

"The sun and moon have been swallowed," Mim announced.

The elevator platform burst into the air and shot through the window of the dome. It flew into the distance, never to be seen again. Rising through the hole left in its absence was an enormous snake. It burst into the room, ramming head first into Thor and then out the nearest window of the tower, taking the thunder god with it. Loki and Fenrir, riding the giant snake, jumped off Jormundgar's back just in time to avoid sharing Thor's fate. Although he arrived in human form, Fenrir immediately transformed into a large wolf and lunged at Odin. The All-Father jumped up from his throne and over the charging wolf, conjuring a spear in midair and cutting a twist flip to land on his feet.

"Do as you must. Fulfill your prophecies," he commanded the other gods, and then he turned back to face the wolf.

Tyr conjured a new spear and then he and Freyr, who was still unarmed, ran at the windows behind them and jumped through the glass, diving down like they were about to land in a pool. The three Valkyries jumped after them, spreading their wings like diving falcons. Brynhildr and Mist caught the two gods while the Kara swooped to the ground where there was a waiting host of hundreds of Valkyrie and thousands of human warriors. Her curly read hair streamed behind her wildly, and she wore the face of an enraged animal.

Mestoph and the others had no choice but to sit quietly and watch everything that was going on, but Persephone screamed. Even the comforting embrace of her beloved shepherd couldn't seem to calm her. Odin and Heimdall fought bitterly, but they were remarkably evenly matched. Despite outweighing the All-Father and having four sets of claws and ferocious jaws, Fenrir found himself in a stalemate against Odin's spear. Fenrir would slash at Odin with a claw and Odin would jump back, over or even roll under the swiping paw. When Fenrir would snap at Odin, he would find himself blocked or smacked by Odin's spear.

Heimdall and Loki were in the middle of an old-fashioned sword fight that had them dancing around the gaping hole the missing elevator had left behind. They both wielded beautiful, though mythologically insignificant, swords that looked similar to Roman spathae. Heimdall fought one-handed without a shield, while Loki used a small, round, wooden shield a little less than three feet across, painted black with a gold rune that looked like a pointy letter B. It already had several slashes and a few chunks missing from the edges. Loki managed to turn a blow wildly to the side with the shield and spun in around to land a slice on Heimdall's right side. It cut through Heimdall's leather overcoat and tunic to reveal a chainmail shirt that went down to mid-thigh. Several rings split and bounced onto the hard floor.

Mestoph wondered if Ragnarok took years because the fights never ended. As soon as he had settled in to what was likely to be a long wait, it became apparent that something was happening outside the tower that was more than just the warriors of Valhalla fighting the warriors of Hel. At first the vibrations were subtle, but with repetition they became closer and more jarring. Just when it seemed the pounding would topple the tower, a figure climbed up the chain that had previously held the elevator platform aloft. It appeared to be another god, though not one they had seen before. The god kicked out his legs to make the chain swing closer to the lip of the hole, which is when everyone noticed that one of the god's legs was encased in an iron platform shoe, as if it was shorter than the other leg.

The god swung over far enough and let go of the chain, jumping onto the floor with a loud clank from his iron shoe. Mestoph and Leviticus braced themselves, but nothing happened. The god looked down at the group of humans with a confused and amused look. Then there was a shaking so violent that the remaining unbroken windows instantly shattered. The short-legged god put his arms out to keep his balance, the metal shoe clanking as he stumbled. There was another earthquake, and then a giant flaming head that looked like it was made of charred wood appeared outside the window behind Metal Shoe.

"Jötunn!" shouted Metal Shoe.

"Titan!" shouted Persephone.

"Fuck!" shouted the shepherd.

Loki smiled at the sight of Surtr and then laughed maniacally behind his shield as Odin let out a string of angry-sounding Norse that was likely some kind of vile curse. Heimdall made a grunting noise but never let up on his assault against Loki, who still laughed even as his shield took a beating. None of the fighting gods stopped to do more than acknowledge the giant staring in the window, seeming to know better than Mestoph and the others what his role in

Ragnarok would be. Heimdall and Loki did spin out of the way when the Jötunn smashed his hand through a couple of support columns, which made the part of the dome they supported sag and begin to crumble away. The Jötunn shoved his hand into the center of the room, nearly knocking Metal Shoe over, and opened his hand palm up. Standing in Surtr's burning palm was Hades, nestled away inside his protective bubble and still glimmering with the blue sparks Loki had imbued him with. Hades and his bubble floated up a few feet, and then the Jötunn pulled his hand back out of the throne room, taking another column with it and causing a quarter of the dome to collapse. Most of the debris tumbled down the outside of the tower or into the long elevator shaft. With his package delivered, Surtr appeared to let go of the tower. Seconds later there was a short but violent earthquake.

Hades floated in his bubble above the emptiness of the shaft in the center of the room and smiled as he looked around the top of the tower. He spotted Persephone, who had gone silent with a look of absolute terror on her face. His smile took a sinister turn when he locked eyes with his wife, and then he floated over toward her, the gods still fighting in the background and paying him no attention. He floated the bubble to just a few feet away from Persephone and stopped, looking down at her smugly. The two wolves that guarded her rose to their feet and began to growl.

"You know, I have a three-headed dog named Cerberus that would love to play with you two," Hades said to the wolves.

The wolves backed down and left Persephone with only the shepherd to protect her. He jumped in front of her and looked up at Hades defiantly.

"Ah, and you must be my darling wife's lover. I'll take you both and sort this out later," said Hades.

Hades waved his hands like a magician showing his

239

audience there were no strings making an item levitate, and a bubble formed around both Persephone and the shepherd. Hades turned and his bubble began floating out of the gaping hole that Surtr had left behind, the smaller bubble containing Persephone and the shepherd following like an obedient dog. Persephone looked back to Mestoph and his group with a pleading look, but they were unable to help. Metal Shoe watched with the kind of interest someone has when visiting the zoo and then shrugged. He looked at the others to see if they were going to do any tricks, but when they didn't even move, he turned his attention to the battles that had continued uninterrupted.

Odin took a forceful slash from Fenrir's claws and staggered back. His robes were in ribbons, and the blue fabric was stained red. Odin caught himself with the spear, but he was severely off balance and realized immediately his mistake. Metal Shoe also realized what was about to happen and took off running toward Odin.

"Father!"

Odin turned to Metal Shoe and smiled. "Avenge me, Vidar," he said as Fenrir lunged, his monstrous mouth open wide, baring all his teeth. Fenrir turned his head sideways and snapped his jaws down on Odin's midsection, cracking the spear he held himself up with. His teeth sank deep into Odin's chest, and blood spurted from a dozen wounds. The wolf tossed Odin into the air, opened his mouth wide, and swallowed Odin whole.

As simple as that, Odin was gone. Vidar stopped in his tracks, his metal shoe sliding noisily before coming to a halt. Fenrir let loose a howl so loud that Heimdall stopped with his sword raised high above his head. Both he and Loki momentarily forgot their fight and looked to find the source of the noise. Loki realized that Odin's absence meant the wolf had finally won his battle, and he began laughing hysterically, jumping up and down in excitement. Heimdall turned to Loki and grunted as he dropped his sword and charged like a linebacker at Loki's raised shield. The impact took Loki by surprise, and he stumbled backward. The two of them went over the edge of the tower and disappeared.

The howling shook Vidar from his shock, and he took off running toward the baying wolf. He grabbed the wolf by his substantial head and jerked it down, slamming it into the floor. Fenrir was dazed and his mouth hung open, tongue lolling out to the side. Vidar looked down at the wolf's open mouth and then at his giant metal shoe with an expression on his face like he had just realized why he'd been put on this world. A giant smile overtook Vidar's face and the god stomped the metal foot down on the inside of Fenrir's lower jaw, smashing the teeth. He then grabbed the wolf's upper jaw and pulled. His muscles strained, as he began to shake with the effort, but at last there was a popping noise like a cork from a champagne bottle and Fenrir's head split in two. There was an ear-piercing boom and brilliant flash as a bolt of lightning struck the top of the tower, sending a spider web of cracks running along the obsidian dome and causing new chunks to fall off from the damaged portion where Surtr had punched through.

"Sweet baby Jesus!" shouted Marcus, as he reared back.

Marcus then looked astonished at his sudden ability to speak again. Leviticus tried to stand up and found he was no longer restrained. With Odin's death, his bonds had broken and now they were all free. Mestoph got to his feet and helped Marcus and Stephanie rise as well. In the rush of events, they had temporarily forgotten their anger and didn't protest. He then walked to the edge of the tower and looked out over the battle below. What he saw was a full-out war. Despite the great height, everything was clearly visible as if they were only a few hundred feet above the plain below.

There were still dozens of Jötnar towering over human warriors intermixed with Valkyries, who would slay an opponent on the ground and then launch in a small group to attack a Jötunn. The gloomy warriors of Hel stayed close to the Jötnar, some a bit too close as they were squished by a giant. Hel's fighters were the old, infirm, or the warriors not deemed glorious enough to enter Valhalla, so they were mostly just fodder anyways.

Spread across the battlefield were also a few pairs of gods fighting each other. Heimdall and Loki had resumed their fight after their fall from the tower, trading blows back and forth in a match that was still brutally even. Meanwhile Freyr, still unarmed, was grappling with Surtr, who couldn't get a good swing at the agile god as he darted in and around the giant's legs. Freyr tackled one of Surtr's legs and with immense strength he managed to pull it out from under him, toppling the fiery Jötunn and taking out dozens of combatants on both sides of the fight in the crash. Thor was locked in a coil of the giant snake's body and bashing at the sinuous creature with his hammer, sending sparks flying from the metallic scales.

Lightning struck the tower again and the floor cracked. Lightning began striking the battlefield, taking out people and creatures indiscriminately. Then lightning struck Heimdall's cabin, sending giant splinters of wood shooting in all directions like arrows and impaling anyone unfortunate enough to be in the way. There was a loud clanking noise as Bifrost began to extend out across the chasm; the controls of the bridge had been in Heimdall's cabin, and having been destroyed, the large counterweights in freefall were extending the bridge. The swarm of Nephilim and Seraphim squawked in frenzied excitement as they saw their chance to enter Asgard.

"We better get out of here," said Mestoph

There was another bolt of lightning that struck the base of the tower, and the entire thing began to sway. Large chunks of debris fell, and the window in the center of the dome shattered. What was left of the dome began to slide to one side. Support columns cracked, and two of them crumpled completely as they took on a disproportionate amount of the dome's weight.

"We better get out of here *now*," said Sir Regi.

The dog walked up to the edge of the tower and looked down. About two hundred feet below them, the bubbles containing Hades and his captives were still slowly descending. The dog reared back, moved forward a few times while growling softly, and then with a yippy bark he stepped off the precipice and soared down. Marcus yelled, trying to stop the dog at the last moment, but it was too late. He ran over to the spot where Sir Regi had been moments before and looked down just as the dog landed on top of the bubble that Hades was riding. The surface wobbled a bit and then the dog sank into the bubble. Hades looked down at him and then up where he had come from, clearly confused.

"Never wanted to live forever anyways," said Mestoph, and he dropped down as well.

"Got any better ideas?" Marcus asked Leviticus.

"Oh Hell, why not?" said Leviticus as he and the other two dropped off as well. Mestoph had already sagged into the bubble when Leviticus landed on top. Marcus's aim was a little off, and he landed on the bubble with Persephone and the shepherd. Stephanie landed on the larger bubble, but it had already started to sag from Leviticus's weight. She hit at an odd angle and bounced off like it was a trampoline. Marcus reached out for her, even though he wasn't anywhere near enough to grab her, and watched as she plummeted down.

"Hades!" said Persephone, as much a command as an

accusation.

The bald god took a deep breath and sighed. He tapped his index finger in the air like he was pressing an invisible button. A bubble formed around the falling Stephanie, and she bounced around inside it several times like a rubber ball. It shot up and joined with Persephone's bubble, and then they continued their slow descent.

"You best remember this, woman," said Hades to Persephone.

"You're abducting me *again* and almost letting an innocent girl die? You bet I'll remember this," said Persephone.

Hades pinched the bridge of his nose and he closed his eyes for a moment. He bowed his head and then looked over to Mestoph and Leviticus.

"Married?" asked Hades.

The two shook their heads.

"Good, don't," said Hades.

The ride down was slow and filled with bickering between Persephone and Hades. The shepherd had yet to say a word, while the others stood there in that awkward silence that was inevitable when confined in the midst of someone else's argument. They did have a remarkable view of the battle below. Bifrost had just reached the other side of the chasm when a blur of black and white wings soared across. They swooped down into the fray. The white Seraphim began attacking the Jötnar. The giants shot sprays of fire at them, sending singed creatures crashing to the ground. Their vast numbers made the casualties nearly inconsequential, and soon Jötnar began falling. Meanwhile the black Nephilim went straight for the Valkyries. Both the Seraphim and Nephilim kept a noticeable distance from the gods and humans. The Vallhallan warriors quickly grouped together and began mowing down Hel's ragged fighters with ease.

Freyr was again darting between Surtr's legs when his luck finally ran out. Surtr swept the leg Freyr was trying to tackle out of the way, which left Freyr exposed. Surtr grabbed Freyr in his massive hand, lifted him up to eye level, and began laughing a slow, menacing laugh. Surtr then slammed Freyr down on the ground with so much force the concussion could be felt all the way up in their bubbles. Then Surtr drew the sword that Loki had given him, which grew to match his giant proportions, and drove the point through Freyr and into the ground below him.

Heimdall and Loki were both beginning to tire visibly. Heimdall's blows weren't as strong or as frequent, and he had either lost or shed his chainmail shirt, while Loki's blocks and counterattacks were becoming clumsier and slower. Heimdall made another overhead slice and Loki's shield finally split in half, straight through the iron cap in the center. Loki's playful demeanor suddenly turned serious, and he looked around him for something to take cover behind. Heimdall seemed to find renewed strength. Loki blocked the swings, but each one jarred him and drove him backwards. Concern and then fear spread across the trickster god's face. Heimdall reared back with all his might, and Loki raised his sword with both hands, the blade slicing into his left hand as he gripped it, but then his sword, too, broke in half.

Loki dropped to his knees. He looked at the half-sword in his right hand and then up at Heimdall, standing tall over him with an impassive expression on his face. This wasn't a victory to gloat over; it was the end of a great adversary and one of the final dominoes in the toppling succession that was Ragnarok. Heimdall thrust his sword into Loki's chest, directly into his heart and through his back, in an emotionless maneuver that he performed out of duty. Heimdall then put his foot on Loki's chest and pushed him off the sword. The god's body flopped back, a spray of blood from the wound shooting up several feet in the air. Heimdall dropped his sword and panted.

Loki raised a hand and motioned to Heimdall. He stepped forward and knelt beside the fallen god. Loki's lips were moving, but from their bubbles they couldn't hear the words. Loki beckoned Heimdall closer, and the white god leaned in. The trickster grabbed the broken sword and jammed it several times into Heimdall's side. Heimdall fell flat onto Loki's chest. With the last of his strength, Loki rolled them both over and thrust the broken blade into Heimdall's heart. He fell to one side, and neither of the gods moved again.

Chapter 19

Deus Ex Machina

The bubbles finally landed and then popped, leaving Mestoph and Leviticus's ragged group with Hades and his new entourage standing on the narrow strip of once lush, now downtrodden grass that served as the battleground for Ragnarok. The bodies of gods, ghoulish men and women, brawny Valkyries, giants, and winged creatures were strewn all across the field of battle. The fight was still raging on, but the numbers had dwindled significantly on all sides. There were only a handful of the towering Jötnar left, directed by their leader, Surtr now that he was free of the pesky Freyr. The giant's sword burst into flames, and he began swinging it at Seraphim left and right as he drove his Jötnar toward the Valkyrie front, which was engaged with the Nephilim. The burning of feathers and the sizzling of their thick blood could be heard even from a distance.

Breaking up the fights, and at times encircling the entire battleground, were the serpent Jormungand and Thor. The hammer wielder had loosened himself from the snake's constricting coils and was now throwing his hammer at it from a distance, trying to keep from getting entangled again. The snake would strike, and Thor would bat his head aside like a baseball. Enraged, the snake would chase Thor through the battlefield, taking out or tangling up anything in its way. This routine seemed to repeat endlessly.

Hades turned and looked at the group that stood before him. He studied at each of them and then addressed Mestoph.

"The free ride stops here. You and your friends are on

your own. If we run into each other again, I won't spare any of you," said Hades.

Hades shot a finger out toward Persephone and the shepherd, and a leash of blue energy shot out of it and lassoed the two lovers. He walked off in the direction of Bifrost, towing his captives behind him like reluctant children. Persephone turned and waved goodbye with a surprisingly chipper look on her face. The shepherd didn't look back and didn't say a word. Then the trio disappeared with the familiar pop of teleportation.

"We came all this way to find Persephone, and there she goes. Now what?" asked Marcus.

"Yeah, now what? What's your great plan now?" Stephanie asked Mestoph. She had obviously had time—and yet another brush with death—to remind her that she was pissed at him and Leviticus.

"Listen, we're both really sorry about things, and if we could change it now we would. But right now all we can do is try to get you two out of here. Feel free to hate us to your heart's content afterwards," said Leviticus.

"Just get us out of here, guys," said Marcus with a sort of pleading neutrality in his voice.

"The bridge! Heimdall said it was the only way across. All we have to do is get to it and we're out of here," said Sir Regi.

It was a simple task in theory, but between them and the bridge were a war and a giant snake destroying anything that had the misfortune of getting in its way. There was nothing to do but start walking and try to avoid combat. Just in case, Mestoph picked up a sword and a helmet from one of the fallen Valhallans; the others followed suite and began picking up odds and ends from fallen combatants on either side of the battle.

"Let's stay together. And watch out for that damn

snake," said Mestoph as he took off running toward Bifrost, pointing his sword out in front of him like a rallying saber.

There were large gaps in between clumps of fighting creatures, which initially made it easy to weave through the battlefield. The path became a maze of shifting masses as reinforcements from one side or another would swell the numbers and close off a path, forcing them to backtrack. A few times the swells of warriors almost surrounded them completely, nearly pulling them directly into combat, but they were able to get between or around the groups and out of harm's way. For the most part both sides seemed to ignore them. However, there were a few overzealous or enterprising barbarians who tried to add a quick notch to their belt by taking swipes at random members of the group. Luck—and the fact that both Mestoph and Leviticus were far more comfortable with swords than they had been with guns kept them alive. Mestoph took a glancing cut to his right shoulder, but otherwise they passed unharmed.

Their luck ran out when they found themselves sandwiched between the converging Valkyrie and Jötnar. Then some of the previously preoccupied Nephilim and Seraphim caught the scent of their initial game: Stephanie. One after another of the winged beasts broke away from their respective fights to dive at her. Mestoph, Leviticus, and the others formed a small circle with their backs toward each other as they tried to fend off the flying creatures. A few of them dove low enough that Sir Regi, who was protectively standing in front of Marcus and Stephanie, was able to bound up into the air and try to catch them like Frisbees, even managing to connect with a few of them, to their surprise. The little dog pulled them down to the ground and tore at them as viciously as he had Father Mike.

The Jötnar now had them completely blocked from the bridge and their only chance of escape. The only thing that kept the Valkyries and Jötnar from engulfing them were the Seraphim and Nephilim, which were now leaving the other mythical combatants alone. They circled above Stephanie and dove down in waves. Having had enough of their numbers decimated by the winged things, the Norse combatants chose to keep their distance.

The Nephilim and Seraphim weren't able to land very many blows individually, but their overwhelming numbers all but made that point moot. Suddenly, a huge hole in the Jötunn front opened up as several giants tried to dodge Thor and Jormungand. It was even effective at clearing out a majority of the flying beasts for a moment. It was just long enough.

"Get out of here!" shouted Mestoph at Marcus and Stephanie.

"Hurry up! We'll hold them off and meet back up at the bridge," said Leviticus.

They hesitated, only for a moment and then took off running toward the gap in between two Jötnar, Sir Regi bouncing quickly between their legs. No one noticed them slip through and out of the fray, not even the Seraphim and Nephilim. On the other side of the Jötunn front, the fighting ended abruptly and Stephanie and Marcus finally found themselves in the clear. It was a clear path to the bridge, not even half a mile from where they stood. They laughed excitedly and smiled at each other, grabbing hands and running for the bridge, while Sir Regi ran behind them barking. In their excitement they hadn't noticed the figure sitting at the edge of the bridge's railing. Arms crossed and idly bouncing one leg, St. Peter was waiting for them with a giant, shit-eating grin.

"You didn't think I'd forgotten about you?" asked St. Peter.

The gorilla stood up and swaggered toward them.

250

"Now!" he shouted.

Reaching up from the mists of the chasm was a smaller Jötunn, though still at least three times the height of a human. The Jötunn waved at them childishly and then dove back off the cliff to belly-flop onto Bifrost. The bridge bounced and groaned and then cracked and buckled. It collapsed, taking the Jötunn with it. Their only escape from Asgard fell silently away into the mist.

"And now this whole ridiculous business ends," said St. Peter as he pointed the gun at Stephanie's head.

"Any last words?" asked St. Peter.

"I love you, Marcus," said Stephanie, squeezing his hand tightly in her own.

Off in the distance, a terrible wailing heralded the agonizing death throes of something large, and then there was a hard thump as whatever it was slammed to the ground. The sound caught everyone's attention, and they turned to see a clean swath across the masses of both Jötnar and Valkyrie, cleared of everything by the body of the giant snake Jormungand—minus its head, which rested upside down next to its roughly hacked upon neck. It looked as if Thor has finally hit it hard enough to literally spin the snake's head off.

All fighting had stopped, even the attacks of Seraphim and Nephilim. They took in the sight of Thor standing near the ripped-off head, glistening with sweat, his hair matted to his face with blood. He was panting, and Mjolnir hung heavy in his hand. He had been victorious over the Midgard Serpent, but the price was that his chest had been pierced with one of the snake's fangs. It had broken off inside him and still dripped with venom. Thor's head hung low and his legs began to shake. He fell to one knee, sighed deeply, and then crumpled under his own weight, falling chest first and pushing the broken fang out through his back near his shoulder blade. A cheer broke out from Hel's army and the dozen remaining Jötnar. The Valkyries and Valhallans immediately retreated. Surtr's sword flamed up wildly, and he began swinging it at everything, including his own people, and catching things on fire. Even the rocks and dirt began to burn.

"Well, looks like it's time for me to go," said St. Peter, and he again trained the gun on Stephanie.

He began to squeeze the trigger when a furious barking erupted from behind Marcus and Stephanie. Sir Regi darted between them and sprang into the air, hitting St. Peter's chest and running up to latch his jaws onto the man's throat. The gun rose as St. Peter swayed backwards, and a shot went off harmlessly into the sky. St. Peter's eyes widened in a terrified panic and he began shaking, trying to throw the dog off. Sir Regi was locked on tight, however, and flopped around St. Peter as he flailed wildly. St. Peter began beating at Sir Regi with his fist and the pistol; the dog whimpered but still wouldn't let go. St. Peter made a thick, wet choking noise and began coughing up blood. Panicked, he stumbled into the railing of the bridge, which fell away. Stephanie and Marcus both ran to catch him, but St. Peter slipped in the dirt and fell backwards toward the chasm before either could get to him. He made a last ditch attempt to grab onto the bridge, but he had yet to let go of the gun. His weak, one-handed grip wasn't enough, and he tumbled into the chasm, taking Sir Regi with him.

Mestoph and Leviticus swung their swords wildly. It didn't matter, since the swarm of flying creatures had become so thick that it was impossible to miss. They were covered in the blood of both creatures, as well as their own from hundreds of cuts all over their bodies. They had to keep pushing through the swarm to find fresh ground; they would be slipping on the sticky black or white goop that served as blood for the Nephilim and Seraphim, respectively.

Mestoph swung and was surprised when his sword didn't connect with anything. The lack of impact meant he overextended the swing, and the gore-slick weapon flew out of his hand, spinning in the air until it stabbed an unlucky Seraph and dropped to the ground with the body. The creatures were quick to take advantage of Mestoph's sudden vulnerability and began concentrating almost exclusively on him. He dropped to the ground and began fumbling around for any sort of weapon in the disgusting muck of sticky blood.

Mestoph caught sight of a fallen Valkyrie less than thirty feet away, her lifeless eyes staring upwards to the sky. Her sword was still gripped tightly in her hand. He scrambled on hands and knees, unable to get to his feet as the creatures began piling on his back and scratching away with their claws. Behind him, Leviticus screamed and charged toward the mob, swatting them away like flies. The brief reprieve was enough to allow Mestoph to get to his feet, and he dashed to the dead Valkyrie, whom he recognized as the red-headed Kara, and grabbed her sword.

"Sorry Red, I need this more than you," he said as he stole the Valkyrie's sword.

Mestoph turned and resumed the wild assault. Then he heard the dinosaur-like roar of Jormungand being slain of to his right. Both the Nephilim and Seraphim suddenly went into a confused frenzy. Half their numbers immediately disappeared, popping like kernels of corn, while others began attacking each other. A few flew wildly in circles and spirals, making a high pitched screeching. The screeching was quickly drowned out by the deep, baritone roars of the cheering

Jötnar and the screams of fleeing Valkyrie and Valalhallan warriors.

"Time to go!" yelled Leviticus.

He and Mestoph dropped their weapons and bolted. They ran toward where they knew the bridge was, but their path was blocked by the body of the slain serpent. He was long enough that it was pointless to try to go around, so they opted to go straight at it and climb over. They were close enough to make out the bruises and gashes that Thor had made with his mighty hammer. Mestoph, trailing only a few feet behind Leviticus, felt a rush of hot air behind him and the swooshing sound of something large being swung. Looking back as he ran, he saw Surtr looming not too far behind him, swinging his giant flaming sword. When the sword hit the ground, it cleaved a giant crack in the earth and a large spiderweb of flames shot out in all directions. The flames grew into walls, and one of them was traveling straight toward him. He veered to the left and called out to Leviticus, who looked back just in time to swerve to the right. The heat was intense, which was surprising to Mestoph since he had lived his entire life in Hell. Leviticus had managed to get far enough away from the flames to avoid being hurt. Mestoph realized his trench coat was on fire. He shrugged it off without breaking stride.

Another wall of flame shot past the two sprinting friends, and this time it ran directly into the body of the snake. It exploded, sending Jormungand chunks high into the sky. Warm, wet bits of snake rained down on Mestoph and Leviticus as they ran through the fortuitous gap in the corpse that had been blocking their path only moments earlier. Mestoph looked back and saw nothing but Surtr and flames. The ground was ablaze, bodies of both sides of the battle were frying, and even Odin's great obsidian and silver hall was burning. Then Surtr charged through the remains of

254

Jormungand's body, heading straight toward the fleeing Mestoph and Leviticus.

"Pick up the pace!" yelled Mestoph.

"That's funny coming from the guy in last place," said Leviticus between labored breaths.

The Angel leaned forward and started gaining speed as they continued to run for the bridge, but they suddenly noticed that Bifrost wasn't there anymore. They looked left and right along the lip of the chasm, but there was no bridge. They were now running roughly parallel to the path that had led them from the bridge to the stairs up to Valaskjalf, but where the path met the chasm it ended into a rocky nub with two figures standing at the edge. Leviticus turned to look back at Mestoph and saw Surtr close in behind them; the giant was beginning to swing his flaming sword again. Leviticus tackled Mestoph, and they tumbled to the ground as the sword swooped above them. Surtr followed through with the miss, then raised the sword up above his head and started to bring it down between Mestoph and Leviticus. They rolled out of the way but were hit by a wave of flames that pushed them in opposite directions.

There were screams from behind Surtr, and from between the Jötunn's massive legs Mestoph saw a small band of twenty or so Valkyries led by the rotund Brynhildr, who looked like an angry bumblebee in flight. Surtr looked down at Mestoph and Leviticus and then back to the charging Valkyries. He let out a deep sigh that blew acrid breath in Mestoph and Leviticus's faces, making them gag. Surtr pointed down at the two of them like he was telling them to stay put and then turned to face the Valkyries, his hand still on the pommel of the sword he had stabbed into the earth.

With his attention diverted, the Angel and Demon pulled themselves to their feet and hobbled off. Mestoph's dreads were singed and a few of the locks broke off like fuzzy icicles when he moved. Leviticus helped him to the remains of the bridge where Stephanie and Marcus stood.

Mestoph heard a grunt of confusion behind him and turned to see Surtr struggling with the sword stuck in the ground. He had driven it down too far and now couldn't pull it free. He and Leviticus paused to watch. The Jötunn struggled futilely with the jammed sword as all of the Valkyries struck him in the chest all at once. Surtr howled, which sent several Valkyrie spiraling to the ground dead or unconscious. Then the giant lost his balance and fell back against the sword. The flaming blade wavered back and forth for a moment, and then there was an ear-splitting ping as it shattered. The sword exploded into an enormous ball of fire that engulfed Surtr, the Valkyrie, and everything else within a hundred yards.

Marcus and Stephanie stood at the edge of what was left of Bifrost Bridge and looked down, hoping it was going to be like the movies and the dog would somehow scrabble up the edge of the chasm and they would all have a good laugh about what a close call it was. After several minutes of staring wordlessly into the abyss, it became obvious that a miracle was never going to happen. Tears began to roll down Marcus's face, and he turned to Stephanie. She put her arms around him and pulled him close, and she began to cry as well.

"He was my best friend, and I hardly knew him…the real him," said Marcus.

They might have stood there forever, had not the exploding snake gotten their attention and broken their embrace. Now they watched an injured Mestoph and

Leviticus run from the giant Surtr as the Valkyries rammed into his chest, knocking him over. Then everything was consumed by an explosion of fire and debris. The ground began to rumble and then it started to crack. Great geysers set fire to anything that Surtr hadn't already burned with his sword. What was left of the bridge crumbed at the edges. Ahead and to the right was nothing but flame and ruin, and neither Marcus nor Stephanie thought being so close to the edge of the chasm was a great idea. Their only option was the small copse of woods at their right, near what was left of Heimdall's log cabin.

They ran for the trees as bits and pieces of rock, charred wood, and metallic splinters of sword began to rain down. They passed a single ash tree, much larger than any of the others, and Stephanie pulled Marcus to a halt. The tree was old and gnarly, puckered with scars that showed it had survived a great deal of chaos and turmoil. Near the base of the trunk there was a gaping wound just big enough for a person—or two—to squeeze through. Stephanie had a sudden flash of her dream about Asgard, and she remembered this tree. She had seen her Grams pointing at it, and inside the hollow she had seen herself peering back out.

"In there," she said, pointing to the opening in the tree.

Marcus looked at her with doubt in his eyes, unsure if she meant what he thought she did. There was such confidence in the look she returned that his doubt disappeared and he nodded his head. There was a great rumble as they climbed into the opening, and an explosion even louder than that of the sword. With one last glance back, Stephanie saw what was left of Valaskjalf, and most of the obsidian cliff it had been carved out of, burst like a dam as a torrent of lava broke through. The volcano beneath the glacier was blowing up, Vesuvius style.

Inside the tree, they curled up together, holding on tight

to each other. There were more explosions, and the meager light grew and then flickered as lava flowed around the tree, catching it and everything else nearby on fire. Despite the flames, the tree never got more than just a bit warm and the dampened rumbling and tumbling created a womb-like atmosphere that, although cramped, was very comfortable. Even though the world was ending, their exhaustion and the tranquility of the hollow made them feel unnaturally at ease. They both felt themselves relaxing as tiny fingers of sleep pulled at the edges of their consciousness.

"Now is probably as a good a time as any to tell you," said Stephanie.

"What's that, love?" asked Marcus.

"I had another dream, more like a brief flash, when I passed out on the bridge. I think I'm pregnant," said Stephanie.

Marcus laid his head against hers, and then they both fell asleep.

They were awakened by a bright light and the sound of running water. Marcus rubbed the sleepiness from his eyes and looked around. They were still inside the hollow of the tree, and Stephanie still leaning against him, only just stirring. She looked up at him and smiled; he smiled back. The aches and pains of being confined in such a small place crept into their joints and muscles, and they both had the sudden urge to get out of the tree. Marcus let Stephanie climb out first and followed her out.

When they left the safety of the tree, they had expected to be met by a dark and ruined wasteland, and for the most part they weren't disappointed. There were several large flows of cooled lava that ran from the cone of the volcano and down over the edge of the chasm. A large icepack was melting around the volcano, sending torrents of glacial water down what was left of the obsidian cliff. The runoff formed several small rivers and streams in between the hardened lava. Although the sky was still cloudy, the unnatural storm had broken and the sun was shining through the gaps in the clouds. Even now, they were already blowing away into the distance. Where the rays of the sun shone through, there were sprouts and sprigs of grass and flowers coming up in between cracks of lava. The large ash tree they had hidden in was the only one that survived the destruction.

There was no way to tell exactly how long they had been asleep, but if the aches and pains were any indication, it had been years. Marcus and Stephanie quietly stretched and drank from one of the briskly cold and refreshingly clean glacial rivers. There weren't any words to express what they felt after all they had been through, and seeing as they appeared to be the only ones left alive, they were content to enjoy the peace and quiet. There was no telling how long it was going to last, after all, and at some point they were going to have to figure out how to get back home.

Home: the idea felt empty to Marcus now. The home he knew didn't feel right in his mind anymore. He had lost his best friend, even if he had gained something else in return, and the apartment he lived in felt empty and cold in his mind. The thought of raising a family was terrifying, but the thought of raising it back home was even more so. Not to mention that he and Stephanie had both probably lost their jobs by now.

Variations of the same theme were running through Stephanie's mind, and the two only had to look at each other to know that they weren't going to be able to go back to the lives they had lived before this. They would cross the next bridge when they came to it, but for now they just walked hand in hand through the new world that had formed around them and enjoyed the silence.

"Hey! Over here! Oh thank God, you guys made it," rang the familiar voice of Leviticus.

In one of the wider rivers that ran down from the glacier was a large chunk of rock that stuck up out of the water like a big thumb. A charred and scarred Leviticus was standing atop the rocky island, waving to Marcus and Stephanie. Marcus sighed at the death of silence, and then they made their way to the bank of the river. It was slightly less than a hundred feet wide, but the water was moving swiftly and there was no way of knowing how deep it ran. Marcus stuck a foot in the frigid waters while holding on to Stephanie's hand and then walked a few steps out. The two of them helped each other balance as they waded across the river, which never got higher than knee deep. When they got to the edge of the island, he noticed that Leviticus wasn't alone. Lying on his back and breathing heavily was a seriously injured Mestoph. At the sound of their voices, the Demon raised his head shakily and gave a pained smile.

"Only the good die young," he said weakly.

Although it probably wasn't a good idea to move someone in his condition, there was absolutely no chance of helping him if they left him on the rock. Regardless of the trouble they had caused Marcus and Stephanie, they had risked their lives to save them in the end. Demon or not, Mestoph deserved at least a chance at happiness. If he died now, there was no telling where he would go or what would happen to him. Finally, Marcus decided to help ferry the ailing Demon across the river, and not just because standing in the frigid waters was beginning to make him shiver.

Leviticus pulled Mestoph by his armpits, lifting his badly burned chest off the rocks and leaving his feet to drag behind him. Both Mestoph and Leviticus were covered in small cuts and gashes, most of which seemed to have been partially cauterized by the flames, but Mestoph had clearly gotten the worst of it. His wounds were sparkling with hundreds of tiny slivers of Surtr's shattered sword. His legs also didn't seem to be working too well. Stephanie grabbed Mestoph by the shoulders from below, and Leviticus lowered him by his legs into Marcus's waiting arms, and then both of them helped Marcus keep his balance in the strong current.

Once on the shore Marcus looked down at Mestoph. "I don't know how far I can carry you, but we'll find help," he said.

Mestoph coughed, and blood came up in little flecks as he shook his head. "No, I'm not going any further. I'm just glad to be off that damn rock with that pussy of an Angel worrying a rut into it," said Mestoph.

Leviticus explained that he had spent the last several hours searching for a way off the chunk of rock that used to be Asgard, but found it surrounded on three sides by the chasm, which was now full of lava, and the volcano on the other, which was also full of lava. If he could find something to make a stretcher maybe the three of them could carry Mestoph around the base of the volcano, but that would eventually mean scaling the glacier, which brought about a whole new set of problems. If they had anything sharp, they might be able to cut down the only tree that seemed to have survived the destruction intact and bridge the chasm, but other than the tips of swords and spears sticking out of the lava, there wasn't a whole weapon to be found.

Neither Marcus nor Stephanie had any better ideas as to what to do. Getting out of there on their own appeared to be difficult enough; adding in the burden of carrying Mestoph seemed to make it impossible. Mestoph's wet coughs made it sound like they didn't have a whole lot of time. Even if they got across the chasm, and even in the unlikely event their horses were still waiting for them on the other side, it would take days to reach civilization. There was also the question of who could help a dying demon.

Mestoph suffered a particularly violent coughing fit, and long streaks of blood ran down the side of his mouth. One of the larger shards of sword debris oozed and bubbled every time he coughed, and he was wheezing thickly now even when he wasn't coughing. They gave up the talk of getting Mestoph out alive and simply tried to make him comfortable.

"I'm sorry," wheezed Mestoph.

"No, it's OK. We survived. We're going to be OK," said Marcus.

"We hurt a lot of people. The shootout, the plane crash, fucking Ragnarok…none of it would've happened if it weren't for us. I knew the risks, and I knew there would be collateral damage, but I didn't really understand what it meant. I'm sorry about that," said Mestoph.

"Well, on behalf of the human race, I forgive you," said Marcus.

He looked to Stephanie, and she hesitated for only a moment. "Me too," she said as a tear formed in the corner of her eye. She quickly wiped it away.

"I'm sorry too for dragging you into this, Leviticus," said Mestoph.

"I knew what I was getting into. I'm as guilty as you are…maybe more so," said the Angel.

"Maybe I'll get lucky and see you on the other side, my friend."

The two shook hands, and then Mestoph fell limply to the ground with a last wheezing gasp. Tears rolled down Leviticus's face. He had never felt grief before; then again, he had never lost anyone. Mestoph might pop back up right away or he might not return at all, but Leviticus would always carry the pain of this moment. He turned to Marcus and Stephanie.

"I really am sorry. For everything."

There were several loud pops as bursts of multicolored smoke appeared behind them. Everyone turned to look, and as the smoke cleared they saw God, Satan, St. Peter, and a tall redheaded man with a shaggy and oddly familiar beard.

Then Mestoph coughed and sat upright.

"God damn it!" he yelled.

Chapter 20

The End of the Beginning of *The End*

God walked toward them, his long flowing white robe billowing in an unseen wind as he looked around in wonder.

"Now *that* is how you do an end of the world," he said.

Satan, dressed in a deep black suit with a stark white dress shirt and solid black tie, was not impressed.

"A little melodramatic don't you think? Considering it's not *The* End?" said Satan.

God shot Satan a disapproving look and waved him off.

"Don't be a spoil sport. As far as the Norse were concerned, it was the only ending that mattered. And boy did they go out with style. Dramatic deaths, epic battles, explosions, and even a little bit of rebirth for good measure," said God, pointing to Marcus and Stephanie.

St. Peter glanced around, confused, and then looked at the shaggy, ginger-haired man and took a quick sidestep, rubbing at his throat. The shaggy man turned and gave him a toothy grin, making a dramatic chomping motion at St. Peter.

"Boys, I didn't bring you back to have you start misbehaving," said God in a fatherly tone.

Although neither had met God or Satan before, Marcus and Stephanie both *knew* who they were seeing and were amazed. Leviticus smiled at Mestoph, who nodded toward God and raised his brows. He knew it was judgment time.

God walked over to Marcus and Stephanie and smiled down at them. He was several feet taller than either of them, but the warm look on his face kept it from being imposing. At that moment He had bushy, curly white hair and a thick but neatly trimmed beard, a lot like Kenny Rogers from *The Gambler*. He put a hand each on Marcus and Stephanie's shoulders and they both felt a warmth and power flow through them. It was similar to the feeling Stephanie had when Heimdall had touched her, but infinitely stronger and warmer. Stephanie felt it in her belly and knew the tiny little seed that grew inside her could feel it as well.

"You two are going to be fine, and your son will live a full life," said God. "I've always been fond of the name Daniel."

Mestoph and Leviticus looked at each other in surprise, wondering when the two of them had even had time to have sex in the last two weeks. God then walked over to Mestoph and Leviticus. Satan had stood back while God was talking to the two humans, but he now came forward to stand next to God. He turned to smile at Stephanie as he passed, giving her a cold and creepy feeling.

"Alright, let's get this over with," said God as he snapped his fingers.

Appearing on the other side of Mestoph and Leviticus were three drastically differing people. One was an ancient woman in a nun's habit who was looking at the Angel and Demon and clicking her tongue as she shook her head in disapproval. Next to her was a short, bald, almost perfectly round, Asian man with a permanent smile on his face. Then there was another man who was almost as old as the nun and wore thick glasses and a red pair of suspenders over a golf shirt and plaid pants.

"Can we get this over with? I've got a game to finish," said the suspendered man in a voice that sounded remarkably like Larry King's.

"Fine," said Satan, and he snapped his fingers.

The ground shook and the recently cooled lava began to crack, sending whirls of heat and steam into the air. The lava and bedrock below began to rise slowly into the air, creating a tall, crescent-shaped wall of porous rock around them. God joined in the interior decorating; he pointed and a black, glass-smooth dais rose up from the ground, followed by two wings of tables on each side that mimicked the crescent shape of the wall. God and Satan began waving around like mad orchestra conductors, and a grim, ultramodern courtroom began to materialize. Seating of black and white, with legs and arms of polished chrome rose out of the ground. A gallery of slate-colored benches formed out of chunks of lava, and as each row formed various people popped into the seats with the rhythmic cadence of champagne corks popping. Some of those people were vaguely familiar to Mestoph and Leviticus, but a few they recognized instantly.

When it was all done, there was a complete and completely stylish courtroom, which would make any primetime legal drama insane with jealousy. The three old and wizened members of Freewill International—Mother Theresa, Buddha, and Larry King—took seats in mesh and chrome rolling chairs at the table at the right hand side of the judge's dais. Three more figures appeared at the opposite side of the dais. One of them looked like every picture of every Greek philosopher ever, seeing as he wore a long, flowing robe and had white, close-cropped hair. He could've been Socrates, Homer, or just a really good period actor. Another figure Marcus instantly recognized was Sigmund Freud, solely because he had an action figure of him on his desk at work that said "So, tell me about your mother," every time you pressed a button on his back. The final man, sitting at the far left of the table, was retired game show host Bob Barker, wearing a pastel pink suit with baby blue pinstripes and a white collar and cuffs. Sitting in Bob's lap was a small, fluffy white Bichon Frise—neutered of course.

While the members of Freewill International greeted and shook hands with each other, God motioned Mestoph and Leviticus toward the defendants' table, the one with black leather chairs, where they nervously took their seats. There were two more empty chairs next to them. Marcus, Stephanie, St. Peter, and Sir Regi were walked to the front row of the gallery. Satan took his place beside God in between the defendant and prosecutor's tables.

A silence spread over all present, and then there was a muffled pop and large roll of light blue smoke from atop the judge's dais. As the smoke cleared, they saw a man in sequined judge's robe of ivory and crimson trimmed in ermine and a royal Victorian court-styled wig of sunshine yellow. The man gave a flourished bow to the gallery, complete with twirling hand gestures, and then greeted each of the Freewill International representatives. He then gave a nod each to Satan and God, who sat down in the two empty chairs next to Mestoph.

Appearing in a triumvirate of weasels going pop were the lawyers for the prosecution, neither of whom Mestoph or Leviticus recognized, and a chubby man in a very conservative suit and a short top hat who stood in front of the judge's dais leaning on a simple wooden cane. The two lawyers took their seats in the white prosecutor's chairs. One of the lawyers was a pale, wiry man of average height with a slightly rodent-like face and large ears; the other was a slightly overweight black man with a wide mustache, short cropped black hair, wearing wireframe glasses. Once everyone was seated, the flamboyant judge motioned to the chubby man in the top hat.

"If you please?" asked the judge in an effeminate voice with a slight Polish accent.

"Oh, right right," said the chubby man in an aristocratic British accent and then turned to address the gallery. "All rise for the commencement of the fifteenth convening of the Freewill Judgment Council, the honorable Wladziu Valentino Liberace presiding. This court is now in session."

"Thank you, Mr. Churchill. And thank you to all those in attendance. Joining me in judgment today are Mother Theresa, Buddha, Larry King, Aristotle, Sigmund Freud, and Bob Barker." Each of those named waved or nodded when called. Liberace continued, "To be judged are the Angel Leviticus and the Demon Mestoph. Representing Freewill International as the prosecution are Franz Kakfa and Johnny Cochran. Representing the accused is the Tetragrammaton and joining him is The Dragon, The Tempter, The Ancient Serpent, The Devil, Beelzebub, Lucifer the Fallen. In the name of brevity, we'll just call you God and Satan. The prosecution may present the charges now," said Liberace sitting down at his dais, sweeping the excess billows of his sequined rob to the side as he did.

Kafka looked over to Cochran, who nodded and stood. "Mestopholes, son of Mephistopheles the Faustus, and Leviticus, son of…well I don't really know who you come from. It's not important. Anyway, the prosecution charges you both with subverting freewill and the unlawful manipulation of Earthly events," said Cochran in a style reminiscent of an evangelical preacher.

"How do the defendants plea?" asked Liberace.

"Uhh, what?" asked Mestoph.

Satan sighed. "You stole an Omen, used it to affect events on Earth for your own gain, and you screwed everything up. Just plead guilty, and we can all be on our way without a fuss."

"Guilty," said Mestoph.

"Your turn," God said to Leviticus.

"Guilty," said Leviticus with confidence. He was certain of his guilt and was ready to pay the price for what he'd done.

The Freewill council began whispering to each other. A few stood up and went to talk to those on the opposite side of the dais. Bob Barker calmly wrote something down on a piece of paper and handed it to Freud, who handed it to Aristotle and then up to Liberace; Bob never stopped petting the fluffy white dog. After a few minutes of discussion, the other council members followed Bob's lead and passed pieces of paper up to the judge.

"The council accepts the plea. The sentence is death for the Demon, voted unanimously with me abstaining" said Liberace, stating the terminal word with a high pitched glee.

Mestoph rounded on Satan. "Whoa, whoa! Wait. You said—"

"Shut up!" yelled Satan, and the sky dimmed perceptibly.

"And for the Angel, in a split decision for which I will now cast the swing vote…Purgatory," tittered the judge.

"Can't you just kill me instead?"

The pianist just shook his head, and Leviticus slumped his shoulders in defeat.

"We also bring the charge of the murder of Father Mike against Sir Reginald Pollywog Newcastle III, also known as Prometheus," said Kafka in German-accented English.

"That son of a bitch was going to kill us!" shouted Sir Regi in his familiar Scottish brogue as he jumped to his feet. Several of the members of the gallery murmured their dissent.

"However," said Cochran loudly, breaking through the noise, "in light of the fact that Father Mike employed kidnapping, excessive force, and unlawful use of a firearm, we dismiss the charge and sentence Father Mike to death. He's already dead, so there's really no paperwork for that one."

Kafka made a throat clearing noise and nudged Cochran,

"Oh yeah, we also charge St. Peter with something or other. We're not really sure what, but I'm sure he did something. We leave his punishment up to you," Cochran said to God.

"Thank you gentlemen, and you Sister. We appreciate your judgments," said God. "However, we wish to bring forth evidence in the defense of the defendants."

"But they pled guilty," said Mother Theresa, looking questioningly at the other council members, most of whom just shrugged. Bob Barker was still calmly petting the dog.

"This is true, but there are extenuating circumstances that the defendants were not aware of."

Liberace raised an eyebrow. "Well then, let's hear these *extenuating circumstances* shall we?"

'Excellent," said God as he snapped his fingers. In his hand, a glass vial appeared holding the now familiar Secured-Signed Prophecy that Leviticus had stolen. God opened the vial and pulled out the roll of e-ink paper. He stood up and walked to the dais and presented it to the council to examine, showing them it was the genuine article.

"These things are useless, as I will show you," said God.

God tapped a digital button on the Prophecy and a keyboard appeared. He deleted all the words of the Prophecy and typed in something that He kept hidden from those watching. He then clicked save and pulled a stylus from His pocket and signed the line at the bottom. He turned the Prophecy so everyone could see, and a bright red button appeared in the center with the words *Enact Prophecy?* He pressed it.

And then they waited. Nothing happened.

"Alright, what did you type into the Prophecy?" asked Buddha.

God tapped a button and then handed it over to Buddha. He looked at it and then did a double take and laughed. He showed it to Mother Theresa, who shook her head disapprovingly, and then to Larry King. Larry read aloud in his distinctive voice: "Satan will instantly turn into a three-assed baboon."

Satan stood, beamed a shit-eating grin to God, and then turned to the gallery. "As you can clearly see, I have not turned into a baboon; three-assed or otherwise."

The gallery chuckled like members of sitcom studio audience.

"These things just don't work. Not yet, at least. It's just a proof of concept at the moment," said God.

"So what does that prove?" asked Mother Theresa.

"I'll take this one," said Satan. God returned to his seat, and Satan began to pace in front of the council with his arms clasped behind him.

"If the Prophecy was null, then the Omen that was meant to play off that Prophecy never activated...even if it was authentic and fully armed," he said, glaring at Mestoph.

"The plane was already destined to crash," Satan continued as he conjured up another Omen and passed it around. "In fact, it was slated to kill everyone on board. So while these two did indeed meddle, they actually saved lives. Something which I doubt even you can really gripe about, Franz.

"Everything else that happened was just a bizarre series of events that ultimately had no effect on humanity. The volcano was going to erupt with or without Ragnarok. Various geological institutes and surveys had shown an elevation of seismic and geothermal fissuring in recent months around the volcano," said Satan as he made stacks of dense research studies and reports from various agents of various governments appear in front of each council member as well as the prosecutors.

"Finally, as everyone on the council is well aware, Ragnarok has been overdue for ages. The Norse pantheon was already all but extinct, and Ragnarok was the fulfillment of a last handful of outstanding prophecies in their mythology. And technically Magnus Magnuson started Ragnarok, not Mestoph or Leviticus," Satan concluded. He walked back to the defendant's table and sat down.

In the gallery Magnus loudly mumbled something about not knowing he was *the* Fenrir. Marcus and Stephanie turned to wave at him, but he was too busy pleading ignorance to one of the passengers that had died in the plane crash to notice.

The Freewill council began to group together in discussion again, arguing more heatedly than they had the first time. Again Bob Barker wrote something down on a piece of paper, passed it up, and sat calmly at the end of the table, now feeding his dog little treats that he pulled from a pocket inside his suit coat. The members of the gallery sat quietly, shuffling around and tapping their feet, trying their best not to be impatient. Finally the council broke their huddle and returned to their seats to write down their verdicts and pass them up. Liberace tallied them and the once again looked up at his audience.

"We've reached a majority, with me again abstaining. In a vote of five to one," said Liberace, with a significant glance at Bob Barker, "we dismiss the charges against the accused."

Mestoph and Leviticus both sighed in relief and patted each other on the back.

"Great. Now if you don't mind, I'd really like to finish that golf game this century," said Larry King.

"I object! This is an abomination, a travestation, a rapification of justice," said Cochran.

"Shut up, Johnny. You know the corruption and stifling bureaucracy that exists in death just as it did in life. Now I'm going to go sit in the woods alone for a few years," said Kafka.

Kafka closed his briefcase and then popped out of existence. Johnny Cochran huffed loudly, looked around, and huffed again when he realized no one was really paying him any attention.

"Yes, Mr. Cochran. We know you're mad you didn't get

to make a grand closing argument and only got to rhyme nonsensical words once. Now, if you're finished?"

Cochran signed and then disappeared.

"Alright, that's enough work for one day. Mr. Churchill?" said Liberace.

The former Prime Minister was fast asleep on the bench, his arms folded across his chest.

"Mr. Churchill!"

The Brit startled awake and then jumped to his feet, mumbling, and threw up a quick V for Victory. He slowly lowered his hand and walked up toward the dais. He cleared his throat and addressed the council.

"Unless there are any other pressing issues?" asked the statesman. "Very well, then, I call the fifteenth session of the Freewill Judgment Council to a close. Court is adjourned," he finished, waving his top hat at the council and then popping away.

Liberace teleported after Churchill, and then there were five simultaneous pops as all but one of the Freewillers left. Still sitting at the end of the table was Bob Barker, who now stood with his dog in his hand.

"I do have one last thing. Mr. Mestoph?" said Bob.

"Yes, Mr. Barker?"

"Fuck you!" said Bob. He flipped off the Demon and then disappeared in a puff of smoke.

"What the Hell was that?" asked Leviticus.

"We've had a few run-ins. Last time we met, he was protesting an animal testing laboratory that I just happened to be running," said Mestoph with a shrug.

God and Satan both stood and turned to the gallery.

"I supposed we should take care of them?" asked Satan.

"Yes, I suppose so," said God, walking toward the rocky railing that divided the gallery from the rest of the courtroom.

"Would those of you who survived the plane crash

please stand?" asked God.

In response, a small cluster of the gallery stood from their seats.

"Hmm, not you," said God, pointing at one man standing apart from the rest of the survivors. He looked around, turned red, and then reluctantly sat down.

"I believe that might be one of yours," said God to Satan.

God turned back to the standing survivors. "I'm afraid that none of you will remember this once you return to wherever you came, but I would like to thank you all for participating. Even if it was just as a formality," he said and then waved his hands as if he were parting the Red Sea. The survivors all disappeared.

"Those who did not survive," he said, looking pointedly at the man who had previously stood with the survivors, "will be returning to your regularly scheduled Afterlives."

And then they too disappeared.

Left behind in the gallery were Marcus and Stephanie, Sir Regi, St. Peter, and Magnus, as well as a handful of Odin's Taint who had fallen during the fighting with the rebels. Neither Fenrir nor Father Mike was present, but no one could really say they were missing either of them. God walked over to the group of Neo Vikings, who were standing around feeling rather out of place.

"I know you follow your own beliefs, but I just wanted to thank each of you for the work you did in protecting those of my flock who came across your path. Although there is a place in Valhalla waiting for each of you," said God, at which point Magnus began looking down at his feet and digging his toe into the rocky ground, "Yes Magnus, even you. That said, I would like to offer you the option of joining me in Heaven."

The Neo Vikings looked at each other for a moment,

then at Magnus, and then back to God. They all shook their heads. Magnus had yet to give an answer, and God looked at him expectantly. The Viking scratched his head for a moment and then looked over at his brothers in arms.

"You all fought bravely and boldly and earned your place in Valhalla, but I don't feel that I did. I was killed by a god in anger for what I did. Go on to Valhalla. I will not be joining you," said Magnus.

The other Neo Vikings voiced their disagreement, but quieted when God lifted a hand to hush them. "While you did trigger Ragnarok by freeing Fenrir, and thus pissed Tyr off to the point that he murdered you, there was never any clear explanation as to who was to free Fenrir and how it was to be done. Someone had to do it eventually, so you played a pivotal though unsung role in your own religion. If you don't deserve entry into your sacred halls, then no one does. Although I'd be honored to have you in my employ, it'd be dishonest to let you come under such false pretenses," said God.

"Very well then, I will join my brothers," said Magnus, smiling for the first time since he had died.

"A wise choice," said God, and then he motioned toward a large rock just beyond the gallery. "Valkyries!"

Out from behind the rock came five of the winged women in full armor, some still spattered with blood from the battle. Each Valkyrie took the hand of a Viking and then jumped into the air. The final Valkyrie took Magnus's hand, and before she spread her wings and jumped he turned back and waved goodbye.

"Good luck, you two," he said to Marcus and Stephanie, and then he was carried into the air and up beyond the clouds.

Once Magnus was out of sight, God turned around surveyed the courtroom.

"No need for theatrics anymore," He said and waved a hand. The accoutrements of a courtroom began to shudder and return to the earth. The benches disappeared, the dais and tables crumbled to dust and rocks, and the crescent-shaped wall began to lower back into the ground.

"Alright, we've all had our fun. I think it's time for goodbyes," said Satan impatiently.

God nodded in agreement and then walked over to Marcus and Stephanie, bringing St. Peter and Sir Regi with him. Marcus approached Sir Regi and gave him a look over.

"All this time, an Angel?" asked Marcus.

"Well, all my time with you," said Sir Regi.

Marcus smiled and then put his hand out. "I'm really going to miss you."

"Oh, come on you awkward bastard," said Sir Regi. The two hugged for a moment, and then Sir Regi gave Marcus a hearty slap on the back. "I'm gonna miss you, too," he said as he turned to Stephanie and gave her a quick hug. "You take care of this guy. God knows he needs someone to."

Leviticus and Mestoph gave Marcus and Stephanie awkward handshakes, as none of them really knew what the protocol was for saying goodbye to people who lied repeatedly and nearly got you killed, but without whom you wouldn't have found happiness.

"One thing," said Stephanie as she turned to look at God.

"Yes, my dear?" asked God.

"If all of it was coincidence or whatever you want to call it, what was up with that storm?"

"Let's just say not everything was a 'coincidence' and leave it at that," said God with a wink. He wiggled his fingers and a tiny version of the pentagram storm swirled above His outstretched palm. "Enjoy Tahiti," said God as he patted Stephanie on the shoulder and then both she and Marcus disappeared.

God and Satan turned and walked toward St. Peter and Sir Regi. God put His hand on Sir Regi's shoulder, and the former Scottie dog smiled even as he was wiping at his misted eyes. If he'd still had a tail, he was sure it would have been wagging.

"There's a place waiting for you in Heaven if you want," said God.

Sir Regi nodded excitedly, and then he disappeared.

"You, on the other hand," said God. He looked straight at St. Peter and then pointed to Satan. St. Peter's face fell.

"Nothing like that," said Satan. "But we do have a job that we think might be especially suited for you,"

"Shit," said St. Peter, and then he too disappeared.

God turned back toward Mestoph and Leviticus. "First thing in the morning, boys," He said, and then Mestoph and Leviticus disappeared.

God and Satan walked off toward the chasm. God put his arm around Satan's shoulder and gave him a friendly pat.

"And *that* is how you destroy a pantheon and get away with it," said God.

"One down…" said Satan.

"End of the World, here we come."

Chapter 21

The Beginning of the Beginning of the Middle of *The End*

St. Peter stood in the doorway of his new office. It was a shithole. Located in the old shipping office of a failed import/export company along the battery of the Savannah River, it had one wall of nothing but old, hazy windows that looked out over an alley that managed to be dark even in broad daylight. The floors were covered in dusty wood that creaked if you even thought of walking on it. Everything in it was left over from the 1950s, when the company had failed. The hat rack in the corner was made of green marbled metal and easily weighed fifty pounds. On one of its rungs hung a rumpled fedora that St. Peter had finally gotten to land by tossing it from the door. He sighed and then sat down at the old cherry wood desk. It was scratched to Hell, had water rings all over, and all its corners were rounded and splintering. The wood slat office chair squeaked as he leaned back in it and put his hands behind his head. He blew a puff of smoke around the large cigar he was smoking, then leaned forward and pulled a bottle of cheap scotch and a highball glass out of one of the drawers. They were the only things in the desk. He poured himself two fingers of scotch, threw it back, and then poured a full glass before putting the bottle away.

He was halfway through the glass of scotch when he heard a knock on the door. He jerked upright and tried to smooth some of the wrinkles out of his shirt. He had been expecting his first assignment, but he was disappointed and not a little pissed off when he saw not God or Satan but a scarred black man wearing a black leather trench coat and an olive skinned man with a hook nose and a long baby blue robe that covered all but the toes of his sandals.

"Mestoph and Leviticus, what a pleasant surprise," said St. Peter, the sarcasm dripping off his words.

He motioned them to sit down in the two simple wooden chairs that sat opposite his desk. They obligingly took a seat and eyeballed the glass of scotch that sat on an otherwise barren desk.

"Don't have any more glasses, but help yourself," said St. Peter as he pulled the bottle back out of the drawer and slammed it down on the desk. Leviticus took the bottle, uncapped it, and took a generous swig. Mestoph took a smaller sip, made a brief grimace at the cheap and rough alcohol, and then lightly set the bottle back down on the table without taking any more.

"So, you're a private detective now?" asked Leviticus.

"That's what the sign says," said St. Peter, pointing to the hazy windows behind him. Painted backwards on the window in big, bold letters was a sign that said "Simon Peter – Private Detective." Smaller lettering below it said "Rock Solid Investigations."

"A private dick," said Mestoph.

"God's dick," said Leviticus, and they both burst into laughter.

St. Peter sighed. He glanced off to one side and composed himself before he looked back at them. The urge to pull out the gun mounted to the underside of the desk and shoot both of these assholes in the head was almost too much for him.

"I take it this isn't a social call, so what do you two chucklenuts want?"

"Well, Mestoph and I, we've been talking and... Well, we think we might have a plan where the three of us could get everything we've ever wanted," said Leviticus.

"What did you have in mind?"

"Have you ever heard of the Sons of Light and Dark?" asked Mestoph.

St. Peter thought for a moment and shook his head. "No, what about them?"

"Well, there's a Prophecy," said Leviticus.

"There's always a fucking Prophecy," sighed St. Peter.

Afterword

There are a lot of people to thank over the embarrassingly long development of this book. To list them all by name would take too long and I'd hate to leave anyone out. So a quick thank you to the friends and family who test read the many iterations of the book, pointed out inconsistencies, missed opportunities, and encouraged me along the way.

This isn't the end of the road for Mestoph and Leviticus. They will be returning in The Sons of Light and Darkness in 2015. To keep up to date on future adventures of the unholy duo be sure to check out my site at www.adamingle.com.

About The Author

Adam Ingle is a basement-dwelling, graveyard-shift nerd by night and an aspiring peddler of exorcised creative demons by day. He lives in a tin can on the side of the interstate somewhere in South Carolina. This is his first novel.

Credits

Cover art was designed by the amazing Pale Horse Design.

Editing was done by the diligent Erin Long of Biblio/Tech.

Made in the USA
Columbia, SC
19 August 2024

40694410R00171